# AMONG
# THE
# GINZBURGS

# AMONG THE GINZBURGS

### A NOVEL BY

## ELLEN PALL

### ZOLAND BOOKS
*Cambridge, Massachusetts*

First edition published in 1996 by
Zoland Books, Inc.
384 Huron Avenue
Cambridge, Massachusetts 02138

The quotations from Don Marquis's *archy and mehitabel* and
*archy's life of mehitabel*, originally published by Doubleday in
1927 and 1933 respectively, are from the 1960 and 1966
Dolphin editions respectively.

The quotations from *The Tibetan Book of the Dead* are from the
1960 Oxford University Press edition (W. Y. Evans-Wentz, ed. ).

FIRST EDITION

Book design by Boskydell Studio
Printed in the United States of America

02 01 00 99 98 97 96   8 7 6 5 4 3 2 1

This book is printed on acid-free paper, and its binding
materials have been chosen for strength and durability.

*Library of Congress Cataloging-in-Publication Data*
Pall, Ellen, 1952 –
Among the Ginzburgs : a novel / by Ellen Pall. — 1st ed.
p.  cm.
ISBN 0-944072-61-5 (alk. paper)
1. Family reunions — New York (State) — Catskill
Mountains Region — Fiction.   I. Title
PS3566.A463A82   1996
813'.54 — dc20   95-43972   CIP

*for* ISABEL

This book could not have been written
without the help of many people.
The author is especially grateful to
Marvin Cooper, Caryn James,
Waverly Fitzgerald, Laurie Simon,
and Richard Dicker.

# AMONG
# THE
# GINZBURGS

# ONE

"Anatole." Sunny Ginzburg Bronski touched her husband's arm. "Please drive."

Anatole sat unmoving, his right hand poised on the stick shift, his left on the bottom of the steering wheel. The Triumph's engine thrummed, sending tiny vibrations up through the spines of its two passengers.

"You might still get pregnant," he repeated. "Say you'll consider one more round at the clinic. Three's a charm."

Anatole's outsized features were arranged to look vulnerable and pleading, and he had turned his head just enough so Sunny got his face in three-quarter view, his favorite. A tiny muscle near his dark right eye twitched. Behind his head, outside the car, thousands of spindly, leafless branches crazed a delftware sky. POSTED. NO HUNTING! read a sign by an old, fat, red mailbox marked "Ginzburg." A few yards up the twisting driveway a peeling, hand-painted wooden placard begged, DEER. CREATURES. SLOW. The road behind them seemed deserted.

Sunny put her knuckles up against her window. The glass was wonderfully cold. She rolled it down. Sharp, dry air prickled the insides of her nostrils. "Drive to the house," she said.

She made an effort to smile and briefly succeeded. "It's almost a mile and I don't want to walk."

"You owe it to me. One more time. Think about it. I'd do it for you if it was my body."

"Anatole, I love you very much, but you wouldn't take a flu shot without calling the C.D.C. first." She gave a short, barking laugh. "Let's not get theatrical here, just go up the damn driveway, okay?"

With a lurch, Anatole threw the car into first. Accelerating grimly, he headed up the narrow drive. Brambles on both sides scratched at the headlights and caught in the bumpers as he shaved the curves. Ruts in the dirt made the car leap. Over the low whine of the motor, Sunny heard the crash of an animal loping off into the woods. She rolled up her window. As they crested the last hill, Anatole stepped on the gas, roared forward, veered, skirted a parked silver Prelude and skidded to a halt six inches short of the house. He jerked the shift into park and killed the engine.

They had stopped outside a red wooden farmhouse, the simple, artless kind of house found on small farms all over the Catskills. It sat on a swell of earth above a wide sweep of fields. For many years, it had been the Ginzburg family's summer headquarters. Now it belonged to Sunny's brother Mark.

The fields around it were covered with short, yellowing grass. The sky was a silent dome clapped over the circling hills; the crisp air smelled of pine. To the west, already dropping toward the horizon, the sun made a pale pink mirror of a distant pond.

"Thank you for that ridiculous performance." Sunny unsnapped her seat belt. "Do you ever think of anything but yourself?"

Anatole turned to answer, then thought better of it. They

both scrambled to get out. Neither noticed a woman's interested face looking out a window at them.

Inside the kitchen, Claire Ginzburg shut off the tap. Sunny and Anatole's Triumph was in the driveway. She hadn't heard them pull in; the running water must have masked the sound.

Her eyes widened. They had certainly come close enough to the wall of the house. As she watched, Sunny emerged from the car. She turned to face Anatole, who was easing himself out on the driver's side. He straightened, his back to Claire. His thick, dark hair, almost shoulder length, churned in a gust of wind.

They moved sideward to face each other over the hood. Anatole leaned forward; Claire could see his large hands pressed against the metal. The hood must be hot after a drive all the way up from the city.

If he spoke, she couldn't hear him.

"I am thinking of us." Anatole's voice was unnaturally low; Sunny had to work to make out his words. "Both of us. Our future. If we give up now, it will throw a shadow over our marriage forever."

Abruptly, Sunny leaned as far forward as she could over the hood. "Don't threaten me." She spoke in a sarcastic whisper. She hated that cheap actor's trick Anatole had of lowering his voice. "This has nothing to do with us. It has nothing to do with our anything. This is my body. And I'm glad to say that, in the state of New York, even a married woman's body remains her own property."

Claire turned from the sink and called across the kitchen in the direction of the open cellar door. "Mark? Sunny and Anatole are here." Then she turned to glance out the window again. Anatole had straightened. "Playing Hepburn and Tracy, I think," added Claire over her shoulder. She glanced out once more, mumbled to herself, "Maybe Catherine and Heathcliff," twisted the tap back on and resumed washing the dust off the wineglasses.

"Sunny, you are being very stubborn. I'm asking that you make no decision for a day. One day, that's all."

"No." She began to back away from the car. "I'm stubborn? You're the one who refuses to realize I'm not going to get pregnant. Not going to get pregnant. No matter what we try, no matter how many times we try it. Understand? But you're such a gambler — with my body, of course — such a cockeyed optimist, such a sport, so ready to give the old dice another roll — my dice, of course — so pathetically hopeful — " She kicked her door shut, blinking down a sudden springing of tears. "Look, if you don't mind, my father happens to be inside this house. I'm going to see him now. Okay?"

She turned away. Anatole watched her hair tremble and snap around her shoulders as she stalked toward the house. Then he went to the trunk, flung it open and hurled their bags into the driveway.

Ignoring the stubbled, rolling fields and the dark trees thick behind them, Sunny marched up the worn steps to the front door. It was unlocked. She yanked it open so hard it bounced on its hinges, then slammed it shut behind her. A moment later, she heard Anatole thud against it, clumsy with baggage.

She raised a hand to the knob, changed her mind and fled to the coat closet under the stairs, standing half inside it. From there, she watched the heavy doorknob wiggle until Anatole finally managed to turn it. He staggered in and dropped the bags. Then, pretending not to see her, he shed his jacket, draped it over the suitcases and made for the kitchen.

"Idiot," breathed Sunny. "Hurtful idiot."

At the whoosh of the swinging door between the hallway and the kitchen, Claire turned again from the sink, shaking her wet hands and glancing around for the dish towel. As she had thought, Anatole's hair was a good deal longer than when she had last seen him. He hadn't shaved today; indeed, a moment later she noticed he still had a smudge of makeup under one eye. He swept halfway across the room, then stopped to execute an elaborate bow. The plume of an imaginary musketeer's hat trailed across the gleaming linoleum. He marched up to her.

"Claire."

Claire stood on tiptoe to lift her face to him, her wet hands high in the air to either side. He was a good ten inches taller than she. Solemnly, he kissed her cheek. His cheek was chilled and rough.

"You look marvelous," he said.

"I can imagine," said Claire, who had not slept through a night for nearly a week.

"Where's Mark?"

"Down in the cellar fetching wine. He'll be up in a minute."

"Are the others here yet? Mimi? Charlotte? Mr. Ham-in-the-Sandwich? I didn't see any cars."

The "Ham-in-the-Sandwich" was Mark's brother, Ira, the middle child of the five Ginzburg brothers and sisters. Mark himself was the oldest. After Mark came Charlotte, who had lived for decades in California; the two of them were known in the family as the Bigs. Sunny and Mimi — the youngest — were the Littles.

"You're the first," said Claire, who had been hoping Mimi

would be first. She glanced vaguely at the refrigerator, trying to remember what else she needed to do, then moved tentatively toward the sink. "Where's Sunny?"

"Sulking in the cloakroom, when last seen." Anatole drifted to the stove, lifted the lid off a pot and sniffed deeply. The kitchen was a long rectangle, with the appliances lined up on one wall and most of the counters and cabinets opposite. It had been redone not long ago; everywhere, spotless white Corian and red baked enamel gleamed. A butcher block table stood in the center of the room, bristling with knives. At the kitchen's far end, near a mudroom, was a breakfast nook with red leatherette banquettes, red-striped wallpaper and a pair of red-shuttered windows.

"We don't have a cloakroom."

"The hall closet, then. The understairs, the where-you-will. The place with all the bobsleds and snowshoes and jackets. What's this stuff, invalid fare?"

"Vanilla pudding. For Mark. He likes it."

Anatole replaced the lid. There was no sign in his face of the argument Claire had just witnessed. His exaggerated features were composed, amiable. Anatole was not really handsome, but he was so accomplished at creating the impression of handsomeness that few people noticed. It was his belief that even Sunny hadn't noticed. Claire thought him very good-looking, though his large hands and feet and his massive Saint Bernard's skull alarmed her a little.

"Pudding for Mark he likes it," he echoed vacantly. "Anyway, Sunny's out there. Please don't mention her. We're scrapping. I'm sorry we — she — barged in without knocking."

"Wouldn't have it any other way." Mark's voice, then Mark, came up the stairs from the cellar. He set down the half dozen wine bottles cradled in his arms and stretched his hand out to his brother-in-law. Anatole pumped it vigorously.

"Mark, Mark, Mark. You old son of a gun, how are you? Sorry about" — he pointed up at the ceiling — "you know. Your dad."

Mark extricated his hand from Anatole's frenzied grip and rubbed it lightly, nodding in acknowledgment. He was a tall man, almost as tall as Anatole, but long-faced, ginger-haired, teardrop-shaped. He had the same high waist as Sunny; all the Ginzburgs had that waist. In the last five or six years, his fuzzy ginger hairline had begun to creep slowly up his gently freckled forehead.

He sucked in his belly, but without any visible result. Anatole *has* to keep his weight down, he thought. It's his job. I would too, if it were my job. Aloud, "It's been hardest on Claire," he said. "She's been doing the nursing."

Claire had gone back to rinsing off the platters they'd need for dinner. Now both men turned to look at her back. The delicate scissoring motion of her shoulder blades was discernible through her yellow sweater. Claire had always been small, but in her teens and early twenties — when Mark first met her — she had been enlarged by plumpness. She was soft and round then, with a dark page boy, shiny brown eyes and blunt, oddly middle-aged features. From the time she gave birth to their first child, though, she had grown smaller and smaller. Her figure dwindled, her cheeks sank. Now her features were fine and sharp. Her graying hair was boy-short, exposing her ears and marooning her eyes in the milky oval of her face. The skin over her cheekbones was delicately scored. A crease had just begun to descend from under her chin toward her convex collarbone.

Anatole went to the sink and draped a heavy arm over her shoulders. "That's the trouble with these helping professions, eh?" he said. "People always expect you to help."

"Bet that doesn't happen to you very often," she murmured.

"Nope." Cheerfully, he clapped her on the back. "People mostly expect actors to be a pain in the butt. I can't tell you how exhausting it is, but one obliges. Where is my wife, anyway? I'm afraid she may be starting a marathon pout. Mark, go out and interrupt her, will you? She's your sister."

Mark looked anxious. His high forehead puckered slightly, and he pulled his short lower lip into his mouth, pinning it there with his front teeth. "Has she been taking it hard?"

For a moment, his brother-in-law stared at him, puzzled. Then, "Oh, that," he said, pointing up again. "Um — mixed feelings, I guess. About what you'd expect. Curious. Sad." He studied Mark's expression for a hint of his emotions. "Perhaps just a teeny, teeny bit resentful. She had kind of shut the old lunatic out of her heart. Hadn't you?"

Mark started to answer, changed his mind and left the kitchen. His sister was not in the front hall, nor the living room. He glanced up the stairs, then out one of the narrow windows that edged the front door. Under a towering blue spruce next to the driveway, Sunny was striding around and around in a small circle. She wore no coat. He started to go out to her, then noticed she was talking. Though the temperature was above freezing, he thought he saw her breath steam in the air. For a little while, he watched. Then, thoughtfully, he picked up Anatole's jacket and put it away.

"That's finished," Sunny muttered into the wintry afternoon. "All finished. Thank God." She inhaled deeply, forbidding herself to cry.

In the kitchen, meantime, as Mark's footsteps had faded away, Anatole said, "I shouldn't have called his father a lunatic, I guess." His voice dropped. "He couldn't have heard me, could he?"

"Meyer?" Claire went to the stove, found the pudding had boiled and began to pour it into thick Pyrex cups. "Not possibly."

"What's your impression of him? You'd met him before, hadn't you? Or hadn't you?"

"Once. In 'seventy-seven. He was . . . gee, sixty, I guess. I would call him . . . eccentric. Entertaining, but completely wrapped up in himself. Not much judgment. He told June some folktale about a demon that scared the bejesus out of her. She was only four or five, and she slept with us for a month afterwards. On the other hand, he and Mark got into a discussion about — the distribution of wealth, I think it was, that Mark says was the single most interesting discussion he's ever had. And then in the morning, of course, with barely a heigh-ho, he galloped back out of our lives. Don't," she interrupted herself, as Anatole dipped a finger into a pudding cup, then slipped it into his mouth.

"Yeck." He ran his finger under the tap.

"It tastes better when it's cold." With a spatula, Claire scraped the last of the pudding into the cups, setting the one Anatole had sullied aside. "This will be yours. Anyway, Meyer seems a bit more able to focus on the people around him now." She pulled a knife from a drawer to scrape the pudding off the spatula. "But he still has quirks. He spent all day Wednesday lying on the floor in his room, because the vibrations were better and he needed to ground himself. And he had us move his bed against a different wall so his head would point north. He brought a suitcase full of books about human electromagnetics and paganism and I don't know what. Of course, he's not really up to reading."

"How sick is he?"

"Sick. Very." Finally, she set the sticky pot on a cold burner and leaned against the counter next to the stove, facing him. "And that reminds me, why exactly is Sunny upset?"

"Oh. Well, naturally, her father . . ."

Claire waited.

"Plus she's got some bee in her bonnet about — Come to think of it, I don't know if it would be discreet to tell you. Sorry about that. Sanctity of the conjugal relationship and everything. Private."

"Anatole, have you been fooling around?"

"Claire, you wrong me. I never fool around."

She looked carefully at him, narrowly; but Anatole merely beamed back, giving her the look he had practiced in his adolescence, while other boys shot baskets or played air guitar in their rooms.

"Hmm," she said.

"I'm looking" — he smiled — "I'm looking at your very lovely left ear — "

Claire turned abruptly, snatched up the sticky pudding pot and dumped it in the sink. Her face was burning. In the three years since Sunny had married Anatole, Claire had come to expect behavior like this from him. But expecting it wasn't the same as knowing what to do about it, or even what he meant by it.

From behind her, she heard him say thoughtfully, "Isn't that funny? About pudding, I mean. Why shouldn't it taste just as good when it's warm? It seems to go against nature."

"Why don't you go out and find the others?" She filled the pot with dish soap and water. "I'll be out in a minute."

"Why don't you tell me more about nursing the Lone Ranger up there?"

Her cheeks had settled enough that she could turn around again. She did so, a huge wooden carving board clapped to her chest. Anatole was lounging against the refrigerator. "Frankly, there isn't much nursing to do. I try to get him to eat and drink,

I wake up and check him in the night. But he's really just weak. He dozes off a lot. You know it's a disease of the bone marrow — "

She broke off as the swinging door flashed open. Sunny was with them.

"Claire."

Sunny crossed the room to her sister-in-law. Claire, she thought, looked awful. Pinched and weary. Drudgelike, especially with the pans and platters on the drainboard behind her. She brushed her cold cheek against Claire's slightly flushed one. Without quite looking at him, she sensed that Anatole was pleased with himself. She backed away to lean against the counter directly opposite the refrigerator, so that Claire could not face both her visitors at once.

"You look terrific," Claire said.

Sunny wondered briefly if this could be so, and if not, why Claire would lie. "You look exhausted," she replied.

Claire smiled. "It's — " She waved a vague hand skyward.

"Well, naturally. Must be H-E–double toothpicks." Sunny paused, looked off into the middle distance and sniffed attentively, as if she thought she caught a whiff of something burning. "Has my husband been trying to flirt with you?" she asked, focusing again on Claire.

Claire looked at her, unable to think of an answer.

"I see. Never mind. He doesn't mean anything by it. It's just that Anatole's like Will Rogers: never met a man, woman or child he didn't feel the need to seduce one way or another. Or was that Mae West? Anyway, how are you, Claire?" she asked, hitching herself up on the smooth countertop behind her. She added, before Claire could answer, "How's Meyer? I saw Mark in the hall, and he said he was still able to sit up and talk and stuff. Should I go say hello?"

"Well, he's sleeping — "

"Oh." Wildly relieved, Sunny opened the cabinet next to her head and looked in.

"I'd rather not wake him, if you can wait, though he'd probably drift right off again. He sleeps for hours. He must sleep twenty hours a day. But he's perfectly lucid once he's up."

"Good." Sunny looked into an orange bowl she had removed from a stack in the cabinet. "I can wait."

Claire took advantage of her momentary absorption in the dish to look carefully at her. Sunny was the beauty of the family, but she had no vanity, and now her complexion was starting to go. There were dark spots under her pale blue eyes and deep parentheses etched around the corners of her mouth. Even in the warm kitchen light, her auburn hair was obviously dyed. She ought to go the whole distance and learn to use makeup, Claire thought. She couldn't really afford to dress that way anymore, either. Jeans and a tailored shirt and a green tweed suit jacket that looked as if it had done time in a thrift shop. Now she swung her long feet, knocking the heels of her heavy boots against Claire's newly varnished cabinets.

Sunny returned the bowl and closed the door on what she had concluded was a modern imitation of Fiestaware. She watched as Claire scrubbed out a pot.

"How's New York?"

"Filthy."

"How's the paper?"

"Faltering."

"Really?"

"No, of course not," Anatole answered. "That's just what management likes to say as Christmas bonus time creeps near. There'll be apples aplenty in Santa's stockings, believe me. Only the little elves will wake up to lumps of coal."

"We had a loss of twenty-two million dollars in the third

quarter," said Sunny. "Advertising linage dropped one point two percent. When I stopped in yesterday, it was suggested to me I might take Vanessa Redgrave to a coffee shop for lunch when I interview her Monday. But enough of life on the culture desk. How's life up here? What's Audubon like these days?"

"Clean," replied Claire, drying her hands. She picked up the first two pudding cups and carried them to the fridge. "Poor. Would you mind?" she added, as Anatole, blocking the door, languidly watched her approach.

He stepped aside but didn't open the refrigerator. Balancing the cups, Claire used a pinkie to pull the handle.

"You don't miss Westchester?" Sunny asked. She hopped down from the counter and crossed the kitchen to carry the next round of pudding cups to Claire. As she passed Anatole, he quickly caressed her cheek.

"Are you kidding?" Claire answered.

Two years ago, when he was forty-five and she forty-three, Mark and Claire had dismantled their suburban lives and moved permanently up to the Catskills, into the house they had bought a dozen years before from Mark's mother's estate. Since the move, although Mark occasionally helped a former colleague write a brief and Claire still did a little private nursing, they lived mostly off their investments.

"I can't imagine Anatole and me in a house a hundred miles from anywhere," Sunny said, noting with interest the unfamiliar brands and flagrantly processed foods (Pop-Tarts, olive loaf) in her brother's refrigerator. "Alone. Together." She shivered as Claire arrived with the last of the pudding, then shut the door. "It's like something out of Stephen King."

"What have you done with Mark, anyway, speaking of Stephen King?" With a sponge, Claire wiped a stray blob of pudding off the counter.

"He went to take our suitcases upstairs. I couldn't stop him," she added, as Anatole blinked pointedly at her. "He insisted."

"I'm not completely useless," Anatole muttered, stamping heavily across the room. The swinging door batted back and forth several times behind him.

"You're not completely useful, either," Sunny called after him, though only when he was safely out of earshot.

"Oh dear." Claire filled the kettle and put it on the stove. Then she and Sunny sat down in the breakfast nook. Outside the shuttered window, a line of heavy pine trees stretched up alongside the disused barn. The grass in the meadow before it was sparse and pale. Nearer the house stood a small rose garden muffled in burlap.

"You missed the leaves," said Claire, following Sunny's gaze.

"I don't think I've ever been up here at this time of year."

"Not really worth a *House and Garden* spread. Kind of betwixt and between."

"It's nice." Conscientiously, Sunny asked after June and Eliot, her niece and nephew. "Will they be home for Thanksgiving?"

"June will, Eliot won't. Junie is joining a sorority." Claire shrugged as if to dissociate herself from such organizations, though in fact she had been pleased. She worried about June, who seemed too young to be away at school. The shrug had been for Sunny's sake. Twenty-five years Claire had been married to Mark, and Sunny still made her feel inadequate. Dull. Not cool. A high school idea, but there it was. Once, at Mark's suggestion, she had told Sunny how she felt. Sunny laughed incredulously and disclaimed any interest in fashion or style, if that was what Claire meant. She said she was sorry if she made Claire uncomfortable. Then they went on exactly as before.

"This younger generation," said Sunny, shaking her head.

"What will they think of next? You're not going to fly them in when Meyer — ?"

She stopped. Down in the city, talking with Anatole, it had been easy to speak of Meyer's illness, Meyer's death. They'd joked about him showing up after all these years to share his last, painful weeks with the family. The sublime crust of it; the pure, sanity-defying egomania of it. Here, though, with Claire across from her and Meyer actually upstairs, things felt different.

Luckily, Claire didn't make her finish her sentence. "He doesn't want a funeral," she said, shaking her head. "He wants to be cremated and have his ashes scattered over moving water. The Hudson, if convenient."

Sunny swallowed. "And when — ?"

"Could be tomorrow, could be two weeks. More likely tomorrow. Once he does start to go, he'll go very fast." Claire had explained all this over the phone, not only to Sunny but to Mark's other siblings. But she had often noticed people needed to hear medical information more than once.

"He's not in pain?"

"Not now."

"But he will be?"

"Very likely not. If he is, we'll be able to treat it."

The whistle on the kettle blew. Claire stood up.

"Tea or coffee?"

"Coffee, if it's easy."

For a while, Sunny watched Claire bustle around, measuring coffee, pouring water. Then, slowly, "Claire, dear," she said, "to the best of my knowledge, my father is a flighty, solipsistic cad who abandoned your husband before he was twenty and never paid you the slightest attention. Not that I'm questioning your judgment, of course, but what on earth possessed you to take him in?"

Claire, who could never remember what solipsistic was, said only, "Let's go sit in the living room," and handed Sunny a cup.

The house in Audubon was a loose, haphazard pile of wood with generous common rooms downstairs and tiny, low-ceilinged bedrooms over them. Its narrow corridors ran off-kilter; its pine plank floors sloped. It had been built in the 1920s by a dairy farmer named Katz. It came into the hands of the Ginzburgs as a result of a wrong turn Ruth Ginzburg took in the summer of 1950.

She and Meyer and the children were up from the city for a couple of weeks that August, staying at a cheesy resort outside Livingston Manor. Driving Mark and Charlotte to a place she had heard they could pick strawberries, Ruth turned up a driveway too narrow to turn around on once she realized it wasn't Overmountain Road. She chugged to the top. Masses of brooding trees ringed smooth, green hills. Cows and sheep looked up inquiringly. In the midst of it all stood a rundown house with a For Sale sign.

Ruth was not a woman much interested in material posses-sions, yet she felt at once a greedy longing. She was then preg-nant with Ira. Mark was six and Charlotte four; Sunny and Mimi hadn't been born. Meyer and Ruth weren't shopping for a house, and they didn't have the money to buy one, but two months later, Ruth's grandmother died, leaving a tiny inheri-tance. The moment she decently could, Ruth phoned the Katzes.

Now Claire led Sunny through the drafty dining room and across the wide front hall into the living room. A spill of late af-ternoon sunlight spread across the long, shabby couches and battered armchairs (for ages, Claire had wanted to replace or at least reupholster these, but Mark was sentimental about them) and seeped into the folds and curves of the bright rag rug. In the middle of the room sat a square coffee table awash in back issues of *The Atlantic, Smithsonian, The New Yorker.* Against the wall across from the front windows stood an upright piano slathered with sheet music. In the high stone fireplace opposite the front hall, lion-headed andirons bore up under a heap of gargantuan logs.

Sunny was about to sit when a clanging wail like a fire alarm sounded. She jumped. "Good God!"

"That's Meyer." Claire set her mug on the crowded coffee table. "Mark rigged that bell in case we were outdoors. I'll go see what he wants."

"Should I go with you?" Instantly, the skin across Sunny's shoulders and chest began to prickle with fear.

"No," said Claire, all nurse. "He may have to use the bathroom and feel embarrassed. Let me see what's happening first."

Reprieved, Sunny sank obediently onto the sagging brown corduroy sofa. She hadn't seen her father in over a decade, and then only for an hour. She could wait a little longer.

The living room was very quiet. Sunny sat immobile, ignoring her coffee, looking vacantly at the overflowing bookshelves, adjusting herself to the unaccustomed silence. Her eye fell on a square of needlepoint Claire was working, lying half submerged on the magazine-swamped table. Not enough stitches had been done to make out the design. Sunny had noticed Claire's shrug in the kitchen. She knew exactly what it was. But was it her fault if Claire felt she judged her?

Claire was so good. Without effort, apparently without having to think about it at all, she encouraged the timid, fed the hungry, tended the feeble. If she had complaints, Sunny never heard them. It baffled her. Where did such goodness come from? Didn't Claire have anything else to do?

Sunny shifted on the couch. About her own goodness, she had several competing ideas. Professionally, she thought, she could lay a fairly solid claim to virtue. She often helped the younger writers at the paper, never stole anyone's story and didn't take cheap shots at the people she wrote about (she did turn them into entertainment — but that, after all, was her job).

Personally, however, she was on shakier ground. Though she loved Anatole and suffered with what she considered saintlike stoicism the countless injuries his personality inevitably threw off when in motion, a deep suspicion told her that he was a much nicer person than she was, that he absorbed her contempt, scorn and impatience as no one else would have done, that his unkindnesses were accidental, while hers were meant. She also suspected she enjoyed the moral high ground she won by appearing to be ill-used.

And it wasn't just her behavior toward Anatole. Sometimes she was shocked by her lack of genuine interest in the people around her. June and Eliot, for example: If she never heard of them again, she wouldn't think once about them. And she did look down on Mark and Claire, so apparently content in their ordinariness, so anonymous, such forces for nothing in the world. She liked that Anatole was famous. She liked seeing her byline in the paper. She was ambitious. She was very ambitious.

Yet she did at least want to be good. Shouldn't that count for something? Why was she so harsh with herself? She would never subject anyone else to such loveless scrutiny; she didn't judge other people. Or rather, she did — but she didn't sentence them. She wouldn't want any ill to come to Claire or Mark. She certainly wouldn't want them killed, the penalty to which she usually sentenced herself in imagination. If she were her own friend, and confessed her nature to herself, she would smile and say, "That's you. What can you do? Relax."

Often, these competing ideas seemed to her to be literally competing inside her. As if each idea were a chariot being driven hard down some cerebral track, the horses panting and steaming, the charioteers ferociously whipping them on. She felt harassed by them, haunted. She would wake in the night and sit in the dim living room over Riverside Drive, examining her conscience.

But in the morning, almost always, she simply rolled back into the flood of whatever it was (hormones? history? Ruth's furious energy, passed along in her genes?) that made her so . . . relentless was the word she most often used to herself. She couldn't help it. She simply would bully or ridicule or demand or extort whatever it was she needed to get whatever (and there was always something) she wanted. If that was so awful to do, she would find herself thinking, Sue me. Fuck you. Get out of the way.

A tap on the window behind her made her turn around. Anatole, gesturing violently for her to come outside. Beyond him, Mark was aimlessly kicking at some fallen leaves. In profile, her brother's torso was perfectly pear-shaped. Bosc pear–shaped.

Anatole beckoned again, gigantically, then waved at the sky. It was indeed a particularly lush, immaculate blue. Sunny shook her head no. Anatole threw up his hands, rolled his eyes, pleaded. Sunny shrugged, raised an eyebrow and turned away from him. Suppose Claire came down and said Meyer was ready to see her? Anyway, she was not sorry to put a little distance between herself and Anatole just now. After a moment, without turning to look, she felt him move away from the window.

# TWO

Claire returned to the living room ten minutes later. Meyer had merely shuffled to the bathroom and back, she said.

"I was literally pulling the covers over him, about to tell him you were here, when I realized he'd gone back to sleep already. Sorry." She picked up her lukewarm mug of coffee and sniffed it.

"Don't be a dope. It's not your fault." Sunny glanced out the back windows. "Anatole and Mark are taking a walk. Why don't you get some air with them before the sun goes down?"

Claire hesitated.

"I'll be here if anyone comes," Sunny said. "And if Meyer rings, God knows you'll hear it."

Secretly, Sunny thought she'd also nip upstairs once Claire was out and sneak a quiet peek at Meyer. But when Claire had actually agreed, put her coffee down, slipped into a parka and struck out across the back meadow, Sunny found herself too nervous even to do that. What if he were awake?

She was still in the living room twenty minutes later, leafing through a worn copy of *The Best American Short Stories of 1953* and mentally drafting a brief review of it, when the sound of a car made her go to the front windows. In the distance, dark against a crimson horizon, Anatole, Mark and Claire stood clustered at the edge of the pond. Closer to hand, in front of the house, a battered VW Rabbit had drawn up next to the Triumph. As Sunny watched, the door swung open and her brother Ira eased himself out from behind the wheel. He paused for a moment to stretch his long back and roll his head.

Of the five Ginzburg children, Ira looked the most fragile. His cheekbones and temples stuck out sharply; on the nape of his neck, the bumps of his vertebrae showed. As he let his head drop forward, a lick of straight copper hair fell over his pale-lashed blue eyes. He combed it back with his fingers, pushed his glasses up his nose, pulled a worn flight bag out from the backseat of the car and shambled toward the house.

Sunny opened the front door and stood on the steps, making goggles of her thumbs and index fingers as he approached. At the top of the steps, he kissed her.

"New glasses," she observed.

"Mmm." He went past her, into the front hall.

She followed and helped him wriggle out of his windbreaker. The air inside felt warm and close, like in a greenhouse, after a whiff of the outdoors. "Nice. They make you look just a tiny bit like Joyce Carol Oates."

"You're too kind." He hesitated, the windbreaker hooked over one finger. "Where do the coats go? Under the stairs, still?"

"Of course. Ira, haven't you been up here since — ?"

"Not for years."

"Actually, we haven't been up much either," Sunny admitted. Ira returned from the closet with something cupped in his hand. "Inchworm," he said, showing her. Ira was an entomologist. "Shouldn't be around this time of year. Very curious."

"Hmm."

"Exactly." He opened the front door again and gently shook the insect onto the steps. "Where's — ?"

"Upstairs sleeping. I haven't dared to go see him yet. Everyone else is out by the pond."

"I saw."

"Want to go up?" Sunny already felt fortified by Ira's presence.

"Maybe in a bit. Let him wake up first." Ira had been inclined to skip this pilgrimage altogether. It was Sunny who'd talked him into it.

"Wasn't Mimi coming up with you?" she asked, as he looked questioningly first toward the living room, then the dining room.

He shrugged. "She wasn't ready to leave the city when I called. Where do they keep the hard stuff, do you know?"

"Alcohol? Kitchen?"

Sunny followed him through the dining room. In the kitchen, he rummaged around until he had assembled the makings for a Scotch and soda.

"You're starting a little early."

"A stitch in time."

"Meyer?"

In truth, even without Meyer, Ira felt that an evening in the bosom of his family called for a drink, but he only said, "It's Friday. What the hell," and returned to the subject of Mimi. "I offered to wait for her, but she wouldn't say how long, and since I have to do some editing on Sunday" — Ira published a newsletter about biological pest control — "I didn't want to get here late. So . . ." He broke ice out of a tray. "She was stammering badly. She said she and Jesse were *talking*."

"Really? What about, I wonder?" Sunny considered her little sister. "Something serious, if it made her choose the bus instead of a ride with you."

Ira poured out the Scotch and screwed the cap back on the bottle. "Maybe 'talking' was a euphemism?"

"Maybe. I often wonder what they have in common. He's not a person I'd care to be — I don't know, stuck in traffic with. What would you make conversation about? Band saws? Moldings?"

"Well, he doesn't have to be someone you would enjoy being stuck in traffic with, does he? He just has to get along with Mimi."

Sunny sensed some warning under Ira's words and immediately suspected this was what he and the others said about her and Anatole. If it was, she didn't want to know it. She followed her brother into the living room.

The moment Ira sat down, he caught sight of a record album in a pile in one corner and leapt up again to examine it. Sunny watched him squat, his long, thin legs sticking out from under him like a frog's. Years ago, it had been Ira who introduced her to rock 'n' roll. He'd bought her the first grown-up album she'd owned, *Meet the Beatles!*

"Country Joe and the Fish," he called out triumphantly. "I always wondered where this record went. And — look at this, Sam and Dave, the Blues Project — this cabinet is like a time capsule."

He switched the stereo on and centered a record on the spindle. A moment later the stately opening chords of "A Whiter Shade of Pale" filled the room.

"Oh, whoops — " Ira suddenly remembered Meyer upstairs, lowered the volume and installed himself in the only armchair in the room, a deep, squashy club chair covered in a flowery brocade.

"Remember that time Mark and Charlotte came home for the summer and the three of you used to sit down here all night, playing records and smoking dope?"

"We never smoked in here. We always went outside. As a courtesy to Ruth."

"'Sixty-five, it was. She knew what you were doing."

"I know. We knew she knew. We were just trying to spare her the embarrassment of knowing that we knew she knew."

"She'd be reading me and Mimi Just So stories or *The Wind in the Willows*, trying to get us to sleep, and all the time there'd be the sound of you guys laughing like maniacs down here. And Otis Redding, and the Animals — 'House of the Rising Sun,' I remember that song especially because I didn't understand it. I thought it was about a family where the son was taking over."

"The Rising Son?"

"Don't laugh. I was only twelve. You're the one who thought Dylan was saying 'Obadiah' instead of 'Oh but I was so much older then . . .'"

"Were you only twelve? You were precocious. I remember you snuck down for a toke a couple of times. You looked so spacy and happy when the smoke hit."

There was a silence while they both thought about dope. Ira had become addicted to heroin four or five years after that summer. He struggled through eighteen months before quitting cold turkey in a hotel room in Tucson.

"*Où sont les neiges d'antan?*" Sunny asked lightly.

"Snow." Ira shook his head. "What a nightmare."

"So."

"So, how's Anatole?"

"Thriving, I thank you."

"Any luck with — ?"

"No. We got the test results at noon today. Neither of the embryos took root." Sunny hoped he wouldn't see she was fighting tears.

"Sorry."

"Frankly, it's a load off my shoulders. The truth is, you're more likely to get pregnant than I am," she went on. "At least with Anatole. Could you please tell him that?"

"He wants you to try IFV again?"

"IVF." Ira had a mental block about these letters; she had noticed it before. It was funny, considering he was a scientist. "In vitro fertilization. Yes, he does. And what I say is, if he wants to spread his legs and have a needle stuck up his genitals after being pumped full of hormones day after day, I'll go into a cubicle and jerk off. Maybe he'll get pregnant."

"Is that how they do it?"

"More or less."

Ira had been sprawled back in the club chair; now he sat up a little. "A needle like what?"

"A needle like twelve inches long. And hollow. Of course, you're floating in space when they insert it, they give you anesthesia. But you know damn well what they're up to. You can feel it." She added in a mutter, "Which they don't admit, of course."

"And how is that supposed to get you pregnant?" Ira asked, sitting still straighter.

"Dear, if you're so interested in this subject, I can lend you a book. The point is, I am not going through it again and Anatole doesn't believe me."

She heard a sound beneath the low strains of Procol Harum, and stood to walk to the side window.

"Anatole, declaiming," she announced. "As I suspected. *Macbeth*, probably. The brief candle speech. He likes to do that at sunset." She peered out again into the gathering dusk. "Yup, that's his strutting and fretting walk. What a guy." She went into the front hall to open the door for the others, adding over her shoulder, "Shakespeare for every occasion. As they rolled me out of the room where they put the embryos in this time, he was trotting alongside the trolley doing 'To be or not to be.'"

By the time Charlotte and Mimi arrived, Mark had lit a fire in the stone fireplace and drawn the heavy drapes across the living room windows. Sunny and Anatole were propped against cushions at either end of the long brown corduroy couch, shoes off, legs stretched out in front of them. Ira had resumed his armchair; at the other side of the fireplace, Mark occupied an uncomfortable oak rocking chair that had belonged (though none of them knew it) to Meyer's mother. On a blue love seat opposite the fire, Claire sat curled, unconsciously massaging her shins. The house was filled with the smell of roasting beef ("I can't believe she wouldn't realize people don't eat meat anymore," Sunny had whispered to Anatole) and the voice of Richie Havens. A basket of cheese straws balanced atop the sea of magazines on the coffee table.

"Yeah, and what's interesting about cotton, what most people don't realize, is that the plant itself has so many pests that fully half the insecticide produced in the U.S. is used on cotton alone," Ira was saying, chiefly addressing Mark. "How's that for 'the fabric of your life'? Plus it leaches the soil, plus third world countries tend to allocate land and water they need to raise food in order to grow it as a cash crop, plus refining it is associated with brown lung and — "

A gust of cold air flooded the living room. Charlotte and Mimi had arrived simultaneously, Charlotte by car, Mimi on foot. They had met, by chance, at the bottom of the driveway.

A moment later, they appeared together in the arched doorway to the front hall. Sunny, who was facing the fireplace, turned around to see what struck her immediately as a living illustration of the effects of age. Mimi was a dead ringer for the

Charlotte of fifteen years ago, except that she had more hips and no freckles. They both had the same pale green-brown eyes, wide cheekbones, slightly pug noses. But whereas Mimi's youthful face was a smooth, luminous, curving disk, Charlotte's had been subdivided by time, sectioned off with deep lines into discrete regions: Upper Lip, Right Cheek, Left Eyelid. And Charlotte was a dermatologist! Her hair, once the color of nutmeg and as glossy as Mimi's, had faded and turned brittle. Her mouth, formerly as full and lavish in its curves as Mimi's still was, had gone pinched and flat.

In seven years, my face will look like that, Sunny thought, and while the hint of mortality was terrifying, she felt a strange comfort, too, in the inevitability of it, the apparently permissible defeat. "Over the hill." It sounded peaceful. Perhaps she and Anatole could develop a new basis for their relationship.

There was a round of greetings. Because no one except Mark had seen Charlotte in more than a year (he had insisted on flying out for her wedding the previous December; everyone else took her at her word when she assured them it would be a typical second-wedding ceremony and not worth attending), she got most of the attention. Mimi was left to shrug awkwardly out of her lumpy, fake-fur coat by herself. She had felt like walking, and the moonlight was particularly bright, so she walked the mile and a half from Audubon, she announced to no one in particular. Charlotte, distributing hugs and kisses, said she would have been here half an hour ago if the car rental agency at Newark hadn't screwed up her reservation.

Fifteen minutes later, their bags in their rooms, hands washed and hair freshened, the two of them were installed in the living room, each in a corner of the nubbly camelback sofa that only Mark was old enough to remember had once been a brilliant turquoise (the competing effects of light and dust had now muted it to a dull aqua). Though they had gone upstairs, neither had asked to see Meyer. In any case, he had been sleeping since the afternoon.

Mimi, her crinkly, coppery hair spread in a glory around her shoulders, sipped a rum and Coke made especially sweet (and afterwards bitter) by the reflection that she probably shouldn't be drinking it. But I need something, she thought. After having said good-bye to Jesse, she felt scraped raw, yet at the same time strangely cleansed. The world had a reddish, painful glow.

Charlotte, severe in a black jumpsuit, meditatively rubbed a lemon wedge around the rim of a tall glass of Perrier.

"How's Ted?" Ira asked, and Charlotte could tell by the slight hesitation between the two words that he had not been entirely sure of her new husband's name. She wasn't offended. She had been living in L.A. so long — over twenty-five years now — that her life there must seem to her brothers and sisters merely a set of names, arbitrary and meaningless, to be learned by rote. For herself, the family she had been born into usually figured in her mind not as real people to whom she was bound by blood and history but as a cast of actors playing out an extended drama on a distant stage.

"A little fritzed," she said. "A little terrified. This is the first time I've left him alone with Kyle over a whole weekend. Kyle's fourteen now, you realize," she added helpfully, "which means he's satanic. The other day I had to sit him down for a heart-to-heart on the subject of why he should not apostrophize me as 'you fucking bitch.' I pointed out he was liable to hurt my feelings, but he argued that if he only said it behind my back, that would be hypocritical. Anyway, he actually likes Ted — so far, at least. Maybe they'll both still be there when I get back on Monday."

Charlotte had expanded upon this subject because she enjoyed shocking Claire. Though she knew it was irrational, she held Claire responsible for transforming Mark (diminishing

him, in her opinion) from a genuinely interesting if somewhat
angry, sarcastic guy into the pious, bland item they now had before them. Claire had drained something from Mark, some
slightly toxic but exhilarating essence. Worn him smooth, like
an old coin. Claire, Charlotte felt, was a Civilizing Influence.

Sunny, knowing some of this, wondered how much Charlotte was exaggerating about Kyle. Surely if children were what
parents said they were, no couple would deliberately have two.
She also wondered, not for the first time, how Charlotte could
have given her son such a tinny, goyische, California name.
Kyle. Why not Scooter, or Bud? Could one imagine a distin-
guished Kyle of fifty or sixty?

She hoped Anatole would not bring up the incident of the
fire.

"I set fire to my parents' bedroom when I was fourteen," said
Anatole. He paused, as he always did, before adding, "They
were in it at the time."

"They were fine, it was a tiny little fire, no one was hurt,"
Sunny said, reluctant to sit through the otherwise inevitable
suite of questions.

Charlotte, who had only met Anatole twice before (once at
their wedding, once when he had flown out for meetings about
a picture that never got made), looked at him with new respect.
"Anatole, what were you thinking of?" she asked.

He gave what Sunny recognized as his "wicked" grin. "Exactly what you're thinking of."

"What a scamp, eh?" Sunny intervened. "You know, Ira,
what you were saying before about cotton — what's the alternative, though? I mean, synthetics are made out of petroleum,
aren't they? So if everybody wore them — "

"Really adroit change of subject, Sun," said Charlotte. "I
hardly noticed. Anatole, we'll discuss this later."

Anatole seemed about to insist on discussing it now when

Mark said, in a tone so startled that everyone turned to him at once, "I just realized something. This is the first time we've all been together since Mom died."

"That can't be," said Claire automatically. "Ruth's been dead more than fifteen years."

"That's what I mean."

For a moment, they all looked at one another in silence across the coffee table, a complicated web of glances. It was true Ira had missed Sunny and Anatole's wedding (he had managed to wangle a small grant for airfare to a biodiversity conference in Nairobi). When Ruth's mother had finally died some years before that, Mark was flat on his back with a slipped disk. There had been no other occasion to bring Charlotte east — Eliot's bar mitzvah had barely sufficed to transport Sunny from Manhattan to Larchmont — and certainly none to move all the rest of them west.

"Not to mention Meyer," added Mark, when it was clear he had been right. "Unless my math is off, it's been twenty-eight years since we were all in the same house with him."

There was another silence while the Ginzburg children pondered what effect this true fact must have had on them. Anatole cast Claire a glance which she correctly interpreted to mean, Mine never got over it. Did yours?

Meyer Ginzburg was the only child of a shy, middle-aged fur cutter and his equally timid wife. He grew up in Brooklyn an astonishment to his parents, a prodigy who could read at three and play the piano at four. By seven he had read through an unabridged dictionary, an encyclopedia and much of Shakespeare. Twelve years later, armed with degrees in English literature and mathematics from City College, he declared himself a poet. By the time he was twenty, he had published a treatise on prime numbers and a collection of what his still-to-be-born children would one day agree was highly derivative (from T. S. Eliot) verse.

Tall and gangling, hunched, with a likable, goofy smile, thick red hair and weak green eyes, he was still jobless and living at home on the autumn afternoon in 1939 when a strapping young second-grade teacher named Ruth Zellerman sat next to him on the A train. Her russet hair bristled with energy; her sharp eyes took him in with a single glance. She stuck her nose into the book he was reading (Hegel, as it happened) and demanded an explanation. When they reached her stop, she said, "Come," and Meyer went. She took him in hand as if he were one of her pupils. The following March, they were married.

Ruth's father, though a good deal less taken with Meyer than was Ruth, gave him a job in the family real estate business and helped the young couple establish themselves in a roomy, dilapidated brownstone off West End Avenue. Ruth continued to teach; Meyer, after reading up thoroughly on salesmanship (he had no snobbery when it came to knowledge and was willing to learn anything), turned over a surprising amount of real estate.

Then came the war. Meyer, who had learned a little Japanese to pursue an interest in haiku, was sent to Alaska as a radio intelligence operator. On a frozen mountaintop, he and a handful of others listened for enemy message traffic. The cold, the long stretches of dark and light, the isolation seemed to agree with him: He wrote a monograph detailing a complex theory of atonal music and completed another book of poetry. Ruth, meanwhile, moved back in with her parents and organized a citywide network of soldiers' wives who pitched war bonds at movie theaters. In three years, they had one leave together. Mark was the result.

After the war, the little family installed itself again in the brownstone off West End Avenue. Any plans Ruth had to return to teaching were superseded by Charlotte's arrival. Meyer resumed his career in real estate as well as his more esoteric pursuits. His interest in atonal music gave way to a passion for philosophy (especially Schopenhauer), which in turn was succeeded by an obsession with psychology (especially Jung). This was followed by theosophy (Gurdjieff, via Ouspensky) and linguistics (Chomsky). His real estate career was pushed more or less into his spare time; his hours with his wife and children were increasingly abbreviated. When he did see them he was often exuberantly playful, a wild and inspired roughhouser with the youngest children. As they grew older, he took to preparing brief lessons on subjects he thought might intrigue them — techniques of calligraphy was one Sunny remembered, papermaking another. He was useless as regarded father-son softball games, moral instruction (at least in any usual sense), household repairs, domestic bookkeeping, discipline. But Ruth saw to these. Meyer's brilliance thrilled her, and she thrived in the vacuum created by his benign neglect. She bought the house in Audubon, learned carpentry and plumbing, laid tile in the kitchen, sewed curtains, hooked rugs. In the city, she took up causes and went on having babies. The family shambled forward, a bit peculiar maybe, but protective of the erratic scholar in their midst.

Then, in late April of the year Mark was nineteen and Mimi three, Meyer, who had never before shown the slightest interest in another woman, met and fell in love with an apartment-hunting twenty-three-year-old from Belfast named Sheila Cassidy. A week later, he left Ruth, moved out of the crumbling brownstone and, with Sheila, set up housekeeping in a fourth-floor walk-up on York Avenue. He asked for a divorce, which Ruth was too proud to refuse, and permission to see the younger children two at a time on Sundays. (Mark was already at Dartmouth.)

That October, Sheila committed suicide.

Sunny, who was ten then, was still not clear as to why Sheila had done this. They had met only three or four times. Sunny remembered an earth-mothery sort of woman with a loud laugh, wild black hair and a rashlike patch of red on either cheek. She had a vague idea that Sheila's Catholic conscience had driven her to it, that she couldn't bear being the cause of a divorce and killed herself (but how Catholic was that?) so Meyer could go back to Ruth. If this was her aim, she failed. He never asked to come back; and if he had, Ruth would have had nothing to do with him. With her father's help, she had already moved the children into smaller quarters on Seventy-second Street and started teaching school again.

As for Meyer, before the year was out, he abandoned the East Side walk-up and left New York for Europe. Over the next two and a half years, he was nothing more to the family than an occasional textless postcard with "Meyer" scrawled across it. Then, around 1966, he phoned. He was in San Francisco, working as a sales rep for a zipper manufacturer. There followed two or three years of occasional phone calls and a flurry of child-support checks. He changed jobs often: He managed a juice bar, proofread for a company that compiled professional directories. His intellectual interests also changed. He had adopted a macrobiotic diet, he told Sunny; maybe she'd like to try it? He had become a Zen Buddhist; it was a discipline Ira might find interesting. He was reading the cabala in Hebrew; was Mimi learning Hebrew? The child-support checks arrived less and less frequently, then dried up altogether.

By the end of the sixties, he had dropped completely out of sight. Years afterwards, the family learned he had joined a commune outside Eugene, Oregon. In the early seventies, Ruth heard through a colleague who had moved west that he was living in Seattle with a very young woman and their infant child. By the time of Ruth's death, he had founded an alternative school in rural Idaho based on the principles of a forgotten nineteenth-century French educator. A year or two after this failed, he paid a round of visits to those of his and Ruth's children who would see him (Charlotte refused). It was the first time they had set eyes on him since 1963.

Sunny had her visit in the lobby of the Algonquin Hotel, a site she chose — she was twenty-four — for its literary associations. She was already working as a reporter for *The Village Voice*, albeit on the lowest possible level, an achievement of which she was extremely proud. But Meyer, now steeped in Maoist Communism, only teased her about it. What was the difference between the *Voice* and *The Wall Street Journal*? Both were marketing tools, both servants of capitalism. He called the celebrated Round Table wits "bourgeois literary mosquitoes," referred to the mainstream press as dupes and lackeys and described most news reporting as "the telling of practically nothing about something that almost didn't happen," a formulation Sunny's then-boyfriend swore he had heard somewhere before but could never trace. Meyer refused to understand how coveted Sunny's job was, what an accomplishment it had been for her to land it. He was still skinny, gangling. His green eyes blinked at her from behind glasses that threw back her own reflection, just as she remembered (though she recalled tortoiseshell and these were wire-rims). But he had painfully embarrassing manners. He ordered tea, then slopped the wet bag onto the tabletop. He scooped a handful of sugar cubes into his pocket. He was interested only in discussing the desperate poverty of Latin American peasants, and the racism practiced against them since colonial times. When she asked him why he had abandoned his children, he shrugged and laughed, as if she had asked what he had for breakfast on March 1, 1951, or what had become of the yarmulke he wore at his bar mitzvah — as if the question were by its very nature preposterous beyond asking.

When they parted, he kissed her and advised her to quit journalism and find an honest job. A few weeks later, she, Mark and Charlotte received letters from him soliciting contributions for a new political party to function as U.S. support for a group of Peruvian guerrillas. Since then, neither she nor her siblings had heard from him at all.

Little as he had had to do with her after age ten, Meyer had left his mark on Sunny's life — indeed, on the lives of all his children, which at the very least were forever divided into Before and After. For Mark and Charlotte, the two phases had much to do with money. Before Meyer left, neither had given much thought to the cost of a college education; afterwards, Mark was obliged to leave Dartmouth and make his way through CCNY and Brooklyn Law on loans from his grandfather, scholarships and, eventually, Claire's earnings. It took Charlotte far longer than she expected to get through school. First she waitressed in L.A. until she'd established California residency, then cocktail-waitressed herself through college and into med school. And she became a dermatologist rather than a surgeon.

For Ira, Before and After had mainly to do with Ruth, who never married again. Ira was thirteen when Meyer took off, and with Charlotte and Mark out of the house, he was both the oldest child left and the only male. Too young to have more than a few shadowy memories of her father, Mimi nevertheless drew the lesson that the props could be pulled out from under your world at any moment. Sunny, among many other consequences, retained an unsettling sense of having grown up in two families, the first large and comfortable, the second small and edgy.

When they had all been silent a long moment, "Fucking hell," Charlotte said. "You're right. Twenty-eight years. Fancy. Listen, Mark, remind me exactly how this touching reunion came about? A hospital in Denver called you?"

"A guy named Tom McBride called. From Boulder, actually, a little over a week ago. He owns some kind of New Age bookstore there, where Meyer had been — well, half employed, half hanging out, from what I could gather. He also slept in the stockroom most of last year. This guy Tom — he seems very nice — he explained that Meyer had —"

Mark hesitated.

"Acute myeloblastic leukemia," Charlotte supplied, cutting off Claire, who had begun to say the same thing.

" — and that he'd already had a couple of rounds of chemotherapy last spring, and a remission. But a couple of months ago, he got sick again and was admitted for another course of chemo. He responded at first, but then relapsed again. Tom and his wife had taken him in to live with them in their house. But they have young kids, and with the prognosis as bad as it is, they just didn't want to be responsible for him till the — indefinitely," Mark finished, after a momentary pause.

"And how did this Tom McBride know where to find you?" asked Charlotte.

"Evidently, Meyer had mentioned spending summers in Audubon. Tom just gambled fifty cents, called information and asked for Ginzburg."

"Then Meyer must have talked about having family in the East?" Sunny's voice came out a barely audible squeak, something that happened to her now and then if she was nervous. Embarrassed, she cleared her throat.

"I guess. To be honest, I didn't want to go into it in detail with a stranger. But it sounded like he talked about us pretty openly. Pretty . . . affectionately."

"I don't suppose Tom had a guess why Meyer didn't call us himself, in that case," said Charlotte.

Unconscious of the action, Mark began to wind the end of his cheese straw into his feathery hair. "From what Meyer himself has told me, he was worried we wouldn't want to hear from him. Especially since he's so . . ." His words trailed off.

"So . . . almost dead?" suggested Charlotte.

"Charlotte," Mimi said, glaring, her normally husky voice tight with reproach.

Charlotte glared back, unfazed.

"So sick," said Claire.

Charlotte set down her Perrier and leaned forward, elbows on her knees. "Sick is one thing. Meyer is a seventy-four-year-old man who is in the final stages of acute leukemia. Let's keep the facts straight, shall we? He'll be lucky to last the week."

"Charlotte," Mimi finally dared to say, "if you don't have any love for him, you could at least have some respect. He is our fa-fa — "

"Father," Charlotte finished.

"Don't fill in her words for her," Sunny said mechanically. They were all supposed to know finishing for Mimi made her stammer worse.

"Yes, our father, after all," Mimi finished.

"And what a father," said Charlotte. "A foxhole father, should we call him? Drops out of sight for a decade or three, gets to death's door, then offers us the dregs of his life. Dad of the year, I'd say."

"You could still be more comp-comp — "

"Composed? Compact? Compliant? Com — "

"Compassionate."

Charlotte's eyes narrowed. "Don't talk about what you don't know about," she said.

Mark was staring at the fireplace. "To be honest, I'm not sure I would have asked him here. I would have sent him money, no question. But . . . it was Claire who wanted to have him come."

"Naturally," said Charlotte.

"What does that mean?" Claire partly uncurled herself.

Charlotte is a knife, Mimi suddenly thought. Claire is a spoon.

The jarring shriek of Meyer's bell made them all jump in their seats.

"Tell you what." Claire rose. "Give me five minutes to tidy him up. Then I'll come down and the four of you go up and then tell me what you would have done if Tom McBride had called you. We can eat dinner afterwards."

She disappeared into the front hall. Mark tossed his cheese straw into the flames. Sunny rubbed her foot against Anatole's, a gesture he understood as a silent plea that he go up too. Mimi and Charlotte avoided noticing each other. Ira closed his eyes and listened to the fire.

# THREE

Sunny searched the bottom of her glass for any remains of vodka tonic. Her head throbbed. "Wow. Wow, ow, ow," she said. "My eyes hurt."

She planted her elbows on her knees and clutched her head in both hands. Anatole, beside her, reached over to massage the nape of her neck. He had stayed downstairs in spite of her unspoken request, as had Mark and Claire, while the others trooped up, Charlotte scornfully in the lead. Meyer had been installed in what was once Mark and Ira's room, the one with the three casement windows; Claire had propped him up against a couple of pillows in the old walnut bed with carved pineapples on its posts.

Sunny hadn't been in this room in years. She wasn't sure if her immediate, breathless claustrophobia came from the half-forgotten low ceiling, or the suffocating memories that seemed to fly at her from every corner, or the shock of seeing Meyer himself. Though she wasn't really able to see him, not yet. What she saw was his condition — the papery, ashen skin, the sunken temples, the looming, hairless skull. The overhead light threw a knife of black shadow across his upper lip, and his glazed green eyes stared out from wells of darkness.

As his children shuffled around the bed, he reached a frail hand to the nightstand and, fumbling a little, put his glasses on. Slowly, barely focused, his eyes moved from Charlotte's face to Ira's, then finally rested on Sunny's. For a moment, she wasn't sure he recognized her. She gazed back, working to keep what she felt from showing in her expression, not daring to attempt a smile. At last, he gave her a tiny nod. His eyes moved on to Mimi. The instant of relief Sunny felt was followed by a lurch of anger at Claire. She, or Mark for that matter, could have prepared them better.

For the next five minutes — all any of them could manage, as it turned out — Sunny could hardly keep her mind on what was being said. Most of her energy was spent resisting the impulse to run from the room. She and her siblings stood like four dolts in a windstorm, buffeted helplessly by clashing gusts of ancient emotion. After what seemed ages, they began as if by common consent to mumble to one another that Meyer must be tired. They left, Sunny first, and staggered down to the living room, where they now slumped in the shabby chairs and couches again.

Mimi looked as if she might throw up.

Ira, dazed, poked at the fire with the tip of his shoe. "He reminds me of this philodendron I forgot to water this summer," he said. "When I finally took it off the hook, it was so light I almost dropped it. Isn't that how he looks? Like he doesn't weigh anything?"

"His eyebrows," Sunny said into her lap. "I forgot he wouldn't have them."

"Did you talk?" asked Claire.

"He was like one of those guys you try not to see in the hospital bed next to your friend who got hit by a bicycle," Ira went on, addressing the fire. "One of those anonymous guys in all the rooms along the hall that aren't the room you're looking for."

"Didn't you say anything to him?" Claire was filled with a strange mixture of contempt, empathy and satisfaction. Even Charlotte, who must have known what to expect, seemed thrown.

"Yes, eventually. We said hello and he said hello," Sunny answered, looking up. "He put on his glasses and asked us how we were and we all muttered that we were fine. Then we stood around some more until Mimi asked him how he was and he said he could be worse."

After a moment, she added, "You should have told us." As she said it, she realized how disconcerted she had been by his voice. That was one aspect of him she did remember clearly — a reedy, slightly nasal tenor that always reminded her of resin. Now it was gone, replaced by a breathy, dry-leaf sound. She wondered whether that was age or illness.

"I did tell you."

"I can't believe that's Meyer." Having seen her father only once since she was four, Mimi had formed her idea of what he looked like mainly from thirty-year-old photographs.

"That's all anybody said?"

"He mentioned today is the anniversary of the battle of Agincourt. St. Crispin's Day," Ira told her. "I think we were a little too much for him, all of us standing around him at once. From now on, we should go up separately."

"He said all our names," added Mimi, trying to sound enthusiastic. No one had used her full name, Miriam, since grade school. Not to mention calling Sunny Sonia.

"Yes, it was a real Kodak moment," Charlotte said. She was so much older than Mimi that she hardly knew her; what little she did know, she didn't think much of. "We all knew each other's names. Almost."

"Why are you so bit-bit-angry, Charlotte?" Mimi demanded. "What did Meyer do to you?"

"Claire, I think we should feed these people." Mark stood up. "Charlotte, come help me pick out some wine, would you?"

Though she had been about to reply, Charlotte followed him from the room, her fists jammed into the pockets of her jumpsuit. Claire went too.

When they were out of earshot, Mimi looked around at the others. "What did he do to her?" she asked.

Ira shrugged and sat again in his armchair.

"The crystal ball is clouding over," Sunny said. "Cross her palm with silver and ask again."

"Was he different to her than everyone else?" Mimi persisted.

More shrugs.

"Gosh if I know. So Meyer's in a bad way?" Anatole asked.

"Public education's in a bad way. Network television's in a bad way. Meyer — " Mimi broke off and shuddered.

"Hey, that's pretty good, Mims." Ira tossed a balled up cocktail napkin at her. "You've been honing your wit."

Unenthusiastically fielding the crumpled napkin, "Thanks a lot," Mimi said. "Would you be kind enough not to throw gar-gar-litter at me?"

"My, my, what a fancy lady," Anatole said. "Now she doesn't want litter thrown at her. What will it be next? Don't dip me in the diaper pail? Fresh Kleenex only, please?"

"How come you're here, Anatole?" Mimi asked. "I thought you were starring in something, or something."

"As a matter of fact, since you ask, I am supposed to be appearing in the fifty-eighth regular performance of *Crushed Velvet.*" He consulted his watch. "In approximately half an hour, eight hundred people are going to be pissed as hell at me, trying to decide if they want their money back or if — since they've already paid for a baby-sitter and dinner out and the tunnel and parking — they'll just go ahead and see it without me."

He jumped up.

"'That arrogant so-and-so,' the men will say," he growled in a voice full of gravel. "'Probably shtupping some chorus boy in a Plaza suite while we hoi polloi eat his dust. Imagine paying forty-five bucks a pop for the chance to see Peter Never-heard-of-him play Broadway for the first and last time.'

"'Now, Morton,' their wives will answer — or George, or Howie — " He assumed the mien of a gently chiding woman. "'I'm sure Anatole Bronski wouldn't miss a performance unless there was some really good reason. He must be ill, like it says on that insert in the program. There is a terrible flu going around.' And, though disappointed themselves, these gallant ladies will vote in favor of giving Peter Whosit a try.

"'He might be terrific!' they'll point out (inaccurately). And they'll add (also inaccurately), 'This is how a lot of Broadway stars get their first big break.'"

Anatole hopped to his left, grew eight inches and peered down. "'As usual, Irene, you don't have any idea what you're talking about.' (Mort grudgingly shows the nearsighted ush-erette the tickets.) 'You've seen *42nd Street* too often, that's all.'

"'Oh, *42nd Street*,' cries Irene. She — "

"You'll just have to break in if you ever want to talk again," Sunny advised Mimi. "He could do this from now till Wednesday. Too many improv classes."

"I think it's won — terrific."

"It is terrific. Of its kind."

"And then they'll go in and sit down in their too-narrow seats with no leg room, with their too-heavy coats crumpled up underneath them," Anatole went on, "and be disappointed that *Crushed Velvet*, a searing drama about the disintegration of a marriage, doesn't have any singing or dancing in it. And at intermission, they'll agree that next time they'll go see *Cats* again. 'Like Morty said we should in the first place.'"

"Anatole wasn't sure if he wanted to come here today," explained Sunny. "On the one hand, his wife's father was dying. On the other, there were eight hundred suburbanites . . ."

"Thank you for that generous and revealing exploration of my dilemma."

"Couldn't you at least have done tonight's show and then come up tomorrow?" Mimi suggested.

"Some thought that would have been adequate," Anatole said.

"He's only missing two shows." Sunny stirred the watery remnants of her husband's manhattan with her index finger. "He'll be back in time for Sunday's matinee; it doesn't start till three. Anyway, there were other factors. We found out today — "

"Sunny, let's not get into that now."

"Well, we might as well say." She drank up. "If we're going to ad — "

"No," Anatole cut her off. Besides his own unhappiness and shame, he knew that the more public Sunny made an issue, the less likely she was to change her position on it. "Not yet."

"Oh, come on, tell," said Ira, who knew.

"Tell," Mimi echoed, and complained, "Everyone has so many secrets."

"Tell us your secrets, Ira," Anatole invited. He sat down again. "And yours, Mims. Mims, you tell us Ira's secrets. Ira, you tell us — "

"I think I'll set the table." Mimi stretched her legs out and flexed her feet. She stood a little unsteadily and started across the front hall. At the same moment, Claire came into the hall from the opposite direction and announced that dinner was ready when they were. Would someone run and tell Charlotte? She'd gone upstairs to phone home.

"Charlotte, dinner!" Mimi bellowed up the stairs, then trailed Claire to the sideboard, distractedly singing a line from "St. James Infirmary": "Let him go, let him go, God bless him . . ."

Hearing her from the living room, Sunny pulled Anatole up from the couch and into the hall after her, leaving Ira alone.

"Can't you get her a job?" she murmured urgently. Sunny was convinced Anatole could get Mimi work if he tried; the fact that he had tried, often, weighed little with her. "She's so good."

He nodded. A jealous flicker leapt in his chest. Sunny was to praise him. "True," he agreed. They hovered near the newel post, listening. "She needs to lose some weight, though. She's gotten downright chunky."

"She's pregnant, you dope." Immediately, Sunny clapped a warning hand over his mouth. "Don't say anything. I don't think anyone knows."

"How do you?"

On the landing above them, Charlotte's feet came into view.

"I don't."

The feet began to descend.

"I mean, I'm sure of it, but nobody told me."

"You have pregnancy on the brain," said Anatole into her ear.

"If only people could get babies that way."

Anatole wrapped his enormous hands around her shoulders and kissed the auburn top of her head. She fell against him a little, closing her eyes.

"Marriage becomes you," said Charlotte, reaching the bottom step.

"I love being married," Sunny said into Anatole's shirt. She could smell the cologne he insisted on wearing and, beneath that, the skin-and-sweat smell she preferred. "Was Meyer awake?"

"Didn't look," said Charlotte.

Sunny didn't believe her, but she was enjoying hugging Anatole too much to search her face.

Mimi skipped in from the dining room. She curtsied. "Dinner is served," she said, and went on to the living room to fetch Ira.

Sunny released Anatole and turned to smile at Charlotte.

"Have you always had that mole?" Charlotte gently touched a long finger to the left side of Sunny's neck, just behind her jawbone.

Sunny's hand flew instinctively to touch it herself, though she knew perfectly well what it was. She thought of it as a beauty spot. "Yes."

"Was it always so thick?"

Sunny pressed it anxiously. "I think so."

Charlotte said, "Hmm," in a quiet, doctorly way. "Keep an eye on it. Have your dermatologist take a look."

Sunny, who had no dermatologist, said she would, and the threesome drifted to the table. They sat, Sunny to the left of Claire's traditional place closest to the kitchen, Charlotte and Anatole opposite her. The mahogany table had been covered with a lacy cloth and set with Claire and Mark's good china (Spode, Sunny confirmed, checking under her plate). Ira came in and sat at what would be Mark's left elbow, Mimi at Mark's right. Reflexively, Sunny edged her chair a little away from Mimi. She liked best to eat alone, though she would never have admitted it. It was an animal instinct. Food should be consumed where others couldn't get it.

Claire came through the swinging door, an enormous lump

of meat steaming before her. Hurriedly, Ira and Mimi slid wineglasses and salt aside so she could set it down at Mark's end of the table. Mimi leaned over to inhale the rising vapor. Sunny's nose sent an unauthorized report to her brain that something good to eat was near.

"First dibs on the mid - mid — No, one of the outside ribs, I like those better," said Mimi.

Mark came in with a bottle of wine and began to circle the table. Claire whisked in and out, fetching vegetables and potatoes. Ira pushed his chair back and relieved his brother of the bottle. "You carve," he said.

Mark raised the shining knife. "Sunny? Rare or well?"

"Actually, neither. I've stopped eating red meat." She gave Claire a glance in which apology and defiance mingled. "Sorry."

Claire, just setting down the gravy boat, smiled her annoyance and offered to rustle up something else.

"No, thanks. My spuds and brussels sprouts shall be my company," said Sunny, "on them to look and nibble by myself."

"Hark, Ginzburgers! thou mayst hear Minerva speak," said Anatole. *"Taming of the Shrew,"* he added, by way of explanation, as he and Sunny exchanged pleased bows across the table. "I had to add the -*er* to Ginzburg to keep the meter."

"I guess these days you really should ask people if they eat meat before you cook for them," said Claire, finally sitting down. "Sorry. We're a little out of the loop up here."

"It's true. In Manhattan at least, the burden of proof has shifted to the meat eater. Like the smoker." Ira sent his plate toward his brother. "Medium rare, please. This will be my first roast beef since — cripes, I really couldn't say when."

Mark neatly lifted a slice from the platter onto the proffered plate. "You can't imagine what a joy it is not to have to care what people are doing in the city," he said. "Isn't that true,

Claire? *New York* magazine is like an anthropological text to us. Sometimes we laugh about it all day long."

"Sometimes we do, too," said Sunny, while Claire nodded.

"I should think you'd go out of your minds with boredom up here." Charlotte handed Anatole's plate to Mark, while Anatole pointed at Ira to indicate that that was what he wanted, too. "What on earth do you do in Audubon month after month?"

"What do we do? What don't we do?" said Mark, cutting Anatole's slice, then laying down the fork and carving knife at last, and digging in. "When a man is tired of Audubon, he is tired of life. Rolls, please."

"No, really, what do you do?" asked Sunny. "I don't mean that sarcastically. We're curious."

Mark and Claire exchanged glances down the length of the table. "Well, let's see. What would we normally have planned for tomorrow, for example? Two Saturdays ago, we went to a pancake breakfast at the VFW. On the way home, we stopped at a house in Roscoe to see if we wanted to buy a corner cupboard they advertised in the Pennysaver. Then we got started on the storm windows. And that night . . ." Mark wrinkled his freckly forehead, trying to remember. "I think that was the night we rented *The Naked Gun*. That was a pretty typical day, don't you think?"

"Pretty typical. And the next day I took an eight-mile run. I try to do that on Sundays."

"And I started reading *The Rise and Fall of the Great Powers*," Mark took up. "And that afternoon, we saw a litter of kittens being born in the back of Lacey's Market. They invited everyone in the store to go back and watch. So you see, we really live very eventful lives."

"Poor cat," said Sunny. "An audience."

"She didn't seem to mind."

"Oh, why didn't you take one of the kit-kit —"

"They're only two weeks old," Mark reminded Mimi quietly. "We might, when they're ready."

"Pancake breakfasts," intoned Anatole, jumping in diplomatically, "impress us. They are wonders of nature. Kittens, however, are another matter. Kittens are born every day, even in New York City."

"Yes. Think of Mehitabel," Ira said.

"Mehitabel!" Sunny dropped her fork. " '*Toujours gai*, Archy,' " she quoted. " 'Always jolly, always game and, thank God, always a lady!' "

" 'Always the life of the party, Archy — but never anything vulgar!' " Charlotte took up, laughing so hard she seemed in danger of snorting a rivulet of wine out of her nose. " '*Jamais triste*, Archy, *jamais triste.*' "

"Mehitabel!" shrieked Sunny. "What a great role model!"

"Remember Archy's interview with the mummy at the Met?" Ira looked to Mark, who immediately recited with him, " 'Little fussy face, I am as dry as the heart of a sandstorm at high noon in hell,' " and dissolved with the others into shouted laughter.

Mimi, who had been too young to take part in the family craze for *archy and mehitabel*, had no idea what the others were quoting (they did seem to be quoting something — something like *Rocky and Bullwinkle*, she thought dimly). She sat torn between wanting to laugh with them anyway and feeling that such a course would be cowardly. She often failed to understand what her siblings laughed about, especially when they got into a riff like this, but she hated to sit unsmiling, looking stupid. In her opinion, as a matter of fact, she wasn't stupid. Jesse said her brains were in her heart, but her own impression was that she took in information through her skin. Brain-information, the kind her brothers and sisters constantly exchanged, came through to her only as muffled noise.

She looked up the table to see if Claire was in on the joke.

From her half smile, Mimi guessed not. But Claire didn't resent being left out; that was the difference between them. Claire had been to college, even if it was only to study nursing, and she could sometimes quote books or play with words almost as well as Mark and the rest of them. Mimi hadn't gone to college at all. After Ruth died, Mark and Claire had taken her in while she finished high school; they offered to help her with tuition, but as soon as she graduated, she shot right back to the city to start her singing career.

She contemplated asking who the hell Mehitabel (if that was the name) might be but decided to let it go. At least their laughter gave her a convenient moment to eat more roast beef, something she desperately wanted to do. Furtively, she slipped two mauve slices from the platter to her plate. Pregnancy was making her ravenous.

"So what's Ted like, Charlotte?" she heard Claire ask as the joking finally wound down. "Are we going to get to meet him?"

"Oh, gee!" Charlotte put a brussels sprout in her mouth and chewed thoughtfully. The idea of introducing Ted to the rest of her family had obviously never occurred to her. "Gosh. I don't know. I mean, you'll meet him sometime. Sure."

"Mark said he's a professor at U.C.?"

"Actually a dean."

Unnoticed, Mimi rolled her eyes.

"Wasn't Alec a dean?" Claire pursued. Alec was Charlotte's first husband, Kyle's father.

"No, he was the chair of the physics department. Ted's assistant dean of admissions. He's much more relaxed than Alec. Very pleasant. Deany, you know. A little bookish. Alec had a lot more testosterone, I think. More Marlon Brandoish."

"Wouldn't that be Brandoesque?" suggested Anatole.

"Brandoid."

"Brandied."

"Whereas Ted's more your Judd Hirsch type, or maybe Gene Wilder. He's pretty funny. He's nice. Frankly, comparing him and Alec feels like one of those wrongheaded term papers I used to write comparing two phenomena that threw absolutely no light on each other. You know, images of illness in Romantic poetry in the context of the history of the microscope. Any two things I happened to be studying in different courses. They're just nothing alike. Ted is nice," she repeated in conclusion.

"Alec wasn't nice?" Mimi heard her own surprised voice ask.

Charlotte snorted. "Are you kidding? He was the world's premier bastard."

"Okay, I'm sorry. I think I was thirteen the only time I really talked to him."

"He was a famous bastard. Is."

"I believe you. Jesus. You people always make me feel so stu — dumb," Mimi suddenly blurted out. "You make me feel like the village idiot."

"You know, I always thought that would be a great name for a coffeehouse on MacDougal Street," Sunny said, after an uncomfortable pause. "The Village Idiot. I can't believe no one's used it."

"What amazes me is how long the phrase has endured. Nobody ever uses the word *idiot* in that sense anymore, or *village* — "

"I want to know why villages had idiots but it was always the town drunk. Didn't towns have idiots?"

"None of you is paying any attention to what I said," Mimi insisted. She had meant her voice to be angry, but it came out as a wail.

"We thought that was a kindness, honey," Sunny told her.

Mimi's pregnancy had made Sunny hate her a little. She hated all pregnant women.

"Nobody's trying to make you feel stupid, Mimi." Mark laid a hand on her upper arm, but she shook it off.

"I realize that." She didn't add, That only makes it worse.

Anatole noticed the way Claire's fork was circling her plate without ever coming in for a landing. He nudged Charlotte with his elbow and began to imitate the gesture to amuse her, at the same time rubbing Claire's ankle with his own, to amuse her. Mimicking other people's mannerisms was second nature to Anatole, who belonged to the school of acting that believes in working from the outside in. (Rubbing women's ankles *was* his nature.) Unfortunately, he was not always in control of his imitations. Twice already since Mimi's arrival he had caught himself stammering, and on the way into the dining room, he noticed he was springing a bit at each step, the way Charlotte did. Moreover, it was Jimmy Damrosch, his character in *Crushed Velvet*, who greeted women with sweeping bows and waves of an imaginary plumed hat.

Claire kicked his foot away and stabbed a chunk of roast beef.

"Doesn't it make you feel weird to have Meyer up there so sick" — Mimi's voice dropped almost to a whisper — "while we're down here talking and eating?"

She had addressed the table generally. At first no one answered. Then Sunny, driven again by envy of her pregnant sister, offered, "It is peculiar, I'll grant you that. It's not what we're used to. Not Anatole and me, anyway. I can't speak for the others."

"I'm not used to it," said Ira, buttering a roll.

"Me either," agreed Charlotte.

At the same time, Anatole incautiously switched from grazing Claire's foot to nuzzling Charlotte's.

"That better have been an accident, buster," Charlotte said, turning to glare at him.

"Freud said there are no accidents," Sunny put in, also glaring at her husband.

"You're all so — flip," Mimi took up again. "At least, that's how you seem to me. He's our father. Doesn't anybody feel anything for him?" Momentarily forgetting that six hours ago she had told him she couldn't understand what he meant by "love" and maybe they were just too different ever to understand each other, she longed for Jesse. At least he acted upset when he was upset.

Sunny, who through the whole week since Mark's call had been fighting the urge to sink into the quicksand of her own father-longing, didn't trust herself to speak again.

After a moment, "Gee, Mimi," Charlotte said, "if you had had the pleasure of actually growing up with Meyer, I think you might feel a lot less conflicted. I personally couldn't care less if he dies upstairs or in Boulder, or of leukemia or a bullet to the head, or in two days or in two years. How's that for feeling?"

"How can you say that? Why are you even here then?"

"Curiosity." Charlotte signaled to Ira to pass the rolls. "Plus I'm planning to see the Futurist show at the Modern. It isn't coming to L.A. I'm sorry if that strikes you as subsentimental."

Mimi pushed her plate away as if she were too disgusted to eat, a gesture that would have been more effective if she hadn't already downed three slabs of meat and gnawed a rib clean. "Can you imagine Kyle saying that about you one day?" she asked.

"Certainly not. I'm a good parent. I can imagine him saying it about Alec, however. Although Alec would never impose his death on Kyle. He's too Waspy."

"What did Meyer *do* to you, Charlotte?" Mimi demanded

for the second time. She put a hand out to Mark. "And don't say it's time for dessert, Mark. Let her answer."

"It's really not that mysterious," Charlotte began. "If you've ever watched Oprah. Or Donahue. Maybe Oprah and Donahue." Ignoring the deep flush flooding up her neck, she went on, "He used to touch me, okay? That's what."

"Piffle," said Mark immediately, while the others stared.

"'Piffle' my ass. How would you know?"

"Meyer? When did he 'touch' you?" Mark threw his napkin onto the table and pushed his chair back as if he were going to stand. "Give one instance."

"I don't want to give one instance," said Charlotte. The scarlet slowly began to drain from her severe, freckled face. "I don't want to talk about it anymore."

"Hit-and-run slander. That's very nice. Anyone else you'd care to defame before we clear the dishes?"

Sunny was looking openmouthed from her sister to her brother. She'd been told plenty of stories about Meyer's peculiarities, but she had never heard a breath of anything like this. She had always thought the trouble with Meyer was that there had been so little of him. What there was, in her recollection, had been rather fun. She focused her gaze on Ira, willing him to look back at her, but he didn't. He was gaping at Charlotte too.

Profiting by the general distraction, Anatole leaned over to Claire's ear. "Wow. Great party," he whispered. He was about to straighten when he changed his mind and kissed her ear. Claire batted him away.

"Slander is when you accuse someone of something they didn't do," said Charlotte, after a pause. "I assure you, Meyer did this. And before I drop the subject altogether, I'd like to add that Ruth of blessed memory was no angel either. She knew exactly what was going on with Meyer and me, and she pretended not to. Even when I confronted her directly, she pretended not to."

"Ruth?" Mimi's eyes widened. Her mouth remained open, ready to deny it.

"Yes, Ruth. I buried the recollection for years, but it came back to me. Meyer the liar. Thank God he left the house before you were twelve, Sunny. That's when he started with me."

Dazed, Sunny echoed, "Thank God." She finally caught Ira's eye, but he looked as baffled as she felt.

"Well, on that note," Claire said after half a minute of silence, "I think we can safely declare dinner adjourned. Why don't you all go into the living room and I'll bring the coffee in there."

Everyone stood and began to drift from the table. Ira and Charlotte helped clear plates; Mark caught Claire as she came around to collect what remained of the roast.

"Sorry dinner ended up this way," he murmured. He stroked her nose with his index finger, a favorite caress. "I know you went to trouble."

"Yes, sorry." From the other end of the table, Charlotte spoke, though she knew she had not been meant to hear him. With an ease learned in her waitressing days, she picked up her own plate and three others and stalked into the kitchen, adding, "So unpleasant," as she went through the door. Inside, Ira was already noisily scraping plates into the garbage. "Bringing up incest at supper," she continued to mutter. "So déclassé."

"She's really very kind," Ira said, straightening to take the dishes she carried. He had been frantically searching his memory for any hint that what Charlotte said could have been true. "And she's been good to Mark. You don't like her because she's conventional, but that's just what he does like."

"No, what he likes is being able to pretend he grew up in a nice big family with basically regular parents, and now he and Claire have a nice little family and are basically regular parents and everything's peachy keen. And she isn't just conventional, she's — "

"Sh." Claire came into the room, and Ira loudly asked her whether the dishes in the washer were clean.

# FOUR

Sunny and Mimi huddled together on the camelback sofa in the living room. They were alone for the moment; Anatole, on a blunt hint from his wife, had announced his desire to go upstairs and unpack. The fire Mark had lit before dinner still burned smoothly, though it was low.

"Do you believe her?" Mimi asked.

Sunny thoughtfully chewed the inside of her cheek. "I believe she believes it. On the other hand, incest is sort of in vogue lately. Not doing it, I mean; remembering it was done to you. And Charlotte can be awfully trendy."

She swung her feet up onto the table and wedged them among the magazines. "She's been through everything, you know — est, Rolfing, Reichian therapy, transactional analysis, behavior modification. Not that I'm against therapy, of course. If it wasn't for psychotherapy, Anatole would be curled up in a closet convinced an evil force wants him dead." She paused for a moment, comparing what she remembered of Meyer with what she knew of Charlotte, then concluded, "No. It's too perfect."

Mimi said, "That's what I think. I think it couldn't be true.

Why would she have moved to the state he lived in, if it was?"

"Well, he didn't live there then," Sunny felt obliged to point out. "He was in Europe when she went west."

"Oh." Mimi took a handful of hair from behind her head and began to twist it. "But still, Ruth would never have ignored something like that."

Sunny knew Mimi was hoping for a confirmation of this sensible hypothesis, but she couldn't offer one. The fact was, Ruth had had amazing powers of denial. She knew when Ira was strung out on dope, but she never acknowledged it, never helped him. She knew Sunny had been wrecked by her father's departure but insisted on the cheerful fiction that "Sunny and Mimi, luckily, were too young to be affected." For years she told people Charlotte was only in California because UCLA offered such a great program, ignoring the half dozen local universities that would have done just as well — ignoring that Charlotte had deliberately gone as far away from her childhood as she could and would never return. When Mark, strapped with school debts, dropped his ambition to do civil rights work — his only motive for going to law school — and instead specialized in insurance law, Ruth accepted it as if that had been his plan all along. Who could say what else she might have pretended not to know?

Sunny looked at her little sister, her wide mouth, her creamy skin, the slight plumpness just starting to develop under her jaw. She was wearing a flowing patchwork skirt made of bits of embroidered velvet and satin, a typical Mimi garment, fanciful, a little like dress-up. A faint, warm scent of vanilla rose from her. Mimi was given to wearing heavy, sweet essences: gardenia, frangipani, orange blossom. Sunny felt a rush of tenderness. "When are you due?" she asked.

"What?"

"The baby."

"I can't believe you can tell that. How can you tell that? It's not even two months." Exasperated, Mimi dropped the twisted lock of hair to push her hands against her abdomen and pull at her skirt.

"It's not your middle, it's your — I don't exactly know what. Is it Jesse's?"

"No, it's the landlord's. He gave me a break on the September rent."

"I hope you're going to keep it. Don't not keep it, Mims."

"Really?" Mimi sat up straighter, peering at her. "You're the last person in the world I'd have expected to hear that from."

"Am I?"

"After Mark, anyway. I thought you'd say I wasn't settled enough to raise a child. And that I can't afford a baby. Which happens to be true. I would have to marry Jesse."

Thirteen years after she flounced out of Larchmont High School to launch her singing career, Mimi still lived in the same railroad flat on Carmine Street. In the last two years, with Jesse Fabrizio managing her career, she had actually recorded an album on a tiny independent label and reached a point where she usually had some kind of singing job one week out of the month. But the power of Jesse's quasi-mystical soft sell had its limits, and the album had never found a distributor. The bulk of Mimi's income still came from waitressing.

From time to time, Sunny or Mark had sounded her out about dropping music and starting a different career, but the truth was, she didn't know how to do anything but sing and wait tables. What she made from that barely paid her bills. Sunny had never seen her in a new dress that wasn't a gift from someone. When they had dinner together, Sunny always tactfully made a preemptive grab for the check.

Inevitably, the idea that she and Anatole could adopt Mimi's baby now entered Sunny's mind. She told herself the thought had indeed been inevitable even as she cringed at the pure acquisitiveness of it.

Although, on the other hand, all kinds of people were raised by their aunts and uncles or grandparents. It was thought to be a kindness.

Except those were usually teenagers' babies. Mimi was a grown-up. She would trot in and out, giving advice and making up rules about their child on the ground that she had borne him. Or her. Telling the kid she was the real mother.

Sunny wondered what a child of Jesse Fabrizio would look like. Not bad. Not bad at all, if it got Mimi's height and hair.

"So marry him," she said. "He's solvent, isn't he?" Jesse was a cabinetmaker with a small business of his own; he managed Mimi's career on the side. "Or doesn't he want to?"

Mimi was prevented from answering by the arrival of Mark, bearing a tray loaded with mugs and carafes.

"Coffee mit caffeine," he offered. "Coffee mitout caffeine. Tea avec caffeine. Tea minus caffeine."

"They all sound so good," said Mimi. "A little of each, please; just mix them together."

"That's pretty amusing, Mimi," Ira pronounced, coming in behind Mark with a plateful of oatmeal cookies. He set them down next to the cheese straws, which no one had thought to remove. "Very good."

"'Very good, Mimi.' 'Very amusing, Mimi,'" said Mimi, patting herself on the head. "Anyone would think I was a cocker spaniel."

"I didn't say it was very amusing, I said it was pretty amusing," said Ira. At the same moment, Mark said, "Don't be silly, Mimi. If you're anything, you're a Bernese mountain dog."

"Oh, that reminds me of something!" Sunny grabbed Mimi's arm and pulled her up from the couch. "Come upstairs a minute."

Uncertainly, Mimi went with her, leaving the men behind. On their way through the front hall, they passed Claire and Charlotte heading into the living room. Anatole would be in Sunny's room. She dragged Mimi through the door nearest the landing — June's, from the decor, but Charlotte's once upon a time. Now Charlotte's overnight case gaped in a corner and a skinny red dress in her style garlanded a chair.

"What?" Mimi looked around, perplexed.

Sunny sat her down on the quilt-covered bed. She took Mimi's hand — laden with cheap silver rings and tipped with surprisingly intact nails — and began, "Listen, you don't know when you'll ever get pregnant again. You're only thirty — "

"Thirty-one."

" — thirty-one, and you think you can always get pregnant another time. But maybe you can't." And Sunny recounted the tedious, humiliating history of their infertility treatment. Until now, she had told no one except Ira. People would only have called six times a week to ask what was happening, then said stupid, comforting things when the bad news came. But at this point, she saw no reason not to talk about it.

"Poor Sunny," Mimi said at the end. She rubbed Sunny's blue-jeaned leg. "Poor Anatole. They don't have any idea why?"

"Well, they have an *idea*. They know it isn't my tubes and it isn't my hormones and it isn't his so-called sperm motility — evidently he's just popping with feisty spermatozoa. In ten years he'll probably marry some twenty-year-old and have triplets. It's just us together. After a thousand tests, they have enlightened us with the stunning diagnosis of 'unexplained infertility.' Let me translate that for you into layman's terms. It means so far I'm not pregnant."

"Poor Sun. This must wreck your lovemaking."

"Lovemaking!" She laughed. "We don't make love anymore; we mate. So many people have been up my crotch in the past year, I forgot it ever had different nerve endings from my knees." She told herself that was enough, to be quiet; but she had kept her anger bottled up for too long. "A man in a lab coat tells me to go in a little room, strip and lie down — I do it like opening my mouth for the dentist. Anatole is more at home getting off into a cup than into me. Our sex life, and I use the term humorously, is a medical experiment. If it wasn't so fucked up, it would be funny." She sighed, dully aware of a kind of relief. "For all I know, it is funny."

"I'm sorry," said Mimi, at the same time assuring herself she could never, never have fertility problems. She just couldn't.

"But I'm telling you not so you'll pity me but so you don't end up in the same boat. You're pregnant now. Have the baby. We'll help you pay for it," she went on — rather recklessly since, in spite of their considerable income, she and Anatole were currently drowning in medical bills. "Have it first and worry about the money later. If Jesse doesn't want to get married, too bad for him. Have it anyway. Maybe you'll marry him after the baby. Life is long."

Mimi smiled but looked dubious. "As a matter of fact, we just sort of broke up this afternoon. I think. I gave him an ult-ult —"

"Ultimatum." Sunny broke down.

"Yes."

"Did you? Poor sweetie." Sunny squeezed her hand. "Was it about the baby?"

"Kind of." She sighed. "He keeps pushing me to get married. But I don't know what he even means by that. His idea of marriage . . ." She stopped and rubbed her forehead. "I'm too tired of talking about it to explain, but it's kind of weird."

Sunny hesitated briefly before asking, "Weird like old-fashioned?" Jesse seemed emancipated enough, but you never knew what lurked behind appearances.

"No, no. The opposite. Weird like not a lot different from not being married."

Sunny considered this. In her experience, not only was marriage different from singleness, it involved a virtual transubstantiation. Her life, her body was no longer hers. She couldn't just say to Anatole, "Look, it's my uterus and my hormones and I've decided not to continue infertility treatment." Or rather, she could say that, but Anatole would have a lot to say back to her.

Another thought occurred to her. "It isn't that he doesn't believe in monogamy?"

"No, nothing like that."

"Or are you worried because of his background? Because he's kind of a different . . . class than we are?"

"A different 'class'?" Mimi was suddenly furious. "Is that what you think about him? This family is unbelievable! *Class.*" Mimi breathed the word so dramatically that for a moment Sunny imagined she was about to break into a musical number. But Mimi merely shook her head and went on. "So Jesse earns his living with his hands. So what do you think I do? I'm a waitress, Sunny. Or do you really mean that he isn't Jewish? Man, for a bunch of supposed-to-be liberals, this family is so prej — so bigoted."

"Sorry," Sunny said.

They sat in a dejected silence. After a while, Mimi muttered, "Forget it."

"If it matters, I was going to say you shouldn't let his — occupation bother you."

"It doesn't bother me."

"Sorry," said Sunny again. She paused, then dared to add, "Or his religion."

"Honestly." Mimi was silent a while. Then, "So, what should we say was the thing you remembered downstairs?" she added.

"The what?"

"Downstairs. Mark said I looked like a Bernese mountain dog, whatever that looks like, and you said, 'Oh, that reminds me of something.'"

"Ah. So I did. Let's say . . . it was an article I clipped about a comic cabaret act."

"Someone might want to read it."

"It turned out I forgot to pack it."

They found Anatole on his way down the stairs, just ahead of them. As they caught up, strains of Country Joe and the Fish, counting and asking what we were fighting for, floated up from the living room.

Meyer Ginzburg lay with his eyes closed, thinking about death. It came toward him now, practically a date on the calendar, like the start of a long-planned journey. He had almost died once before, when a train he was on in '64 derailed outside Cádiz. He recalled most vividly an exhilarating sense of liberation. Lately, he had been reading all he could find about the experience of dying — quite a lot, thanks to Tom McBride's collection. What he had read, he liked. Others who almost died, but didn't, reported all manner of pleasant travel, lights, sensations of wholeness, profound understandings, even encounters with dead relatives. Meyer was not especially eager to be reunited with his clingy, fearful parents, but there were friends dead more recently he would very much like to see. And they might be around still (as his mother and father, both of them gone these forty years, probably would not?), only partly digested by whatever process it was that took over when this life ended.

That he had a personal, immortal soul Meyer was convinced. He could not have said where it had been before it came to be his, or if all humans had them. He was skeptical with regard to reincarnation, which counted such a curious preponderance of former sovereigns among its theorists. If all humans did have souls, he didn't know what other living creatures might be so endowed, how far down the evolutionary chain they went. And about the purpose of the whole system he had no opinion whatever. But that he was in part composed of an entity separate and distinct from "Meyer Ginzburg" — that "Meyer Ginzburg" was only a nickname, an assignment, an interlude for this entity, which would endure long after "Meyer Ginzburg" was gone — of this he was sure.

It wasn't his illness that had brought him to this conviction, though the conviction did make the illness more interesting. Apart from the train wreck, he had had many out-of-body experiences. Zen meditation particularly seemed to have the effect of nudging his — call it a spirit — out on its own. He'd often found himself looking down at the top of "his" head as he floated around just under the ceiling, calmly aware that the silent body below him was a fiction, a little tale that had to be told before a larger drama could go on. Not a digression, because the drama itself proceeded by the telling of such tales. But only one part of a greater whole.

Meyer sighed, suddenly seized by an urge to turn from his side onto his back. He opened his eyes, hoping to distract himself, but all that lay within his nearsighted view was the nightstand, on it a pile of books topped by his folded glasses. Tom had presented him with dozens of books the night before he left, many of them about death and the worlds beyond. On the plane east, he had read three quarters of *The Tibetan Book of the Dead*, which he had somehow missed reading before. He wasn't quite sold on its assertion that you could escape the cycle of death and rebirth by following its precepts. On the same principle as Pascal's wager, however, he planned to give it a shot.

But though the book was beside him, he hadn't been able to finish it. Almost since his arrival, he had felt so exhausted that the moment he opened a book and found the right paragraph, he fell asleep. That was the worst of AML — how weak and light-headed he sometimes felt.

And yet, on the whole, he thought himself lucky in his manner of dying. The treatments had been harrowing, but the disease itself was tolerable. Frustrating, humiliating, but painless. And Ed Agutter, the young doctor from Community General, in Harris, who was overseeing his case now, had promised he could die here. He would not be sent to the hospital, with its imperious hands, its torturing tubes and machines. He hoped he would die conscious, not so drugged for pain that he missed the experience. Mark had reviewed the living will he brought from Colorado and assured him it was valid here.

He closed his eyes again and felt once more the itch to turn onto his back. He hadn't told Mark or Claire, but he felt much weaker today than yesterday. The other four were coming, and he didn't want them greeted with such news. Still, it was a fact.

His mouth twitched as he remembered the expressions on the faces of the new arrivals when they had come up to say hello. He must look even worse than he thought. The baby — Miriam — seemed nothing short of horrified. Well, they had shocked him too: They were all ten or twenty years older than the way he thought of them. Ah well. *Tempora mutantur, nos et mutamur in illis.* Times change, and we with them. Even after a week, he had not fully equated his middle-aged, paunchy host with Mark, his son. A very nice person, Mark, albeit as routine as toast.

Concentrating, Meyer finally pulled himself over onto his back. There were footsteps on the stairs; muffled strains of rock music and an occasional word or two in one of his children's voices floated up to him. He opened his eyes. In the middle of the ceiling above him hung a lamp covered by a globe of milk glass. Claire had turned it out, but it caught a faint gleam from the hallway where the door stood slightly ajar. When he closed his eyes again, the globe appeared in his mind's eye, glowing. It blossomed into a huge snow dome, pristinely pale. From that mushroomed the alabaster roof of Kubla Khan's stately pleasure dome. A drifting cloud passed over it, then over Meyer. That was the way sleep came to him now, like a soft, fat cloud swallowing a mountaintop.

# FIVE

Charlotte and Anatole sat on the cold, rotting steps of the barn, cocktail glasses in their gloved hands. A silver half-moon shone down on them, its brightness obscuring the stars. For a while, Anatole watched moonlight gleam off the shifting ice in Charlotte's vodka.

Then, stealthily, he turned to look at her face. Her stern profile, both like and unlike Sunny's, was softened by the night. The curve of her eye glistened. She seemed to be watching the house. Anatole also had been watching it, though it was too far away to make out more than shapes moving in the yellow windows. Several people had passed into the kitchen, and a minute ago he had seen someone moving upstairs. The flickering fire in the living room made its windows seem to shimmer. High above it, smoke rose from the chimney.

Anatole wondered why Charlotte had agreed to come outside with him. He had invited everyone in the living room for a walk, but only Charlotte accepted. Sunny, who had emerged from her tête-à-tête with Mimi looking mildly shaken, said it was too chilly for her and continued to pick an argument with Mark about Israel.

"Seems like it got warmer," Charlotte now said suddenly, breaking the silence.

"So it does."

"Global warming?"

"Or the wind dying down." He rattled the glass in his hand. "Or this stuff."

"No, it's global warming. Poor Kyle. By the time he inherits our house, it'll be submerged."

Charlotte heard herself giggle and looked at her glass. Half the vodka gone, and that on top of a couple of glasses of wine at dinner, plus some Courvoisier afterwards. She, who rarely drank.

"So tell me about trying to burn up your parents," she invited, turning to face Anatole. "Where did you grow up? I can't remember."

Anatole's thoughts had turned to the applause the second-act curtain of *Crushed Velvet* would be getting right about now. All evening, on some semiconscious level, he had been involuntarily tracking the progress of the play. Occasionally, a key moment would surface to full awareness (now the curtain is going up, now the set is revolving to the bedroom), each a small, bitter stab. He was glad to have his attention returned to Audubon.

And so he told her about his childhood outside Worcester, Massachusetts, his father, a shoe factory foreman, his piano-teacher mother. He had a way he usually told this story — certain pauses, certain self-deprecating jokes. Ordinarily, he dwelt on his father's gloomy cynicism about America, his mother's opposing, almost manic cheer, the wars they fought over him and Laura, his older sister. He told about being called Ronski Bronski in school, and how he had vowed to drop the name Ronald as soon as he grew up. When he came to the fire-setting episode, he generally played it as a three-minute, Marx Brothers–style farce, taking all four roles himself.

Tonight, though, "My father escaped the Holocaust by passing as a Gentile," he heard himself begin. "That's probably why I got interested in acting."

This obvious connection had never occurred to him before, all his years of therapy and acting workshops notwithstanding. Charlotte accepted it wordlessly. He went on, explaining how the rest of Max Bronski's family had been killed, how Max wound up in Massachusetts, how he met Lil. And then stolid, relentlessly prosaic Worcester, and the boxlike house they lived in, the piano students, the shoe shop. Laura's scoliosis. Lil's miscarriages. How he learned at seven both he and Laura were adopted. Lil's visits to the sanitarium. Charlotte sipped her vodka and listened. He was not at all sure she was interested.

When he stopped, having gotten himself to Juilliard, she asked, "What about setting their bedroom on fire?"

"Oh, that." Anatole laughed at himself for forgetting, a long, almost delighted laugh. "I don't think I meant much by it. They were in their bedroom, more likely fighting in whispers than making love. I was outside, raking leaves. Their room was on the ground level, just on the other side of the wall where I was making a heap. All of a sudden, I got mad — more about having to rake the leaves than anything else, probably. I whipped out the Zippo every teenager carried — remember when people used refillable lighters? Remember buying flints?"

"Remember when people smoked?"

"And I set the leaves on fire. I'm sure I never expected the house itself to catch, but it did. There was an old wooden holder thing for the garden hose, and it went up like a matchstick, and then the shingles caught. So I got scared. I yelled for my dad. My dad ran out yelling 'Ron, Ron!' I ran in yelling, 'Mom, Mom!' My mother dragged me out again, my father ran

in yelling, 'Laura!' . . . We were all beside ourselves for a
minute or two. Almost literally. Then my father called the fire
department and they put it out and that was that."

"You weren't punished?"

"That was the funny thing. My father was usually very strict.
But I think he was so" — he paused to find the right word —
"so baffled by why I would do such a thing, that he just let it go.
He never even scolded me."

"Ron, huh."

"Yeah. I lifted Anatole from Anatole France, after I read
*Thaïs* in eleventh grade."

Charlotte said nothing, then unexpectedly gave a little jump.
She drew her breath in sharply.

"What?"

"Look." She pointed into the meadow that lay between them
and the house. "No, there." She guided his chin with a suede-
coated finger, cold from holding the glass, turning it slightly
until he saw what she meant: In the silver light, a rabbit crouched,
immobile in the short grass. It knew it had been seen.

"Go on, little bunny," Anatole called softly. "We won't hurt
you."

"Let's not look at it." Pointedly, Charlotte turned her head
to gaze straight at Anatole, who did the same in reverse. They
held still some seconds, noses an inch or two apart. Anatole felt
Charlotte's breath on his chin.

"I think it left," Charlotte said finally, swiveling her eyes to
check. She turned her head away. "Yes."

Anatole, still feeling her warm breath, wondered if she could
possibly not be thinking about sex with him. He didn't see how
she could not. He remembered how severe she had been at dinner, how astringent, how scornful.

"What was your childhood like?" he asked. "I mean, I know
a lot from Sunny. But for you — you're so much older."

"Thank you."

"I like that you're older," he said, truthfully. In fact, just at this moment her slightly greater age — her professional title, her bitter self-knowledge, her harshness, her complacent anger — all of it was making him almost dizzy with desire. It occurred to him that she must have stretch marks. His head swam.

"My childhood . . . ," Charlotte started, and stopped. "My childhood sucked eggs. What do you mean, you like that I'm older? Older than whom? Why did you say that?"

Anatole looked at his hands.

"Well, aren't you a piece of work?" Mindful of splinters, Charlotte carefully slid over until she was a good two feet from him on the steps. "Does Sunny know about you?"

"What there is to know. There isn't actually much." He kept his gaze trained on his hands a moment longer, then lifted his eyes to hers and smiled. Charlotte met his look and leapt to her feet.

"Man, if Ted did this to women, I'd chain him to the bed-post," she said. But he noticed she didn't walk back toward the house. She walked away into the field. He stood and followed her.

"Was it true what you said about Meyer?" he asked. "Did he really molest you?" He realized he had adopted her bouncy step again and made himself quit it.

"Of course it's true." She strode a little ahead of him, enjoying the action of walking, the coordinated motion of her own smooth musculature, the sturdiness of her bones, the quickened pressure of air against her face and her faint awareness that Anatole was watching her walk.

"What was it like?"

Anatole's inquisitiveness was rarely fueled by a desire to know another person better. What motivated him was the wish to learn the feeling itself, the experience of another person. Because — as with a mannerism — you never knew when you might be able to use it. His was an acquisitive curiosity.

Most people failed to discern this, at least at first. Flattered and touched by what they mistook for sympathetic interest, they told him what he asked not just willingly but gratefully. Charlotte sensed the difference at once, but her nature was such that she noticed it with relief. The friendly solicitude of others made her uneasy, prickly, suspicious. Anatole's cold selfishness, by contrast, reassured her.

She cast her mind back. What had it been like when Meyer had touched her? The fact was that, despite her assertion at dinner, she was not entirely sure he had. She could summon up the corridor outside his study where it had first happened, the electric lights on in all the rooms because the afternoon was so gray, her stunned realization that he was not simply placing his hands on her shoulders but had slipped one over her chest — her new, tender, desperately vulnerable chest — but was what she remembered a real event or an imagined one? If it had first been imagined with sufficient vividness, might not a fictional recollection have much the same half-gauzy, half-nauseating tenor as an actual one? But if she'd imagined it, where had she imagined it? In school, during a flute lesson, at night in bed? She couldn't remember a framing memory. So it must have been real.

Still, it was with a guilty sense that she might merely be passing along misinformation that she told Anatole, "It was sickening. Because I knew it was wrong — I don't mean morally wrong, but wrong like the wrong answer, like 'What's wrong with this picture?' Like an object falling upwards. Part of me, my girlhood, you could say, froze forever. At the same time, I was very proud to be singled out by this important man. The most important man in the world, as far as I knew. And excited,

because at twelve you're just a mass of synapses. At least, I was."
She was still walking ahead of him, talking into the night. The
uneven ground was slightly damp, and their heels sank into the
earth a little with each step.

Anatole hurried to keep up with her, though he was careful
not to draw even. When she started speaking, he had realized
the ice clinking in his glass might remind her he was there (they
both still carried their glasses) and dumped his drink into the
field. Now he heard hers clink as she took a deep swallow. The
only other sound was the dim whir of cars on the Quickway,
plaintive through the acres of leafless trees.

He wanted to know what exactly Meyer did, and what she
did in response. But, afraid to push too hard, he asked instead,
"How many times did it happen?"

"I'm not sure. Three? Half a dozen?" None? "I know I told
my mother, I remember that."

She did remember, too, more clearly than the rest of it. But
had what she told her mother been the truth?

Anatole wasn't interested in this telling-the-mother scene.
There was no role for him in it. As Charlotte walked on in silence, he decided to go for broke.

"What did he actually do?"

She walked faster. "What did he do? I'm not sure I want to
discuss that. A man like you — " She stopped and wheeled
around to face him. Anatole found himself brought up short.
"A story like that might turn you on."

He looked down at her. In his eagerness to hear what she had
to say, he had utterly forgotten his momentary attraction to
her. Not that he wasn't willing to be reminded of it at some
time. But first he wanted the information.

"Tell me," he said, so gently and persuasively that only her
uncertainty whether there was anything to tell made her hesitate. He toyed with the notion of moving away from her, to

relieve her of the pressure of his physical proximity, but an instant later he understood that what she wanted was for him to move closer. He did. He noticed she was at least an inch taller than Sunny. His mouth was on a level with the bridge of her nose.

"Tell me," he repeated.

Charlotte became aware simultaneously of her heart thumping high in her chest and of the fact that Anatole was no longer drawn to her, was merely, deliberately, manipulating her. The tawdriness of the last ten minutes — a married woman standing in a dark field, flirting (and not very successfully, either) by discussing child molestation with her sister's husband — struck her, and she laughed.

"There's nothing to tell, really. I probably made the whole thing up," she said, to deprive him of the secret he thought he had received. "I was a very perverse young girl, you know. I've always been perverse."

"I don't believe you."

"Ask Sunny."

"I mean about making it up. You just said it was true."

They stood, facing each other in the middle of a field whose edges stretched invisibly into the night. Anatole tried to smell the answer.

Charlotte shrugged. "I say a lot of things," she said.

"I hope I never have a little girl like you." He took a step backwards, almost stumbling over a tussock.

Charlotte gave a sharp laugh and finished the rest of her drink. "I'm sure God will grant such a modest request."

In the living room, Country Joe and the Fish had been replaced by *Blonde on Blonde*, and Sunny, Mark and Ira, having disposed of the Middle East, were making sharklike circles around the subject of each other's lives. Half an hour before, somewhere between Lebanon and Iraq, Mimi and Claire had both declared themselves exhausted and gone up to bed.

"How many hours a week do you work?" Mark asked Ira.

"Never counted." He squirmed sideward in his chair until his legs hung over the arm nearest Sunny, who lay flat on the brown corduroy couch, arms folded over her chest as if in death. Mark had resumed his rocking chair.

"What about you, Sun?"

"Depends on the week. Fifty. Sixty. Thirty."

Mark rocked forward to peer at her. "Right," he said. "Name one week you worked thirty hours."

"What's your point?"

"My point is, life is short. You should work to live, not live to work."

Sunny shoved a cushion under her head so she could see over the arm of the couch. "Oh, Mark, I hate that kind of inside-out formulation, those sort of — mirrored metaphors. 'It's not the size of the man in the fight, it's the size of the fight in the man.'"

"When the going gets tough, the tough get going," said Ira.

"If guns are outlawed, only outlaws will have guns."

"You can take the boy out of the country, but you can't take the country out of the boy," Mark contributed.

"I'd rather have a bottle in front of me than a frontal lobotomy," added Sunny.

"Live simply, that others may simply live," said Ira.

"Actually, I sort of like that one," Sunny said. "Not that we do it, of course. Anatole and I must be some of the most complicated livers in the country." She was thinking especially of IVF, which required $8,000 and the assiduous care of a dozen professionals to accomplish what two teenagers could do by accident in the back of a Range Rover.

"I live simply," said Ira.

"No one who lives in Manhattan lives simply," Mark said. "I couldn't believe it the last time I was there. Just riding the subway is a moral dilemma. How much do you pay — only the fare? The fare plus fifty cents for the guy playing the violin on the platform? The fare plus fifty cents for the violinist plus a buck to someone dying of AIDS? If you're going to pay all that anyway, why not take a cab? But if you take a cab, the money goes to the cabbie."

"And you get there half an hour late," put in Sunny, whose every day was a decathlon of deadlines.

"I can't afford to take cabs," Ira said.

"Sometimes I think New Yorkers are tired all the time because we expend so much energy trying not to see New York," Sunny said. "Not to see the schizophrenic screaming at his dead wife. Not to see the sleeping body under the cardboard on the park bench. The brown pool of whatever it is — coffee, you hope — on the subway seat next to you. The guy hurrying down the hall to catch the elevator whose door you're trying to shut so you can get to your desk. The garbage in the gutter. The guy spitting in the gutter. Heck, a couple of months ago, I saw a guy in the gutter, stark naked at eleven in the morning, singing the executioner's little-list song from *The Mikado*. It takes energy not to admit experience like that. It exhausts you."

"Not only exhausts, hardens," Mark said. "That kind of constant exposure to pain forces a person to narrow the scope of his compassion. You can't afford to care for everyone, so you choose one or two things to care about — your apartment, your wife — and the rest of the world can go to hell."

"But what's the alternative?" asked Ira. "If everyone who could afford to leave the city cashed out the way you did, no one would be left except the poor."

"I don't see the moral superiority of keeping your compassion wide by avoiding the spectacle of suffering," Sunny seconded. "'I cannot praise a fugitive and cloistered virtue, unexercised and unbreathed, that never sallies out and sees her adversary, but slinks out of the race where that immortal garland is to be run for, not without dust and heat.' *Areopagitica*," she added. "Milton."

"*Areopagitica* is about censorship," Mark complained.

"Isn't what you're proposing a kind of self-censorship?"

"Don't be ridiculous. Anyway, I ate my share of dust for twenty years, working in New York. I wouldn't do it again for all the yen in Tokyo."

"That's because you don't need all the yen in Tokyo. Or any yen, I suppose," Sunny told him. "And because you hated your work. Ira and I love our work. Don't you love your work, Ira?"

"I do," Ira confirmed. "I even love your work."

Sunny noticed with shame that she received this joking praise with a little thrill of pleasure. Ira never mentioned her writing to her anymore; no one in the family did. In the early days of her career, someone used to call her every time an article appeared.

"Plus which, Ira's work makes the world a better place to live in," she said now.

"Better for bugs," said Mark.

"Better for everyone."

Ira rolled his legs back over the arm of the chair and slouched deeply into the cushions, his feet thrust under the coffee table. "Mark believes environmentalists do more harm than good," he said.

"Not more. As much, maybe. I think there are some excellent environmental initiatives. The drive to reduce solid waste, for example."

"What can you possibly have against environmentalists?" Sunny grabbed another pillow and propped her head up further.

"For one thing, people who react with outrage to the very idea of criticizing them," he said. "For another, in spite of current fashionable rhetoric, a lot of so-called environmental legislation simply discourages traditional entrepreneurship, and that means fewer jobs for people who need them. And I don't just mean in the U.S. — now we're trying to force developing countries to live by standards that would have crippled us. Everyone thinks of environmentalists versus captains of industry — David versus Goliath. But when captains of industry suffer, the little cogs and wheels suffer too. More people are poor and hungry, more do without adequate health care, infant mortality rises . . ." A lecturing tone Sunny detested had crept into Mark's voice. "Everything in life is choices. You purchase one kind of good at the price of a different kind of evil. What I don't like about the environmental movement is its rigid application of a single measure to every situation. Does it hurt the environment? isn't always the pertinent question."

"That's nice. That's an interesting point of view. As a matter of fact, that's the way I feel about the League of Women Voters. Here are these intelligent people, all kinds of murder and mayhem is going on all around them, children are being shot in the streets, babies are being born with AIDS," Sunny went on, the sarcasm in her tone slowly gathering momentum, "and all they can think about is, Is everybody voting? Does everybody know the issues? Narrow-minded fanatics, you know?"

"Sunny — "

"Or take Oxfam. 'People are starving, people are starving.' What a bunch of whiners. Do they ever make a statement about nuclear waste? No. Do you ever hear a peep out of them about prison conditions, or First Amendment rights? Not a word, not one fucking word. Just, 'Give us money, people are starving,' like that was the only thing happening in the world. Yeah, Mark, I can really see what you mean."

Mark was laughing by now, but Sunny's voice rose angrily. "I'm serious. If people like Ira didn't raise environmental issues, who do you suppose would? You think some capitalist is going to come up with a patentable widget to restore the ozone layer? Or maybe General Motors will figure out how to sell sunlight and market a solar-powered car? If Greenpeace and the ERG and the NRDC and the World Wildlife Fund didn't question the way we live — "

"Let it go, Sun," Ira said.

She paused, looked at him and in the silence realized how shrill she had become.

He raised his eyebrows and repeated, "Let it go."

"You're so smug, Mark," Sunny muttered. Savagely, she pulled the pillows out from under her head so she was flat on her back. Mark was always condescending, given the chance, but he was especially so to Ira. As a little boy, Ira had been the family fuckup (a title Mimi had since inherited): dreamy, sloppy, a breaker of cups and furniture, a forgetter of homework and teachers' notes. That was the Ira Mark knew, and the one Sunny believed he preferred. In those years, Mark himself had played the family role that should have belonged to the distracted Meyer: Ruth's confidant, her sounding board, her co-conspirator.

But for four years after Meyer's departure, with Charlotte in California and Mark first in college, then married, Ira was Ruth's confidant. He helped her with budgeting decisions, deliberated with her over whether Sunny should skip sixth grade, whether they should take in a boarder. As best he could, he protected his younger sisters from vengeful teachers, bullying classmates and each other. And, sometimes, Ruth. When Mark came to visit, Ira deferred to him and stood aside; but they both knew the scepter had been passed.

That Ira, Ira the Good Son (that instar, as Ira himself referred to it) was a pale, solitary, peculiar-looking boy with an unusual enthusiasm for insects. He ended with the advent of rock 'n' roll Ira, drug-torpid Ira and, finally, strung-out Ira. After kicking heroin, and almost right up until Ruth's death, Ira struggled with all the questions he had postponed during adolescence. He was hardly more competent then than the dreamy little boy he had once been.

In the vacuum Ira left, and especially during Ruth's illness, Mark resumed and expanded his old role as Ginzburg paterfamilias. He shepherded his mother through the medical establishment, phoned all over the country to learn the latest thinking on cancer of the bladder, pulled every string Claire could find to get her to the best people, consulted with her surgeon, comforted her, was with her when she died. He was an associate then, working a sixty-hour week, and the father of two children. But there was no one else to do it. Charlotte was in California, swamped in the last year of her residency, Ira useless, Sunny paralyzed with fear and too young anyway, Mimi barely out of grade school. In the politics of the family, it was a Phoenix-like resurgence; and having managed it, Mark clearly did not mean ever to be eclipsed by Ira again. Since then, he had reserved his very loftiest pronouncements for his brother — even after Ira had gotten himself into school at Stony Brook. Ira's redemption had been grim, a daily struggle to take one further step into what he called the respectable world. He had finished his B.S., then, at last, his master's. But far from making Mark proud of him, Sunny thought, these achievements had only heightened Mark's condescension. The past eight or nine years had been even worse: Ira had followed his ideals into a career, while Mark had felt compelled to scrap his for money.

"You must respect Meyer no end," she added sullenly after a moment, "if you don't believe in putting work first. He's practically a lily of the field."

"Actually, as flowers go, lilies work just as hard as the next guy," Ira remarked. "I don't know how they got such a bad reputation."

"I do admire that about him, in a way." Mark's high forehead gathered into thoughtful pleats. "Although in his case, obviously, it wasn't so much a gift for living as an inability to tolerate responsibility."

"That's a charitable interpretation," said Sunny. "I would have said complete self-absorption."

"Unwillingness to tolerate responsibility," refined Ira, who had put in his time on this issue. "Unwillingness."

"I wonder if he regrets deserting us." Sunny sat up at last and burrowed into the cushions at the end of the couch nearest the fireplace. At the same time, on some preverbal, preconscious level, she began to wonder where Anatole was.

"Ask him."

She peeked over the pile of throw cushions at Ira, who had made this suggestion. "Maybe I will."

"I can think of quite a few questions somebody should ask him. Since he's here. But maybe you already have, Mark," he added, with a hint of his old deference. "Have you talked to him much?"

Mark shook his head. "It's stupid, because he's been here five days now, and I really do want to know some things. But when I get up there and open my mouth, I feel like I'm kind of —

prying, I guess. After twenty-eight years, you know, you start to figure the guy's life is his own business. I wouldn't want him asking me questions about my private life.

"The things I want to know," he went on, "are like why did he have a family at all? Why did he get married? Because he was always a kind of weird father, even before he left. Don't you think? Not that he would ever have molested Charlotte," he added, cutting off Sunny, who had begun to speak. "I have a daughter too, now, and I know what that means. He was never like that."

"I always thought he got married because everyone got married in those days," Sunny said. "And after you got married, you had children. Not an altogether stupid custom, when you think about it," she added, looking significantly at Ira. Several doctors had intimated that she and Anatole might have had no trouble if they had started earlier.

Not that they knew each other earlier.

"Claire keeps warning me I'll be sorry if I don't talk to him now." Mark stared unhappily at the unsheathed records they had been playing earlier. *Blonde on Blonde* was over, but the stereo panel was still lit up. "What did you think we should ask, Ira?"

Ira took a deep breath, then removed his new glasses and started to clean them with the hem of his sweater. "Oh, just a couple of basic questions. Did he love us? Did he love Ruth? What was it about Sheila Cassidy? Why did she kill herself? Where is the child he had in Seattle? Not that the answers would make any difference, but as a matter of history, I think he owes them to us. He probably doesn't even know the answers."

"I think those are important questions," Sunny told him. "I think you should ask him."

"I don't know. I feel like someone who was blind for thirty years and then suddenly could see. They'd probably still keep their black socks in the leftmost compartment of the second drawer anyway, and the brown socks in the next compartment over, and the blue ones next to that. They'd still probably read in Braille, at least for a little while. You have to learn to see, get used to it. I mean, I know he's there, but I don't feel ready to speak to him. Maybe I'm scared, the way people are who get out of jail after a long stretch."

"I'm scared. I'm scared if I talk to him I'll start to love him again," said Sunny, hoping that saying it flat out like that would keep it from happening.

"Claire's right." Mark began to drum his fingers against his knees. "We'd be crazy not to take advantage of having him here."

"On the other hand, think how much we might learn that we don't want to know." Since marrying Anatole, Sunny had become increasingly convinced that certain questions were better left unasked. For example, "Do you hate me sometimes?" Or, "Am I starting to look old?" In your heart, you knew the truth, but hearing it said seemed to transform it from a relatively inert state to a hideously active one.

She was about to explain something of her theory when Anatole himself stamped in, alone, full of the wholesome righteousness of those who have been outdoors while others lounge by the fire. He kissed her flame-warmed cheek, sat down at the old piano, played a couple of quick arpeggios and jumped up again. Then he dropped down by Sunny's feet, and the conversation turned to the phase of the moon.

# SIX

After climbing the stairs with her, Mimi followed Claire into Meyer's room. She stood just inside the doorway and watched as Claire went noiselessly to the bed. Meyer was sleeping. His mouth was open, and a whistle accompanied each rhythmic exhalation. Claire tiptoed away a moment later, his water glass in her hand.

"Forgot to bring up a clean one," she murmured as she went by. Mimi trailed her along the hall to the back stairs and down into the kitchen. From across the house, through the open door to the dining room, she heard Ira's voice saying impatiently, " — but the Palestinians can't be expected to . . ."

"Honey, I don't want to speak badly of Charlotte," said Claire suddenly, dumping the water into the sink, "but what she said about your father . . ." As she turned to open a cabinet and select a clean glass from the depleted supply, Mimi could see her tired frown. She filled the fresh glass, then turned again. "Just remember, there are two sides to every story, okay?"

"Not to worry. In my opinion, Charlotte is not too tightly wrapped. Or maybe she is too tightly wrapped. That's more like it." Suddenly, "Claire, does Meyer have any money?" she went on, in a different tone. "Could he have afforded to go somewhere else to be taken care of?"

"You mean like a private nursing home? No, not that kind of money. In fact, Mark thinks he probably owes the McBrides something, although they wouldn't hear of our sending a check. But Medicare would have paid for a hospital. If Meyer had wanted to be in a hospital," she added reluctantly.

"Oh." Mimi's voice went flat. "Then he didn't really have too much of a choice about coming back."

"Not too much. Not if he wanted to stay in control of his care. He might have had other friends he could go to," she pointed out, with a brightness Mimi immediately recognized as forced.

"Right." She was silent awhile, watching Claire fill a blue glazed bowl with apples and pears to bring to Meyer's room. Across the house, they could hear Sunny telling a story about a reporter sent to Germany.

"Jeremy Levy, his name is — you know his byline. So these two men come up to him on the street one night in Essen and say, 'Herr Levy?' 'Yes?' They hand him a folded note and run away. He opens the note — a swastika and the words 'We're back' in German. And this was before reunification!"

"Claire, how much pain is Meyer in?" Mimi asked.

"He's not in pain," said Claire, suppressing her annoyance. How many times was she supposed to explain this?

"But eventually he will be?"

"Probably not. I do have a painkiller ready if he needs it. If worse comes to worst, Dr. Agutter will prescribe morphine. He won't suffer, if that's what you're worrying about."

Mimi said, "Good." She was glad to know Meyer wouldn't suffer, even though Claire made it sound like he was a pet they were putting to sleep. In a moment, Claire snapped off the kitchen light, and they went upstairs again. As they passed out of earshot of the living room, Mimi heard Mark's loud, angry voice saying something about Louis Farrakhan.

"Claire, how did Mark ask you to marry him?"

Claire smiled. "He didn't, exactly. We were together so long, it got to be something we figured we would do. And then one day, we did."

"But when you did, you were sure he was the right person for you?" Mimi prodded.

Claire looked curiously at her profile. It was largely for Mimi's sake that she had urged Mark to fly his father here — so poor Mims could get to know him a little. But up until now, poor Mims hadn't seemed very interested. She had arrived late and hadn't even asked to see him then.

"I don't know. I'm not sure I believe there is a 'right person.' I think there are probably all kinds of possible futures with all kinds of people, each of them right in a different way. Why? Are you thinking of getting married?"

"No," said Mimi firmly.

In Meyer's room again, Claire woke her patient, felt his forehead and checked his pulse. She offered the fruit — which he declined — or anything else he might like: an egg, a little roast beef, a cup of chicken broth. But no. He couldn't eat. "I'm a bit wambly," he said.

"A bit — "

"Wambly. Shaky, queasy. Probably from the Norwegian *vamla*, to stagger."

Claire pressed her lips together. "I see. At least drink some water, then." She propped him up against her arm and gave him the water; Meyer sipped slowly, tiny sips that left the glass nearly full when he lay back again.

"Look who's here," said Claire, smoothing his quilt. "Mimi."

"Miriam," Mimi added helpfully.

Meyer smiled at his youngest daughter. It looked to Mimi as if the smile cost him an effort. "Hello."

"Hello."

His gaze traveled from her face to a stack of books on the night table beside him. Their spines were facing him, away from Mimi, but she could read half the title — The Ti Something the De Something — of the paperback on the top. Claire consulted her watch.

"You've had a couple of hours sleep," she said. "Maybe Mimi will sit and keep you company for a while."

Mimi forced herself to look into the hollow eyes that flicked tentatively to her again. "Would you like me to stay with you, Fa — Meyer?" she asked.

She had been foolish to attempt to say *Father*, a word that had made her uneasy as far back as she could remember. It suggested to her a mix of *fear* and *fur*. And *farther*. She did a little better with *daddy* because that occurred occasionally in blues lyrics, but she had no recollection of ever having called Meyer Daddy. Even the name *Meyer* seemed to her to be full of buried meanings.

"Unless you're too tired . . . ," she went on, letting the words fade away.

Both women looked hopefully at Meyer. "Yes, stay," he said, though his voice was so weak as to be barely audible.

"Then I'll leave you two alone." Claire disappeared, pulling the door halfway shut behind her.

Mimi felt a touch of the panic she sometimes got just before going onstage. Her father's eyes had closed. He lay on his back, hands at his sides, his pitiful chest rising and falling almost imperceptibly. She didn't see how he could already have fallen back asleep, but he looked as if he had. Perhaps that could happen when you were so sick.

She sat down on a ladder-back chair that had once been part

of a set in their city dining room and listened to her father breathe. It was a sound she didn't recall having heard before. Everything else around her was perfectly familiar. The room, the one Mark and Ira had shared during the summers when everyone used to come up here, had a bathroom connected to it, and an enormous closet. Ira once threw a pillow at Sunny that hit the brass standing lamp by the dresser. The lamp still had a dent where it fell.

The double bed with the polished pineapples sticking up from the head and footboard had belonged to Ruth — to Ruth and Meyer, Mimi supposed, before that. She counted backward. Her birthday was in April. She might have been conceived in this bed. She looked at it more attentively, trying to imagine the night of her conception. Had either of them intended it? Had the springs squeaked under them? Had Ruth come? During her illness, Ruth had once told Mimi she'd been surprised how little she missed sex with Meyer after he left. Mimi hadn't wanted to know about this. She didn't ask what it had been like before, when Meyer was there. Sunny claimed to remember occasional thumps and suppressed moans coming from their bedroom in the city (Sunny and Charlotte's room was on the other side of the wall). Sunny's theory was that Meyer was one of those men who didn't think about sex until you reminded them, then liked it — "did it," they would say — and forgot about it again. Mimi had known such a man. Maybe that was what Sheila Cassidy had done — waked Meyer to sex.

Anyway, there was something impersonal about birth, just as there was about death. Anyone could die if the wrong germ got hold of him, or if the M5 bus whacked him while he wasn't looking. It didn't have to be a germ you had a special affinity for, or a busline you ever took. And it didn't matter if this was the bed where she was conceived or not. Maybe not even if it was this person's sperm that did it.

A familiar tug in her midsection made her realize she was hungry again. How was that possible? She tried to imagine having this baby, then walking away from it when it was three. That was what the man in the bed had done to her. Of course, he was a man. But she couldn't imagine Jesse just wandering off forever from his child either. Even if she didn't marry him.

The shallow breath was interrupted by a dry cough. Meyer's head turned toward her on the pillow. His eyes opened. They were a faded jade green. He stretched a hand out — toward her, she thought for a heady moment. But no, for the water glass. He fumbled at it. Mimi stood and gave it to him, but he seemed unable to raise his head to drink.

Uncertainly, "Should I — ?" She made a scooping gesture with her right arm.

"Please."

Trying to remember how Claire had done it, Mimi slid her hand behind the pillow, under his head. Her heart thumped. She looked at the naked scalp so close to her, a few inches, the head now leaning on her arm. She said to herself, "This is my father. My father has a bluish scalp with three large freckles on it. My father has long earlobes. His head is the shape of a cough drop. He smells like fresh sheets."

Meyer drank.

"Enough?"

"Mmm." Gently, she let the pillow down to the bed again. His head rolled a little as she withdrew her arm. She sat down, aware of the blood still pulsing hard through her.

"So, Mamie," he said, his voice still exhausted and faint.

"Mimi, actually."

"Mimi." A long pause. She wondered again if he had dropped back to sleep. Then, "I'm sorry," he said.

"Oh, that's okay." She said it without thinking, then wondered whether he had meant sorry for getting her name wrong or for missing twenty-eight years of her life. There was no way to know.

"Good. Good," he repeated with an obvious effort. "So tell me about yourself. Are you happy?"

"Happy?" Without warning, a thrill rippled through her. Her father cared if she was happy! "Yes!" Happy? Jubilant! Her forehead wrinkled as she concentrated all her attention on his next words, determined not to miss a syllable.

"That's fine. And — let's see, you're a singer?"

"That's right."

"And what do you sing?"

"Blues, usually. But almost anything, really." She didn't want him to think she was narrow. Maybe he didn't like blues. "Standards, jazz, showt-showt-songs from musicals. Whatever."

"The human voice is a marvelous instrument. Maybe later you'll sing for me." Meyer tried to lick his narrow lips. A wave of the awful light-headedness that had plagued him recently rolled through him. What had he just said? Something about singing. Confused, he examined the face of the young woman before him for a clue. Ah! Miriam. She sang. "Tell me some singers you like." His voice came out in a whisper.

Mimi's mind went blank. She could not recall the name of one singer, male or female, living or dead.

"I love Elisabeth Schwarzkopf, myself," Meyer said, his thoughts once again clear and swift. "I met her one time, in Europe."

"Did you?" Who was Elisabeth Schwarzkopf? The only Schwarzkopf Mimi knew of was Norman.

"The way she sang Schubert lieder . . ." Her father's sentence trailed off.

"Yes," said Mimi, lost. 'Schubert Leader'? Was that the name of an opera? A composer? Later, Ira told her what Meyer must have meant, but at the time she wondered if he was quite sane. Sunny had always referred to him as a nut, but Mimi had never taken the epithet for a diagnosis. Perhaps his illness was making him delirious. For a moment, she wished Jesse were here. He would help her understand this.

"Schubert leader," she repeated finally, trying not to make it sound too much like a question.

"Oh yes."

She floundered around for what to say next. If only she could think of the name of a singer she liked! That would bring the conversation back to recognizable ground. But all that occurred to her were pianists and drummers, even novelists and actors. She was still floundering when she realized Meyer had lost interest in the subject anyhow and was now plucking feebly at the quilt, which had slipped down off his shoulders.

She was on her feet in an instant. "Let me help you." Reverently, she took hold of the quilt on either side of his chest and eased it up. When she let go, her heart was thudding again.

"Thanks." His eyes closed and his head dropped to one side. Even as she stood there, his breathing seemed to change. She waited a minute, her blood slowly settling, then switched the bedside lamp off. After hesitating briefly in the shadows, she turned to go.

But as she crossed the threshold, Meyer murmured, "Hold it," stopping her in her tracks. "What's the password?"

"What?"

"I give you three guesses. It's the name of a fish."

Mimi's heart seemed to freeze for a moment. This bit of Marx Brothers shtick was one of her tiny store of memories of her father, who used to grab her and run her through it as she left a room. She still remembered the night she finally saw

*Horse Feathers* on television and learned where it had come from.

"Swordfish," she whispered, and fled. She alighted briefly in the room that was hers for the weekend but decided she was too rattled to sleep and hurried downstairs. In the front hall, she discovered her passing wish had been granted: Headlights swept the windows. When she went to look, she saw a gleaming white van marked BEACH STREET FINE CABINETRY pulling into the driveway.

# SEVEN

The kind of fight Sunny liked started with her charging Anatole with some undeniable misdeed (he had left her entirely alone at a party where she knew no one and he knew everyone; he had tucked their quarterly tax check into the inside pocket of his suede jacket and sent it off to the cleaners), then pointing out to him how this particular wrong was part of a whole pattern of wrongs, a mere inch or two in a fault running the whole length of his character. Mute with culpability, Anatole would meekly listen while she paraded before him the history of other such incidents in their life together. If she was lucky, he would literally hang his head in shame.

When she had exhausted her anger — and since she had the rare gift of being able to recall precise examples of his past sins even in the heat of present rage, this was usually many minutes later — he would apologize. He would swear to mend his ways. And he would cajole her, first until she allowed him to kiss her, then until she kissed him.

Why she got such satisfaction from proving her husband was unfit to live with, Sunny couldn't have said. She did wonder. Mostly, she thought, it had to do with the pleasure of being right. Since childhood, she had loved to be right. So, the more wrong Anatole was (perhaps), the more right she felt.

For his part, Anatole also enjoyed Sunny's favorite kind of quarrel, though there were others he liked better. It wasn't that he took any delight in being her whipping boy. But he admired Sunny's technique in presenting her case. It fascinated him that she could remember the exact circumstances of incident after incident in their lives. He listened spellbound as she conjured up weather, articles of clothing, meals, conversations he had completely forgotten. These were fossils of his own life, and Sunny possessed them, and he did not.

Except for certain sensations and emotions (which he remembered forever with architectural precision), and the rough outlines of unusual events — as well as those bits of language and mannerism he continually scavenged — Anatole forgot his personal history almost totally from day to day. When it fell to him to have to say what he had done yesterday, he usually resorted to trying to think what day of the week it must have been, then working back from there to what activities he would logically have been engaged in. He was especially prone to confiding a problem to a friend, then confiding the same problem to the same friend a day or two later. If someone asked him how his Thanksgiving had been, he would frown and mumble, "Thanksgiving, Thanksgiving," casting about wildly in his memory for some taste of stuffing or texture of cranberry sauce that would give him a clue. He had always experienced life this way; until he got involved with Sunny, he assumed everyone did. There was nothing defective about his memory per se: He could learn lines as quickly as the next person. He simply discarded the details of his life as he went along.

Whereas Sunny retained them. Marvelous, to know whether you brought flowers or wine to a dinner party eight months ago! To be able to say who sat next to you and how late you went home! Anatole's instinct to defend himself gave way to wonderment as Sunny retailed first one rich anecdote, then another and another, like a furious Scheherazade. He found it curiously flattering, gratifying, that she would have stored up his very words on such and such an occasion and could repeat them now, however scathingly. It was like being given the earlier day back to live over again.

But the kind of fight he relished — and the kind it appeared they were going to have tonight — began with Sunny laying down some sort of law ("If you accept one more engagement without consulting me, I swear I won't go anywhere with you for a month") and ended with Anatole throwing an absolute tantrum in response. If he could manage to make her feel guilty — if he could catch hold of that tiny dropped stitch in her self-confidence which, when pulled, would unravel row after row of her ego almost effortlessly — then she would allow him to storm and sob and wheedle and moan to his heart's content. And comfort him afterwards. It really was hardly a fight: Once he got started, it was shooting fish in a barrel.

Tonight's round began the moment they were alone together upstairs. Without thinking about it, Sunny had been growing increasingly annoyed by Anatole's absence the whole time she was talking with her brothers. By the time he returned, she was too irritated with him to let him flop down and join the meandering conversation. He hadn't been in the living room five minutes before she yawned, said she was beat, took him firmly by the hand and led him up the stairs to their room.

"I'm giving up trying to have a baby," she announced, leaning on the door as she closed it behind her. "Not only am I not going to try IVF again, I won't even pee in a cup. I won't check to see how gummy I am. And on Monday, I'm going to call an adoption lawyer."

Anatole chose his line and got to work. "Just like that," he said.

"No, not just like that." Sunny drew him down on the bed next to her. It was really two twin beds that Claire had pushed together, and the green spread on it was too narrow and stuck out over the sides like fins. She spoke in a low, carefully controlled voice. "I've had two hysterosalpingograms, an endometrial biopsy, a tummyfull of hormones, four IUIs and two flings at IVF. Not to mention a lot of lesser ordeals I would prefer not to mention. If I weren't afraid to add it up, I would also point out how much all this has cost. So, no, not 'just like that,' but 'after all that.' Okay?"

Even as he pushed ahead to take his advantage, Anatole felt sorry for his wife. Truly, it wasn't fair that her body had to be poked and pinched and scraped, and worse, while next to nothing happened to his (although his secret conviction that the biological fault lay with her mitigated the inequity somewhat). Nevertheless, the situation was desperate.

"Sunny, I haven't wanted to say this — "

"No."

" — because I've felt it could only increase the pressure on you — "

"Oh, please. Please, sweetie, no." Flooded with prescient gloom, Sunny buried her face in her hands.

" — but the plain fact is, as you know, I am adopted."

"Oh, Anatole."

He felt a warm upswelling rise through his chest as the prospect of giving way to his emotions for the next hour or so opened before him. It was an old, old sensation, but one that never lost its sweetness.

"I have no blood relatives in the world," he went on.

"Well, you do have some, probably. You just don't know where they are," Sunny muttered into her palms. Two or three months before their wedding, Anatole had finally gotten up the nerve to ask Max and Lillian what they knew of his origins. They had been fully as hurt and angry as he expected, and they'd suspected Sunny of having incited him. But even with their unhappy assistance, his search had come to nothing.

"The point is, if we don't make a blood relative, I never will have any. That I can find," he added hastily.

Sunny looked up at him through a gap in her fingers. "Of course I realize that," she said.

"You've never mentioned it."

"I couldn't bear to. I thought it went without saying."

"Which was fine as long as we were trying. But if you really mean to quit — "

"I really do."

"Then it's hopeless." And, as they had both known he would, Anatole dropped his head into his hands and started to cry.

Sunny patted his broad back and made soothing sounds.

"You don't know, it's like I'm not connected to anything," he blurted out, between muffled sobs. "I feel like a — like a branch sticking out from a tree that isn't there. I want to be connected to something. Please, please, Sunny."

Still patting him, smoothing tears into his cheeks, "But it doesn't work, sweetheart," she said. "You know that. It would be one thing if I'd even gotten pregnant, say, and miscarried. But we haven't gotten that far. I didn't even respond very well to the Pergonal, you know? People get a dozen eggs, and we only got three the first time and two this time. So — "

But Anatole had stopped crying, and Sunny could feel a new tension in his back. When he lifted his massive head, she saw in his face an excitement she immediately mistrusted.

"Yes, but that's why" — he sniffled deeply, more to create a dramatic pause than because he needed to — "that's why I think we should try with donated eggs."

Sunny stared at him, as it seemed to her, from across a sudden chasm. He literally looked smaller to her, though neither of them had moved.

"Excuse me?"

He took her hand, which she instantly snatched back. "Ovum donation," he persisted. "You know. There's a fifty percent success rate. Fifty, Sunny. And we're due for some luck."

"Why should we try ovum donation? Why don't we try sperm donation? There's no reason to think my eggs are in any worse shape than your sperm."

"Sun, let's not be petty. The point is, Dr. Calder said — "

"Dr. Calder — Dr. Colder — Dr. Killed-her is a smug son of a bitch who never had a hysterosalpingogram in his life."

"But if we have a baby with a donated egg, it'll be my baby," Anatole said, before dissolving again into sobs. "It'll look like me. You can't understand. Here you have four people — five — who look like you, and are like you. But I don't have..." His words faded wetly away as he wept for his genetic loneliness.

Helpless, Sunny took his head and shoulders into her lap and bent over him, cooing and petting. "If we did do that," she finally said, "it would be your baby but not mine. I'd be having some other woman's baby."

He raised his head a little. "No, because you would carry it. You'd nourish it from the moment of its conception, almost. It would be our baby. Ours," he finished passionately, before diving again into her lap. He lay there, from time to time giving a gentle sniffle or sob.

As she cradled him, Sunny tried to imagine what it would be like to be pregnant with a fetus composed from another woman's egg and Anatole's sperm. For starters, it would make her ordinary jealous fantasies about him and other women pale to the point of transparency. There was something deeply perverse about the idea of providing the very womb where the fruit of your husband's liaison with a stranger could develop. It was like inviting him to make use of your bed for romantic trysts.

But that was ridiculous. The "other woman" would be nothing but a microscopic dab in a dish of agar. She forced her thoughts on. How wonderful to be able to do such a thing for Anatole — not only to make a family with him but actually to make family for him. What a bond between them!

On the other hand, what a horrible favor to ask of her. Sunny had never been one of those women who long to be pregnant. On the contrary, as he very well knew, she dreaded pregnancy — a fact she guiltily feared might be partly responsible for her failure to get pregnant. She didn't want her body distorted; she didn't want her poor back to have to support a fifteen-pound hunk glommed onto her front; she had no curiosity about labor, let alone delivery. She didn't even especially long for an infant. Infants were far too vulnerable: They terrified her. A child was what she wanted. If she could have gone from not-pregnant to mother-of-a-toddler, that would have been perfect.

Although, since she couldn't . . .

But she didn't even like to have overnight guests. Wouldn't she find it intolerable to have someone else's baby tucked under her skin for nine months? She would feel like a crock pot. Let some other woman carry the baby. Perhaps the woman whose egg it was. A surrogate mother, yes!

Except that was trafficking in flesh, paying someone to give up a baby. Besides, it could lead to hideous legal troubles. And with Anatole as well known as he was, the whole story was practically guaranteed to come out in public. She shivered a little at the idea of a *National Enquirer* article (an inside page, not the cover; he wasn't that famous).

She had reached this point in her thoughts when Anatole, finally lifting his head from her lap and leaning it instead against her shoulder, asked as if idly, "Did you ever find out if Mimi is really pregnant?"

"Almost two months," she told him. "But her baby wouldn't be either of ours," she added, misunderstanding. "It's Jesse's and hers."

"Damn," said Anatole.

"Well, you wouldn't expect it to be anyone else's," Sunny said reasonably.

"No, I mean . . ." He sat up, away from her. "Is she going to have it?"

"I hope so. I tried to encourage her to."

"Don't. It would be better if she didn't."

"Why? What are you talking about?"

Anatole turned on the bed so he could take both her hands and look into her eyes. "Darling, wouldn't it be great if we could use an egg from Mimi? Then the baby would have almost the same genes as our own would."

"Anatole, are you serious?"

"Completely. People do it all the time, you must have read about it. But the problem is, she can't give us eggs if she's pregnant. That's why it's better if she doesn't have the baby, see? Otherwise we have to wait a whole year to get started. And if she decided to nurse, who knows how long."

"Oh, I see. Gee, I guess you're right at that. Mimi can't be using her ovaries herself when we need them. That would be unfair."

"Don't be sarcastic, Sunny, please. This is very important to me."

Sunny's hands, lying in his, twitched involuntarily as his tightened.

"What on earth makes you think Mimi would consent to give us eggs? You know she'd have to go through all those shots and hormone manipulation and monitoring, not to mention the retrieval itself, which I wouldn't wish on — "

"She would do it. She'd do it for you. She idolizes you."

"She doesn't idolize — "

"If you asked her, she would do it. You know she would."

Privately, Sunny thought this was probably true. But she wouldn't ask Mimi, even if she weren't pregnant. In spite of what the doctors said, Sunny wasn't convinced fooling around with a woman's hormones like that couldn't have long-term consequences. To say nothing of short-term. When she had asked their initial infertility specialist whether Pergonal had any side effects, he had answered, "It could blow you up! Your ovaries could explode. But if you can take it," he added without irony, "I can take it."

For that matter, just tonight, Charlotte had gotten her nervous about her mole. Her beauty spot. She touched it again, assuring herself it had been exactly the same for years, but said nothing. Anatole, too, was silent awhile, facing her on the bed. Finally, he sighed.

"If only Charlotte were a little younger," he said wistfully. "I guess she is too old?"

"To grow eggs for us? By ten years or so, yes, lucky for her." Sunny wrenched her hands away from his once more. "But, I know! We can get the egg from Mimi, fertilize it with your sperm, and then implant the embryo in Charlotte. Because we know she can carry a baby to term, which we don't know about me. Then, Mark and Claire can raise it until it can talk and walk, Ira can give it a moral education and when it's all ready to be a little person, perhaps we'll have it visit us. How does that sound?"

"You're getting hysterical," said Anatole, feeling cheated. By his reckoning, it was still his turn to be hysterical.

"Oh, am I? Why shouldn't I? You know what hysterical means? Having to do with the womb. These are literally hysterical options. Human beings were never intended to face such options, Anatole. I would collapse with joy, I'm telling you, if I could wake up and find myself a peasant in a nice quiet shtetl, with the rabbi telling me to pray to God for fruit from my marriage. When you think about it, praying is a much more sensible way to deal with infertility than to ask your sister — "

"Keep your voice down. Don't rave."

"A much more human way to deal with it, and in our case, in all likelihood, a much more useful way — "

"Sunny, thousands of people who couldn't have babies otherwise have had them because of infertility treatment."

"Thousands of women. Thousands of women," she repeated, with bitter emphasis. "People don't have babies, Anatole. Women do. If men had babies, the whole process would be infinitely more respectable. Giving birth would carry at least the prestige of launching a successful business venture, don't you think? You'd probably get a title of respect, like 'Sir.' Exotic first-person tales of childbirth would be published in magazines with titles like *Hard Labor* and *Delivery!* Doctors would broach the idea of hormone injections with serious, considered discussions — "

"Sunny — "

"Instead of casually tossing off, 'Oh, of course, your testicles could explode — '"

"Sun — "

"And people like you wouldn't think they could poach on people like Mimi's reproductive tracts as if they were — as if they were swimming pools the owner wasn't using, or some kind of backwoods wilderness no one would notice if — "

"Darling, you'll wake your dad."

"My 'dad!' My 'dad.' That's exactly what I'm saying, don't

you see it? Meyer Ginzburg gets to be my dad for the rest of his life, no matter what, just because one night he got his rocks off with — "

"Okay, Sunny, okay." Anatole put his arms around her and pulled her to him. The focus of her anger having shifted from him particularly to the male establishment generally, she allowed him to envelop her and sat not unhappily nuzzling her cheek against his flannel shirt.

"It's been a long day. With a lot of bumps," he said after a while. Contentedly, she felt the words rumble in his chest. "We don't have to make any decisions tonight. Let's climb into bed and get sleepy, okay?"

She rested against him awhile longer, then murmured a bit tentatively, "Didn't adoption work pretty well for you, sweetie?"

"What?"

"I mean, you knew you were adopted from the time you were seven, but it didn't wreck your childhood, did it? And God knows Max and Lil couldn't have loved you more. It isn't such a terrible alternative. Is it?" She added, as he failed to answer, "If we had to resort to it, I mean."

But Anatole wouldn't be drawn into any more discussion. "Come on, I'll get your nightie," he said kindly. "Pick up your little feetsies, Marie, and tickle the ticking." This was a line from a play Anatole had done at Juilliard, many years before Sunny knew him, but they often used it as a code to mean go to bed. He added indulgently, "You may skip brushing your teeth."

The moment Mimi saw Jesse had arrived, a small rocket of hope fired inside her and she was aware of the blood pulsing in her ears. She opened the front door and found him on his way up the steps. In the yellow porch light, his complexion, usually a mellow ivory, looked slightly jaundiced. His black hair, parted down the middle and combed smoothly back into the tiny ponytail he'd recently taken to wearing, blended into the night behind him. He was short for a man, barely an inch taller than Mimi, and more muscular than he looked. His brown eyes had a tranquil glow that suggested an inside track on certain spiritual verities — a glow which had been a large part of his early appeal for Mimi but which she had come to understand was mostly an accident of nature. Really he was as confused as anybody else.

In the city that afternoon, after he left her apartment, Mimi had sobbed and screamed. But she had also made up her mind she would not call him. For two weeks, ever since she'd told him she was pregnant, he had been trying to get her to marry him. But his ideas about marriage made her want to cry.

The way he put it was that he didn't believe in the "transforming magic" of weddings. They were to each other what they were. Maybe they'd move in together one day. Maybe they'd pool their finances. Naturally, he would pay her childbirth expenses and take a hand in raising the baby. But it was sentimental gobbledygook to believe a ceremony could make them one flesh or bind them eternally. You had only to look around to see that. For an easy example, both their parents were divorced. Yet didn't she think both couples had gone to the altar in all sincerity? Which went to prove his theory: Not only was the traditional idea of matrimony unrealistic, even dishonest, but the more starry-eyed you were when you went into it, the more likely it was you'd come to grief. No couple could promise their feelings would stay the same for fifty years.

On the other hand, marriage was a socially recognized institution every child had a right to be born into. Jesse's best friend when he was growing up in Baltimore was illegitimate, and that boy had suffered for it all the way through adolescence. It would be cruel to do that to their child. As for an abortion, if

Mimi had any such ideas, she should never have told him she was pregnant in the first place. He was shocked when she said she'd assumed he would want her to have one. (In fact, she had thought he would demand it.) They loved each other. That was more of a head start in life than a lot of children got. They would manage. But she must marry him. He was ready any day she named.

Mimi had at first been deeply touched by Jesse's proposal, peculiar as it was. Their relationship had its faults, but it had also lasted longer than any she'd had before. Jesse knew her better than any previous lover. He was faithful. He was tender. True, he was kind of a pain in the neck about things other people never even thought about. He had ideas about how cooking should be done, for example, and how the house should be cleaned and even where they should sit in a subway car — ideas that had to be followed just so. If they weren't, he became hopelessly anxious and unhappy. Still, he believed in her talent. He enjoyed her singing and had helped her career. Where her brothers and sisters were cool and supercilious, he was warm and direct. Where their humor was dry and wordy, his was goofy and physical. Most important, she felt he was genuinely committed to her on a level deeper than either of them could talk about or control, a level perhaps even he wasn't fully aware of. This was her instinct about him, and she knew her instincts were usually right.

Nevertheless, she didn't see how she could marry him. Marriage meant joining your life to someone else's. It was surrendering your individual identity to a shared one. As Mark and Claire had. Even her mother, Mimi felt, had never really been divorced. Legally, of course, she had; but that was a technicality. She never made a new life after Meyer left. From the day she left her parents, she lived and died as Ruth Ginzburg — wife or ex-wife hardly mattered.

At the same time, though, Mimi couldn't really refute Jesse's arguments. How could you promise to love someone for the rest of your life? She couldn't have promised to — to love New York for the rest of her life, or scrambled eggs, or even music. Suppose she had had to promise to love the blues forever? Could she take such a vow? It would be more like making a wish if she did. And that was what Jesse was saying about marriage.

Still, she was sure he was wrong. In the end, his logic only made her head ache. She told him he could either marry her for real or not marry her at all, but he was not to call unless he had made up his mind to one or the other. And so he had left her apartment.

Now, in the yellow porch light, he smiled uncertainly at her, his dark eyes shining. She heard her own breathing, sharp and shallow. Would he have dared to come up here if he hadn't come around to her point of view?

It felt colder now than when she had arrived. The wind had sprung up again. Mimi closed the door almost all the way behind her and hugged her arms against her chest for warmth.

"Sorry about the fight, baby," he said. He reached out to take her hand.

But she edged back. "What are you doing here? Did you change your mind?"

"I had to see you. Mim, we can't let it end this way. I think we need to talk more."

"Talk?" Disappointment stabbed her. She turned the knife on him. "We've been talking for days. That's why you drove all the way up to Audubon?"

"I know it's a bad time. I'll go home right away. Just — How's your father?" he interrupted himself.

"He's dying."

"But have you been able to speak with him at all? Are you getting to know him?"

"Jesse, it's past eleven. I'm turning into an icicle, no one invited you, and this is a family-only get-together anyway. See what I'm getting at? I told you I didn't want to see you unless you were ready to get married for real — "

"But that's what I don't understand," he broke in. "How can you think it's more real to make a bunch of fake promises than to say we'll do the best we can?"

Tears started to her eyes. She didn't try to hide them; she was beyond doing that with Jesse. "You know, I'm going to have a baby," she said. "I don't have time for your stupid, academ-dem-so-called logical arguments." She started to back away across the threshold into the house.

"Oh, Mim, have mercy." He hesitated for an instant, then crossed the steps and put the flat of his hand against the door just above her head. "At least let me come in for a minute. It took me almost three hours to get here."

Since he was pushing the door at the same time as he said this, it swung open and they tumbled into the front hall together.

He closed the door behind them.

"Mims, you okay?" Mark called from the living room, where he and Ira were still talking.

She brushed the tears away from her eyes. Jesse took her hand and kissed it as they went inside.

# EIGHT

Charlotte gave up trying to sleep and reached for the watch she had left on the bedside table. Its hands glowed blue in the dark: almost one o'clock. When she and Anatole had come in from their walk two hours before, she had felt suddenly exhausted. She went upstairs without saying good night to anyone, climbed into bed and read drowsily for half an hour — Barbara Pym, for the plane — then turned off the light. But her easy descent into sleep had been too good to be true, not a miraculous adjustment to East Coast time but merely a bout of grogginess brought on by a day of travel and too much to drink. All she had done was lie in the dark, worrying about Ted and Kyle (would Ted stick with her through Kyle's adolescence? Why should he?) and guiltily wondering why Mimi made her feel so savage.

She sat up and switched the light on again. It struck her that when she had last slept in this room, she had been a teenager; she supposed she could wait another hour to sleep here again.

She checked her math. Yes, she had been nineteen. Ruth sent her a ticket so she could fly home for the summer. She got a job making beds and cleaning at Milt's Retreat in Roscoe to help cover her next year's tuition. Mark worked there too that summer, as a waiter.

Ruth had still been obsessed by the failure of her marriage. It was two years after Meyer's departure, but she talked about him as if only months had passed. Looking back, Charlotte thought perhaps her mother had spent the first year or so in shock. Then all the memories came tumbling out, and she talked about Meyer by the hour.

When Charlotte had been home a week or two, she started to suspect that this was the reason her mother had paid to fly her in: so she would have an adult female to talk to. At first, Charlotte was merely resentful, but as the weeks went on, she developed a gruesome fascination with being privy to her mother's most personal recollections.

"You know, when we were first married, before you and Mark, your father and I used to go out every Saturday night to dance," Ruth would say, having intercepted Charlotte when she came in from Milt's and hijacked her to the kitchen. She would shove a bowl of boiled potatoes in front of Charlotte to be mashed, or hand her a carrot and a grater, while she herself deftly separated egg yolks, melted butter, pounded flank steaks. "Did I ever tell you that? I can't remember. I banged my ankle today, and it made me think of it. Meyer was a terrible dancer, mind you, but we used to have such fun. You know, it's not true what they say — that you can tell from the way a man dances the way he'll be in — " Here, she would break off and pretend to study the open, gravy-stained page of *Joy of Cooking* for a moment. "Anyway, once you all arrived, we didn't have much time for that. Pour out a half cup of milk and warm it up, would you? I want to whip those potatoes."

In retrospect, Charlotte thought those monologues had been Ruth's way of sifting through the past, looking for the detail of her marriage she had missed at the time — the event, the oversight, the flaw that would account for its breathtaking termination.

Charlotte made a face in the darkness. She was wide awake, no doubt about it. Stupid to have drunk alcohol. She rarely did so anymore. No wonder she had made such an ass of herself with that handsome lunk. What had she said to him? Something about getting him aroused, or turning him on. Either way, undoubtedly something tactful.

Shivering, she slid out of bed and wrapped herself in the scarlet robe Ted had given her for her birthday last year. She would go down to the kitchen and phone him. In fact, she amended as her stomach growled, she would go down and scare up the rest of that roast and phone him. Dinner had been so early for her, she hadn't eaten nearly enough.

She turned the knob and slipped quietly out so as not to wake the others. The upstairs corridor was dark, but a light showed under Mimi's door, next to her own, and she thought she heard a low murmur of voices from behind it. Sunny and Mimi, maybe — they seemed to be pretty thick. She had started downstairs, where the last one to go to bed had thoughtfully left the front hall light on, when on impulse she turned and instead went down the hallway to Meyer's room.

The door was open. She could see him in the faint glow cast by a plastic night-light plugged into the wall near what she realized after a moment was one of the ladder-back chairs from their old dining room set in the city. His face was a pale streak in the dimness; his thin chest pumped fitfully up and down. A pile of books sat on his night table. On the windowsill near his headboard, within arm's reach of the bed, Claire had placed a bowl of fruit, hoping to tempt him. What a patsy Claire was, thought Charlotte. Like one of those birds who sit on other birds' eggs. For her own part, Charlotte had declined even to discuss Meyer's case with the doctor in Boulder. After three decades of leaving his family to their own devices, he could take care of himself.

She went closer, hovered a few feet from the bed, peered down at him. "Meyer," she said aloud, angrily. It was a disgusted declaration, not an apostrophe. She didn't expect it would wake him.

But his eyes opened at once and stared into hers.

Her jaw tightened. At the same time, she felt a little ashamed. "It's the middle of the night, go back to sleep," she said.

"Charlotte?"

She nodded.

"I don't think I really was sleeping. Sit and talk," he whispered, then yawned. "What's the middle of the night to people like us?"

But she didn't want to sit. A wave of fury that threatened (she felt) to drown her unless she spoke her mind crashed in her head. "Did you molest me when I was twelve?" she demanded.

Meyer smiled, sleepily, politely. "Did I what?"

"You heard me." Her voice was low but harsh, urgent. "Didn't you used to touch me? You used to touch my — chest. Admit you did."

His head moved weakly against the pillow. "Charlotte, are you serious?"

"Am I serious? I should smother you with the pillow and get it over with."

His head wobbled and fell onto his left cheek, so that he was facing the night table. It crossed his mind that he might be having a dream. He had noticed lately that the line between sleep and waking was less solid than it used to be. "I don't know what you're talking about," he mumbled to the lamp.

"You deny it?"

"Of course I do. What gave you such an idea?"

"It's not an idea," answered Charlotte, more uneasily than she let on. "It's a memory." Abruptly, she stepped back and dropped onto the chair.

Meyer blinked and forced himself to focus on Charlotte. She didn't look like a dream. With an effort, he pulled his thoughts together.

"A memory of what, exactly?"

Charlotte's hand encountered a Kleenex in her robe pocket. Absently, she rubbed her nose with it. She thought of Dr. Kates, the therapist with whom, three years ago, her recollection of the incest had surfaced. At the time, she had told Kates it might be a fantasy — was a fantasy. But Dr. Kates said that was resistance.

"In the hallway outside your study." Her voice faltered. "A rainy afternoon. You came out just as I was about to knock and come in."

"And?"

She bent her head so that her hand, still with the tissue in it, kneaded her forehead. She had gone over the corridor incident so often that it was like a stone worn smooth by water: Whatever distinguishing features it might once have had were gone. Now all that marked it was its smoothness.

"And I'm sure something happened that shouldn't have." Her voice sounded slightly overwrought to herself, pleading.

"Maybe I smacked you by accident with the door?" he suggested.

Charlotte said nothing. Meyer, a flicker of anger running through him, contemplated trying to sit up but decided against it.

"Charlotte, you don't know me, and that's my fault," he began again. "But I give you my word I never — "

"Why?" she broke in, so loudly that even in the extremity of her feelings, she worried she had wakened the house. She warned herself to lower her voice. Teardrops fell from her eyes straight onto her lap. Her father's suggestion, offhand as it was, had tripped a perfectly clear, perfectly ordinary memory. He had opened the door into her elbow while she was holding a glass of warm milk. The milk was for Sunny — then called Sonia — who was in bed with a cold. It had spilled all over Charlotte. She saw now what she had been wearing: a pink angora sweater, a gift from Grandma Zellerman. Beneath it was her brand-new training bra. She felt the hand of the saleswoman in the dressing room at B. Altman, checking what was under the wretched garment "for fit." Jesus Christ.

"Why did you leave us?" she demanded. "You killed us. You flew away and left us for dead. Like we were furniture. Like we were books you couldn't be bothered to finish. Why? We never did anything to deserve it."

Now she buried her head in her hands. She had trained herself during her marriage to Alec to cry without making noise. She sat breathing jaggedly in and out, the plush robe absorbing the falling tears. Meyer, his anger gone, stretched out an arm to her, the nearest he could come to getting out of bed. Her head down, she didn't see him.

"That's right. It's true, it was nothing you did, nothing. You were splendid. It was me."

Charlotte wept on.

"'After such knowledge, what forgiveness?'" said Meyer, but the words rang strangely in his ears; soon he couldn't tell whether he had said them aloud or only to himself. He must be drifting toward sleep again.

Meanwhile, Charlotte sat beside him. Whereas before she couldn't keep quiet, now she found she couldn't speak. She blotted her face with the Kleenex and repeatedly blew her nose. When, at length, she looked up again, her father was asleep. One stick-arm hung off the bed in front of her.

Still almost panting, she smoothed the lapels of her robe and ran a hand through her tangled hair. Slowly she stood, took his arm by its wasted wrist and tucked it under the quilt. He had not molested her; she was sure of that now. What he had done was leave her. He had run off with a teenage slut from Dublin and left his own daughter to rot. She dabbed her eyes again with the wadded-up Kleenex, now thoroughly revolting, then noticed a box of fresh ones on the nightstand and plucked out a handful. She sat once more and listened to the sporadic, distant whoosh of cars on the Quickway.

In the summer, the leaves used to absorb the traffic noise and make it inaudible, even at night. Now she pictured the trucks and cars speeding by and, encased in them, the weary teamsters, disappointed lovers, distraught parents frantic for formula or children's medicine. Would she have to tell the whole family that Meyer had never touched her after all? How humiliating. Perhaps a general announcement at lunch, to get it over with . . .

Through the dimness, she squinted at Meyer's sleeping form. What had become of the looming colossus of her imagination? All her life, the mere knowledge that he was downtown in her grandfather's real estate office, or east across the Atlantic, or out west, or up north on a commune, had colored that point of the compass for her, made it a direction of mystery or menace. Unconsciously, she had used his whereabouts (or, often, his last known whereabouts) to orient herself, if only in opposition to him. When he was in Europe, she had fled to California. Twice she had married men notable for their lack of resemblance to him. When Kyle was born, she had set herself the goal of giving him a childhood nothing like her own.

And here before her lay the very pole of which her life was to be the antipode, the fiery furnace in which her heroic resolves had been forged, as near to a heap of dust and ashes as living man can be.

She stared at him. His wretched chest, a wrinkle under the quilt, jerked up and down. "So that was your best," she said in a low murmur, thinking of Alec and Kyle. Alec had never been able to put Kyle first, though Charlotte had seen him try. It occurred to her she could still call the doctor in Boulder and ask for a few details of her father's case.

Then, because she knew she would never sleep now, she went to the bathroom across the hall and splashed her eyes before going downstairs.

There was a light on in the kitchen. Ira was there, reading in the breakfast nook, his hands wrapped around a yellow mug. He wore a plaid robe and white tube socks. His fine copper hair had lost its neat part; slender clumps of it, held together by static electricity, drifted this way and that. Charlotte watched him for a moment. She found herself unexpectedly delighted to see him. She was feeling curiously relieved, chatty, almost light-headed. She cleared her throat, and he looked up.

"Good morning. What are you reading?" She crossed the room to look at the open book before him. "*Insects, Experts, and the Insecticide Crisis.* That looks like it would take a person's mind off his troubles. Can I borrow it when you're through?"

"You can take it now. I'm rereading it, really."

"Oh, no. I couldn't."

"What troubles did you want your mind taken off, anyway?"

Charlotte opened the refrigerator and looked in. "My empty stomach, for one thing." She wondered how pink her eyes and nose might still be. "For two thing, for me it's ten-fifteen, not one-fifteen." She lifted the Saran-Wrapped remains of the roast out, then started to hunt for mayonnaise and bread.

"Did you know certain beetle larvae can eat their weight in food in twenty-four hours?" Ira asked, watching her extract two slices of bread from the middle of a loaf in a plastic bag.

"No. What a very appealing thought, though." She unscrewed the mayonnaise jar top. "Thank you for sharing. Do they like roast beef?"

"Charlotte, have you talked to Meyer?"

"You mean since we all went up?" she stalled. "No," she said flatly. "Have you?"

"Yeah, a couple of hours ago. Mark and I went upstairs to give Jesse and Mimi some privacy — "

"Jesse?"

Ira looked briefly confused, then realized Charlotte probably had never heard Jesse's name, and certainly had missed his arrival. He explained and went on, "Mark and I went upstairs so they could talk. Mark went to bed, but I peeked into Meyer's room, and he was awake — looking at the door, I guess, because our eyes sort of met, without either of us meaning them to. I really thought about going on down the hall, frankly. I frankly wouldn't be here at all if Sunny hadn't leaned on me."

Charlotte had found a sharp knife and was sawing at the beef. She paused. "Really? Mark leaned on me."

"Well, there you are. Or here we are, more exactly. Anyway, I did go in. I sat down next to him, and, you know, I asked how he was feeling and all of that. And I told him I had some questions for him about the past."

"Yeah?" Charlotte screwed the lid back on the mayonnaise and put it in the fridge. She took her sandwich and sat down across from him with it. "What did you ask him?"

"That's just it." Ira slumped back into the leatherette booth, his head framed by the folded red shutters. "I didn't. When it came time, I looked at him, this scrawny skeleton, and I opened my mouth and I said, 'Oh, they can wait.' Like I was telling the cleaners not to bother delivering my shirts till my pants were ready. What a fucking coward."

Her mouth full, Charlotte shook her head sympathetically, chewing.

"So he said, 'Okay,' and I went on to tell him about the article I'm working on now with ladybugs and this organic farmer in Virginia, and eventually he fell asleep, and that was that. And I've been sitting here ever since, trying to figure out why I did that."

"And?" Swallowing, Charlotte leaned forward to glance into his mug, saw that it contained warm milk with a skin on it, made a face and leaned back.

"And I don't know. Partly, as stupid as it sounds, it was pride. I didn't want to lower myself to ask."

"Mmm-huh," said Charlotte, through a mouthful of sandwich.

"Partly, it was human pity. I mean" — Ira looked briefly, guiltily at his sister, then at the smoothly rounded edge of the maple table — "whatever he's done in his life, he's very near death now."

Charlotte said nothing.

After a moment, "But another, a big part of it," he went on, "was that I truly didn't want to see him look miserable and defensive and small. I thought he might say he was sorry, and on some level, I really didn't want to hear that. Even after all these years, some part of me still wanted to hang on to an idea of him as a strong, tough guy. An adventurer, a freethinker. A man with a mysterious right to fuck us all over because he felt like splitting. Like Jack Kerouac or somebody, someone with a kind of cosmic *droit du seigneur.* That was the image of Meyer I made for myself when I was thirteen, and that was how I got through the first years after he left. I identified with him." Ira shook his head. With the tips of his fingers, he toyed with the bottom slats of the shutters beside him. "I pretended he was waiting till I was a little older, till he could come back and take me with him on his travels. When that fantasy exploded — around the time we learned he'd been in the States for months and never called us — that's when I got big into drugs."

For a moment, he was silent. He picked up the second half of Charlotte's sandwich and took a bite.

"Remember that week I spent with you in L.A., in 'seventy-one?"

"Dimly."

"I'd been looking for him in San Francisco. I didn't want anyone to know. I thought Ruth would be hurt."

Firmly, Charlotte reappropriated her stolen sandwich half. "Did you find him?"

"No. Not my fault, really, since, as it turned out, he was in Oregon." He watched her take a bite of her sandwich, then asked, "You don't remember that week? You were just starting med school. I remember you telling me about some patient who had come into an emergency room hallucinating he was a fish. I was such a nut job in those days, I remember thinking, Maybe he is. That sounds cool. Fins, gills, seaweed . . . I could get into being a fish."

"You're kidding."

"Oh, I was a lot crazier than that," he said lightly, without elaboration.

"I remember you. You weren't crazy," said Charlotte. "You were a drug casualty."

He shrugged. "Same difference. I still couldn't make a plan

or hold down a job or maintain a decent relationship with a human being."

"Hey, that reminds me. How come you don't get married? You can certainly do all that now."

"Maybe I don't want to."

"Do you date people?"

"I get my share." He took a sip from the yellow mug. A warning flash in his blue eyes persuaded Charlotte to change the subject. Ira had always been mysterious about women. One of the things she did remember about the week in '71 was that he didn't come home at all one night. She'd found him on her porch the next morning when she opened the door for the paper, his clothes rumpled, his skin and hair musky with sex. When she asked where he'd been, he said, "With a girl," in a tone that made it clear she had already asked too much. Even Sunny said she never knew who, if anyone, Ira was going out with. She said he had never introduced her to a woman without stipulating she was "just a friend," and he rarely appeared with even these women more than once.

There was an awkward silence between them while Charlotte swallowed the last of her sandwich and washed it down with a swig from the yellow mug. Finally, "Well, so anyway, how's your life turning out?" she asked.

"You mean since nineteen seventy-one?"

"Nineteen seventy-one, nineteen eighty-one. Nineteen ninety-one. How's your career, do you like what you do?"

It interested Ira that Charlotte would not hesitate to ask this question, whose bald generality pointed up so plainly how seldom they talked. Chronologically, Ira fell squarely between the Littles and the Bigs. But he was much closer now to his younger siblings than to the others. It was a fact he always felt compelled to obscure or soften by a pretense of active connection. If he had wanted to ask how Charlotte liked her work, for instance, he would have said, "So how's your new office? What made you decide to move?" Something that indicated, by a few specifics, that he was at least aware of some of the details of her life — even though she would know, since they hardly spoke to each other from one year to the next, that it was Sunny who kept him posted.

But a perfect stranger could have asked him Charlotte's question. He felt more liberated than offended by what he would have deemed a lack of finesse in himself, and he answered with greater honesty than he would have otherwise. "I like the work itself," he said, "the bugs, the reading, the biology. Although it is a little weird to study something just so you can kill it better, which is what a lot of entomology comes to." He pushed his new glasses up his nose; he'd been trying not to notice that they had a tendency to slide down, but it was getting difficult to ignore. "That's the trouble with ecological systems, though. In order for someone to gain, someone else has to lose. Nature, red in tooth and claw, you know."

"So which part do you not like?" Charlotte glanced sidelong at the kitchen clock and realized she probably wouldn't get to call home after all. That was okay; she'd spoken to Ted from the airport, and to Kyle before dinner.

"Well, kind of also nature, red in tooth and claw, I guess. The office politics, the fighting for money, people's ambitions, interorganizational backbiting . . . People think do-good, non-profit offices like the Environmental Resource Group must be filled with fine individuals working tirelessly together toward a noble goal, but the truth is, these jobs are so fucking hard to get that only the most competitive, single-minded, aggressive, ruthless sons of bitches make it. Do you know, I don't have a single friend in my office? No, I shouldn't say that; I have quite a few friends, but there isn't one I'd trust for a fair shake if our interests happened to collide. The only people I really like are the support staff."

"What about you? Are you trustworthy? Or have you become ruthless too?"

"I'm . . . Yeah, I'm probably ruthless. I mean, you start thinking, This is my career, this is my livelihood. These are my bugs. If I don't get this grant, my little newsletter could go down the tubes. You know the *Earthwise Pest Control Monthly Gazette* isn't funded by the ERG. They just give me office space and let me use their logo. So I'm always walking a tightrope. Shoestring, actually."

"But you're doing it for the cause, that's the point. Ultimately, you are 'doing good.'"

"Maybe. I hope so."

"Of course you are. What other motivation could you have?"

Ira laughed. "You are looking at probably the most personally ambitious member of our family," he said. "I include Sunny. Don't be fooled by this mild-mannered exterior, or the harmless sounding *Earthwise Monthly*. Pest control is a hot topic, and after throwing away ten years of my life, I'm damned if I'm not going to make a name for myself in something. I'm probably a worse asshole that way than Mark ever was."

He didn't add that, sincere as he was about his mission, he was also plagued by a persistent idea that he wasn't especially good at his job, that someone else could be doing it much better. Especially when he received grants, a sense of fraudulence gnawed at him, of having pulled the wool over the donors' eyes. Not that he wasn't energetic or dedicated. He was. But so much of his work seemed to be public relations. In order to get anything done, it was necessary first to convince people of your own singular importance. Even in Bangladesh, where he had done his fieldwork, he found it necessary to assume a cold, almost arrogant demeanor toward his superiors to gain their attention. Using the same technique, he had now managed to persuade plenty of people to believe in him. But their confidence only made him feel more of a fake.

"Oh, get out," said Charlotte. "Eyewash. Hooey. If you only wanted to get ahead, you'd be working for Dow Chemical, or American Cyanamid, or whoever it is who's the enemy."

"You're sweet, Charlotte, but I'm actually too much of a snob to work for them. And you couldn't make a name for yourself that way anyhow. They're too big and faceless. How's your career, anyway? I hear you're kind of a bigwig these days, professionally."

"Oh, yes, indeed. I'm the Napoleon of the Southern California Dermatology Group." She stood up and wandered back toward the refrigerator, looking for more to eat.

"But you like it?"

"Very much. People think dermatology is all acne and Retin-A cream, but there are some very serious skin diseases." She found a package of Oreos in a cupboard and returned to the table to open it. "The skin in general is quite interesting." Having carefully bisected a cookie, she offered him the half with the filling on it.

He declined.

"But unlike yourself," she went on, delicately licking at the icing he had refused, "I seem to have come completely to the end of my ambitions. I noticed it about two years ago, when I was offered the chance to take over the practice of a very prominent retiring colleague. I said no. And here is a theory I'll offer you about it, since you're a man of science. Also about two years ago, I started to get my period quite irregularly. I still get it, but it's more and more erratic, and twice now I've had what I'm quite sure are hot flashes. My gynecologist tells me this is the beginning of menopause. I'm a bit early, but not terribly, and it's normal for your cycle to be odd and patchy like that for quite a while before it gives up altogether."

She went on, leaning forward, "My theory is, as my estrogen has gone, so has my ambition. In fact, I'm a thousand times calmer in every way now. Isn't that remarkable? Don't tell anyone I said this. But these days when I look back on my twenties, and even most of my thirties — in particular, my entire marriage to Alec — I see it all as a huge hormonal misunderstanding. The depression, the frenzies, the *pain*. That was my life. All that money spent on psychotherapy, all that guilt over emotional extremism. Hormones."

Ira said, "Yow."

"Exactly. Nobody will admit to this. It's one of the great secrets, like how you will never know if having children made your life better or worse. I feel as if I just got off a thrill ride that lasted thirty years. Despite the fact that menopause is the first great knell of mortality for a woman, I am more serene now than since . . . Than ever, come to think of it. No wonder Jewish men thank God daily for not creating them women."

She took another Oreo apart. Ira accepted half. For a while, they gnawed in silence.

"Ira, I lied a minute ago when you asked me if I talked to Meyer," Charlotte said. "I did."

She took a deep breath. She might as well start by telling Ira as anyone. Blushing, she confessed her error.

Ira listened in rapt silence, astonished by the spectacle of one of the Bigs admitting to a grave personal mistake. Even Sunny never admitted to more than a minor miscalculation — at least not to Ira — while Ira had had to confess his failings to the family over and over again. He found the turned tables so delightful, he almost didn't care whether Meyer had done it or not.

"Oh, that's okay, Charlotte," he said magnanimously, as she brought her story to a close. "Anybody could get mixed up about a thing like that." A bit awkwardly, he patted her freckled hand. "Sure."

He found the experience of pardoning and soothing her so enjoyable, he did it again.

"Not to worry. No harm done," he said jovially, splitting another Oreo for her and offering her the side with most icing.

# NINE

Mark was having a nightmare. The toaster oven would not work. Wrathfully, he twisted the dials, pounded it, shook it in both hands. As it exploded, he woke with a jerk, rolled over and sat up, panting.

Claire woke and reached for his hand.

"My heart," said Mark. In the darkness, it seemed to him to pound like a fist trying to get out of his chest.

Claire sat straight up. "Does your left arm hurt?" she asked, fumbling for his pulse.

"Oh, no. Sorry, I'm fine." Apologizing again, he explained what had wakened him. Claire switched the bedside lamp on. It was three-thirty.

Mark described his dream. Claire laughed.

"Let it go," she said, when he had finished. "Don't think about it."

"It wasn't funny in the dream," muttered Mark. "I was livid."

"Oh, Mark. Poor little woolly lamb." Sometimes at night, Claire told Mark to imagine he was a small lamb grazing in a lush field in summertime. It had always helped him sleep, especially in the years before he retired. She yawned. "You're under too much stress, that's all. I know the perfect antidote." She patted his thigh and slipped out of bed.

While she was downstairs, Mark stood up and pulled the covers straight. Carefully, he folded the top sheet back over the blankets so that the chain of flowers Claire had embroidered along the hem would show. He shook out the pillows and smoothed them before climbing in again. He thought of reading — *The Rise and Fall of the Great Powers* lay unfinished on his night table — but instead he merely sat back expectantly against the headboard, the soft sheet draped so that his paunch almost disappeared. Sometimes it worried him that Claire called him a little woolly lamb. He was nearing fifty, a retired partner in a well-regarded law firm, the father of two grown children. Lately, he had been thinking about running for county office. He wondered if the faux-Tudor fortresses of Larchmont, the broken-down trailers and aluminum-sided ranch houses of Audubon hid other midnight lambs. It was the sort of thing psychiatrists would know, he supposed. But Mark had never gone to psychiatrists, or been friendly with any.

The still-vivid image of the exploding toaster oven flashed again in his mind's eye. He did like to be in control. Machines that didn't work, cases that got out of hand, paralegals who wouldn't take orders, even the vagaries of his own stomach could fill him with indignation. He did his part; why didn't everyone else?

His mouth twitched. Charlotte's ridiculous accusation about Meyer had annoyed him. Too much time in the sun, that's what it was. All the same, he liked having her here. Having all of them here. Throughout most of the evening, he had felt an electric buzz, a kind of excited satisfaction that had partly to do with a pleasant consciousness of his own hospitality. But there was also a sheer, sensual joy for him in seeing them gathered, and especially — since hearing was his strongest sense — in listening to the sharp confusion of their voices.

Even when they argued, their particular inflections, the way they all pronounced certain sounds, delighted him. There was a Ginzburg family *r*, rounder and richer than most, that almost approached an *l*. They all had a flat, deadpan way of batting questions to one another, and a peculiar, dry lilt when they said something funny. There was a timbre, a low vibration in all their voices that came down to them from Ruth, and before her from Isaac Zellerman. Like a cross-generational *basso continuo*, thought Mark. Neither June nor Eliot had it. No one did now, except himself and Ira and their sisters. He missed it.

Mark's thoughts paused and shifted as a yawn overtook him. Tomorrow for sure, he told himself, he would go in to Meyer and ask some hard questions, have it out with him. That was why he was having nightmares, he knew: because so far, he had not been able to bring himself to talk like a man to his father. The minute he got into Meyer's room, some anachronistic deference, a socially programmed code of respect for the elderly, kicked in, and he found himself asking what he could fetch to please Meyer, or listening courteously to whatever was on his mind. Everything he said came out either stilted and formal or bizarrely childish. Even at the airport, when he and Claire picked Meyer up, Mark had been mortified to hear himself yelp "Daddy!" at first sight of him. Here, he often made Claire come into Meyer's room with him; when she left, he found an excuse to follow her out. But not tomorrow. Tomorrow would be different. Otherwise, he would never forgive himself.

When Claire returned with a cup of pudding, he accepted it gratefully, spooning the smooth, cool custard into his mouth with slow concentration.

"Make me talk to Meyer tomorrow," he said, when it was

mostly gone. "I mean really talk to him. Make me stay in there with him alone."

"Okay."

"Don't let me weasel out."

Claire smiled, listening to Mark's spoon clicking against the thick glass. "Okay. Don't worry."

She watched him run a finger around the inside of the glass and lick it. Then she set the empty cup on the dresser, kissed him and turned off the light. Ten minutes later he was on his stomach, hands outflung and clutched around the top of the mattress, legs splayed, ginger hair wild around his head, mouth open. He always slept this way: desperately, like a drowning swimmer.

It was almost four when footsteps going past her door woke Sunny. She was afraid of the dark and had left the light on in their closet and the door cracked open. In the faint glow, she could see Anatole's face, homely and uneven now that no emotion organized and drove his features.

She turned onto her back and scanned the shadowy ceiling. When exactly had the embryos the doctor deposited inside her died? Right away? That was her worst fantasy — that her body manufactured some kind of lethal baby-poison. But maybe they had survived awhile — a week, perhaps. Maybe one had. The doctor said the embryos floated around at first; they didn't even try to take root until they had been in the womb several days. About twenty-four hours after the last two were put inside her, Sunny tripped over a pair of slippers she had been too tired to put away. She went flying forward for what seemed a long time before she stopped herself with a hand against the wall. The medically senseless notion haunted her that this little jolt, this brief pitching forward, had shaken the embryos out of her uterus.

Before they did the transfer, the hospital gave you a Polaroid of your embryos sitting in their petri dish. Your name was scratched into the glass of the dish; Sunny supposed they gave you the photo as proof that your own egg and sperm had been placed inside you. After their first IVF attempt failed, she learned not to take the Polaroid home.

Despite her exhaustion, she began to be aware of a certain nervous energy creeping into her limbs. This was a side effect of the hormones, which at other times made her irresistibly sleepy. Now her blood seemed to be itching inside her veins. She closed her eyes and tried to focus on her breathing but only felt the swelling surge of restlessness more clearly. Useless to hope it would go away. She slid out of bed (carelessly, jostling Anatole, since it was his fault anyway that all these chemicals were still racing around inside her), put on her robe and slippers and went into the bathroom.

This bathroom had three doors, one opening into the room she had come from, one into Meyer's room and a third to the hallway. She peed and washed her hands, then stared idly into the mirror while she debated whether or not to flush the toilet and risk waking Anatole or Meyer. As usual, she experienced a dull shock at the sight of her eroding jawline. She'd spent too many years sticking her chin out to emphasize the length of her neck when she was young. Now the skin was hopelessly stretched. She had just moved on to a survey of the lines around her eyes when a low sound — a sort of whispery moan — from behind the door to Meyer's room made her turn and listen.

It came again. She put her ear against the wood. Was he dreaming? Calling for help? She tied her robe a bit tighter around her, then slowly, gently turned the knob and nudged the door open.

Her father was awake and facing in her direction. In the

wedge of light from the bathroom, she saw that his eyes were shut and his lips pursed out. He was meditating. What she had heard was his mantra, chanted aloud in his thin, skittering-leaves voice.

She almost retreated, but Meyer sensed her presence and opened his eyes. Even in the half-light, she could see his face was pinker and more animated than when they had all come up together. She expected him to be embarrassed. She was embarrassed. She hadn't been alone in a room with her father since she was ten. But he only smiled slightly and asked, "Did I wake you? Sorry."

She shook her head no.

"Come in," he invited, adding, "Everybody else has. Charlotte was up here a few hours ago, and you just missed Claire."

"Really?"

"Really and truly," said Meyer. "I feel downright frisky, God knows why."

Sunny hesitated a moment longer, then entered the room. "I don't want to wake my husband," she explained as she softly pulled the bathroom door shut behind her. Meyer's room was now very dim, lit only by a night-light. Sunny felt her way to the chair by his bedside and stood uncertainly near it.

"Sit."

She sat.

"Do you meditate, Sonia? I believe I taught you how."

"No. You didn't, and I don't." Sunny asked herself if she was going to sit here and let him talk to her as he used to do on the phone when she was fourteen, asking if she'd ever read Spinoza, or advising her to check out No drama, or who knew what.

"I think you would find it most helpful," he was going on pleasantly, meanwhile. "There are many ways to med — "

"What did you do in Europe?" she demanded abruptly. She

would not be spoken to this way. She would not. She was a reporter. She would interview him.

"In Europe when?" he asked.

"In Europe in nineteen sixty-three. 'Sixty-three through 'sixty-six. Sheila Cassidy had died in October," she prompted, as she would a skittish subject. "You left the States in November and — what did you do?"

"I went to Paris." He closed his eyes, smiling a little. So Sonia was still a journalist. Good for her. "It was the low point of my life. I fell in with some Moroccan housepainters and learned to smoke hashish."

"And it was the low point of your life because your girlfriend had killed herself?"

"Yes. And, of course, I had lost my family, too. That was very difficult."

Sunny decided to deal with the question of Sheila first and come back to the family later. In particular, she meant to confront him point-blank with Charlotte's absurd allegation and see what he did. For now, "Why did she kill herself?" she asked.

"Ah." Meyer had opened his eyes. He rolled his head away so he was looking at the ceiling, or perhaps at the pineapple on the nearer bedpost. "According to the letter she left, because she was happy and wanted to die happy. So one morning while I was out showing office space to a couple of travel agents, she hopped into the tub and slit her wrists."

"She wasn't concerned that if she died happy, that meant you would be wrecked?"

Meyer smiled again. "Madame, not one man is selfless; I name not one, Madam," he said.

"What?"

"It's a palindrome. Let me think." For a few seconds, Sunny sat listening to his breath — quick, but deeper, she thought, than before dinner. "Truthfully, I don't hold that against her," he said finally. "She was a poet, a real poet. Not like me. Divine. Also very young. And a drinker. And a little crazy."

"And where is her poetry?"

"Burnt before she died. She asked me to burn the few copies I had, too. She had never tried to publish it. Oh, Lord." Meyer gave a long sigh and let his head fall so he was looking at his daughter again. "Sheila was a comet. She was a comet. It's funny how seldom I think of her."

Sunny tried to imagine it: the volatile girl, raucous and sentimental, far from her family, alcoholic, in love with a brainy, bony, erratic, married man twice her age. Home alone with a bottle of whiskey, a match and a razor blade. She tried to imagine Meyer finding the body in the East Side walk-up. The tub, she seemed to recall, had been in the kitchen. At the same time, she thought of Ruth: brisk, zealous, exhausting. Tough even at her most affectionate. Especially at her most affectionate.

"You must have been besotted with her," she said.

"I was."

They were both silent awhile. Sunny thought Meyer might be falling asleep. For the first time, it occurred to her that those aspects of Ruth's personality which had driven her children wild might also have acted upon her husband. Previously, Sunny had always thought of Ruth as the control, Meyer as the variable. But perhaps he had felt starved for tenderness, as Sunny had. As they all had.

And then there was the business of Ruth's energy. She had been one of those people who can simultaneously hold down a job and cope with five children and repaint the dining room and study Italian and host an exchange student and also lead a crusade to force the city to build a new playground. And still answer the phone with zest. One of Sunny's clearest childhood memories was of Ruth, hugely pregnant with Mimi, knocking together a set of bookshelves for Ira's room while a vat of homemade clam chowder simmered on the stove. At the time, Sunny had only felt the good fortune of having such a marvelous mother. It wasn't until she was a teenager that she started to feel the pain of her own comparative inadequacy.

Not that it excused him, but it was no wonder Meyer had found himself drawn to a needy, violently romantic young woman.

Suddenly, he spoke. "It wasn't until after she died that I realized I had given all of you up," he said. "Until then, I didn't even really know I had stopped loving Ruth. I liked her; I admired her, certainly. Everybody did. But I could never have lived with her again as man and wife."

He rested a moment before going on. "Not that I knew all that at once, of course. It took time. That's what I did in Europe. That and travel. I went all the way to Londonderry, to meet Sheila's people. But once I got there, I decided against it. If they had her temperament, they might have killed me. Ah, Sheila *mavournin*."

"I thought her name was Cassidy."

"*Mavournin* is an Irish word for darling. Anyhow, I went back to London. Then Antwerp, and Geneva, Barcelona, Rome . . . I made friends. I read, washed dishes for money, and I learned how to cook. I was an excellent short-order cook in half a dozen cuisines before I returned. I thought a lot about the past. When I was sure I could never go back to it, I hopped a freighter for San Francisco."

Sunny watched as her father tried to wet his lips with his tongue. It was hard to think of him as a forty-six-year-old man — as anything but a wasted invalid. It might only have been a trick of the scarce light in the room, but she thought the healthier pink she had seen in his cheeks when she first came in had faded. She was exhausting him. All the same, "But didn't you regret abandoning your family?" she asked.

"Regret?"

To Sunny, he sounded vague, as if he had never heard the word before. Yes, regret. What are you, fucking Edith Piaf? she wanted to say. But she suppressed this and, as she would in an interview, rephrased her question instead. "I mean, do you wish at all that you had done otherwise? Come home, maybe not left with Sheila in the first place. Lived out your days as Meyer Ginzburg, real estate broker and paterfamilias."

He was silent a long time. At last, "Are you looking for the truth?" he asked.

Sunny answered promptly, "Yes," then wondered if this were so.

"Okay." His breathing was definitely more labored than when she had come in. "No. Not in the sense you mean. Sure, I regret not knowing you all. I'm sorry I hurt you children, and Ruth. I wish I could at least have written letters, visited you. I thought about it, but I never could seem to do it.

"It's difficult to explain," he resumed, after a brief hesitation. "I would have felt dishonest if I had tried to patch together what I myself had broken. Broken not by chance, you must understand, but deliberately, with a will that surged up from my deepest nature."

He paused to collect himself and rest his voice. Now he felt tired. Extremely tired. But he was also interested in his own story. "In a way, I divorced you all. After Sheila, you see, I began to realize my whole married life had been a strange and, in some ways, a dreadful aberration. I had allowed Ruth to relieve me of the burden of my own selfhood. When she first came upon me, I had no idea how to explain myself to the world. In the world of books and ideas and poetry, yes, I was comfortable. But in the outside world, I was a ship drifting out to sea. No job, no prospects, no discernible form. I was glad to let her tie me up, moor me, make a tame animal of me. I was grateful to be her clumsy, comical performing bear. I thought she had helped me put down roots, make a life for myself. Then Sheila came, and I found that, on the contrary, nothing at all attached me to that life. I just came clean away in her hands." He stopped and lay panting awhile. "Sonia," he said.

"Yes."

"You mustn't think I never cared for you. While I was with you, I loved you all."

She heard a skeptical "Mmm" rise from her own throat. She was burning to argue with him. How could he speak of divorcing his children when they had had no voice in the decision? What did he mean, he "never could seem" to visit them? But it was clear she had already worn him out. He lay almost gasping, his eyes closed, his mouth gradually slacker. After a minute she stood, then crept through the bathroom into her room.

Curled on his side, facing the wall, Anatole was snoring. Stealthily, Sunny fumbled through her overnight case until her hands found a small notebook she had packed. She fished a pen from her purse. Driven by habit, she tiptoed back to the bathroom and wrote down everything Meyer had said.

# TEN

The Ginzburgs woke on Saturday to find Audubon engulfed in a violent rainstorm. Water thudded from a dark sky, rattling the windows. It bounced off the tin gutters with a noise like cap guns.

Scrabble weather, thought Ira automatically, opening his eyes, a thought from summers thirty years ago. Nervously, he reached for his travel alarm. He'd been up past three the night before, lying in the dark, his mind ticking over and over the events of the evening.

It was six forty-five.

Less than four hours. I'll be exhausted today, he thought and immediately corrected himself: I'll be surprisingly clear-headed and energetic today. I will pass the day in a state of unusual acuity.

He repeated this idea as his muscles quietly announced a variety of kinks and aches that had been twisted into them during the night. Ira had great faith in the shaping power of thought over sensation.

And indeed, as he brushed his teeth a few minutes later, it came to him with absolute clarity that he should never have allowed Sunny to talk him into coming up here. He had long ago cauterized that part of himself where Meyer had once been attached. To him — to his wiser self, at least — Meyer was nothing more than the gap through which he had fallen into addiction. His immediate instinct when Mark had called to say their father was "coming back" had been to hang up the phone and not pick it up for a month. And a very healthy instinct, too, he reflected bitterly, watching foam rise from his teeth. He had an image of himself, a cartoon figure being sucked into a vacuum cleaner — the vacuum of his need for Meyer. Meyer's absence. His unbearable death.

Ira spat out the foam and rinsed his mouth with scooped handfuls of cold Catskill water. Rinsing his mouth of toothpaste was a sufficient pleasure to distract him briefly even from these thoughts. Since he'd quit drugs — a long time now — Ira had learned to notice and savor a wide array of ordinary gratifications. Some of these were pleasures other people recognized: the heat of a swallow of fresh coffee pulsing down his throat, the relief of lifting his glasses from the bridge of his nose at the end of the day, the color and shape of tulips massed outside the Korean markets. Others were subtler: the smell of ink from his fountain pen; the snug grip, like tiny jackets, of his high-tops around his ankles. Even the routine business of emptying his mailbox when he came home yielded at least two pleasures: first, in anticipation, the thrilling possibility of who-knew-what intimate missive written days ago and sealed until it should blossom in his hands like a flower; second, after (as almost always happened) the box proved to hold nothing but bills and appeals for money, a faint but pungent triumph at being an adult among adults, a person whom charities and campaign funds might reasonably petition, who might be expected to order boots from a catalog or purchase a time-share in Cocoa Beach. When you had been an addict and drifted around as Ira had, even such a sheaf of mail as that emitted an exhilarating scent of success.

He went to the small bathroom window and looked through the rain to the abandoned barn. It was cold enough outdoors that his breath made a cloud of mist on the window. With his index finger, he drew a squiggly vertical line flanked by two straight lines. It was a symbol he often made, though he didn't know its meaning. His ex-wife, Suzanne, once said it stood for their union, the squiggly line an *S* for her initial, the verticals *I* for Ira. But in fact he had drawn the hieroglyphic since high school.

Though they had been married less than a year, and that twenty years ago, Ira still thought of Suzanne often. They met in a drug counseling program in Flagstaff, Arizona. For a while — at least as Ira recalled it — they were happy. But Suzanne went back to junk. He had last seen her nodding out against the refrigerator in the kitchenette of a place they were renting over someone's garage.

In his room again, dressing, Ira suddenly realized that he could have told Charlotte about Suzanne last night when she'd asked him why he hadn't married. Somehow he had never mentioned Suzanne to his family, an unintentional omission each passing year made harder to correct. Even Sunny didn't know. The fact was, Ira had still been married that week he spent at Charlotte's.

He remembered going out to a jazz club and picking up the first woman he'd slept with since his wife. Jody, her name was. He had gone with her to an apartment in Westwood she shared with two other students. In her bedroom, he had flipped her over on the narrow bed, pulled her skirt up and gone at her from behind.

He was easing a turtleneck down over his head as he thought of this, and the recollection caused him to freeze for a moment in agonized self-disgust. Then the moment passed. His head popped through the turtleneck, his hands wriggled into the sleeves. For twenty years — since Suzanne — his sexual desires had disgusted him. In the last ten or twelve, they had grown to be a virtual torment. He simply could not link sex with affection. The cheapest, coarsest, most idiotic pornography aroused him; tenderness did not. If his aesthetics had been as primitive as his erotic tastes, he sometimes taunted himself, his walls would be covered with paintings of kittens on velvet.

He had kept his sexual life and the rest of his life absolutely separate. If any of his colleagues or friends could have read his mind, he would (he believed) have killed himself at once, humiliated beyond endurance. He was considered in the office a model of male emancipation, respectful of his female co-workers, vigilant against sexual harassment, so leery of impropriety that he sheered off from even the blandest flirtation. Yet for two years, he had maintained an almost wordless liaison with a graphic designer named Kyoko, arriving at her apartment every Wednesday evening at eight and leaving before midnight. He had no idea what her life was like except for those hours, no knowledge of her family or other lovers or how happy or miserable she was with the arrangement. It wasn't that he did anything violent to her, or she to him. In the range of human activities, he sometimes sought to console himself, what they did together was probably not even very interesting. Still, it appalled him.

As he pulled his socks on, he realized for the first time that those few hours in Jody's Westwood apartment had had a permanent effect on him. Not the sex, but the apartment itself. It was a modern, undistinguished place — ugly, cheaply built, furnished with the usual brick-and-board bookshelves and Salvation Army effluvia. But everywhere was evidence of study: textbooks and novels, notebooks, loose-leaf binders, pads of graph paper, dictionaries, maps, empty tea canisters bristling with pens and highlighters. On the desk in Jody's bedroom — equipped with Tensor lamp and ashtray — lay an open copy of the *Aeneid* surrounded by loose pages of closely written notes. Tiny handwriting decorated the margins of the book. Even in the middle of the night, the humming snugness of the place struck Ira. At the time it made him jealous, angry to think this woman should be so protected from the forces that battered him every day. But later, etched in miniature and embedded in his memory, the image of those rooms had become an emblem, a symbol of peace and industry. A goal toward which he had begun a long and painful trek.

Ira gave a long sigh as he swung out into the corridor.

"What was that about?"

Mimi, swathed in a terry-cloth robe, was on her way into the bathroom next to his room. Her hair was unbrushed and had gotten matted down on one side during the night. Her eyes were pink. Her complexion had a curious patina.

"Oh, a little of this, a little of that."

With her eyes, Mimi indicated Meyer's closed door. "Him?"

He shrugged. "What are you doing up?" They spoke in murmurs, since all the doors except the one to Mark and Claire's bedroom were closed.

Mimi, well known in the family for sleeping until noon, shrugged in her turn. Then, in a burst of candor, "I'm preggers," she confided. "If it's not peeing, it's puking."

Ira fought down a reflexive desire to demand who had knocked his sister up and go punch him out. "Are you going to have it?" he asked instead.

"That's the sixty-four-thousand-dollar question."

He looked inquiringly at her stomach. "How far along?"

She told him. "Let me — ?" She pointed suggestively at the bathroom door. He waited outside for her. When she emerged, he invited her into his room.

"So. Playing Beat the Clock?" Ira watched in admiration as his youngest sister plumped down on the bed and snuggled into the corner where his sleep-crumpled pillows were crushed. Whatever her weaknesses, she had the gift of making herself comfortable. The notion of flopping down on somebody else's unmade bed made Ira anxious — in the case of his sister, almost queasy. Mimi, unself-conscious, clearly expected him to plop down on the foot of the mattress, or even sit beside her.

There was a small maple student's desk near the bed, with a rather rickety chair. Ira turned the chair around, sat down and rested his feet on the edge of the bed. The outline of his long toes, crooked and curved against one another, could be faintly discerned through his thin black socks.

"Beat the calendar," Mimi corrected. "I still have a couple of weeks to decide."

Ira smiled and restrained himself from praising this modest bit of wordplay. It was true that he thought Mimi stupid, an opinion he and Sunny often debated. Sunny contended that Mimi suffered from *pigletisme*, a syndrome she had named after Piglet in *Winnie-the-Pooh*. Victims of *pigletisme* were afflicted with excessive enthusiasm, said Sunny. Excitement and (often) affection made them say or do the first thing to come into their minds. This sometimes gave them the appearance of being stupid.

In any case, Ira suppressed his immediate response and asked instead, "I presume Jesse is the father?"

"You pres — assume correctly." She gathered a thick rope of hair beside her left shoulder and started to braid it. In a few words, she explained where Jesse stood on the matter and where she did. Though they had sat up talking until two last

night, nothing had been settled between them, and (except that
all the fizz had gone out of her ultimatum) nothing had changed.
Having finished, she gazed at him hopefully. As if, Ira
thought, he might happen to know the answer to her dilemma.
Her expression reminded him of the look a friend's Irish setter
had once given him after dropping a dead squirrel on his feet.
"Would you like me to talk to Jesse?" he suggested. But he
felt, and sounded, doubtful. "Sometimes a third party, someone
who's not involved . . ."

"You're nice to offer," Mimi said, "but it's really between he
and I."

"Him and me," Ira corrected before he had time to stop
himself.

Mimi's creamy face darkened instantly. "Oh, him and me, he
and I. Us," she said, her voice dropping into a thrilling, con-
temptuous register. She would never have said "he and I" if she
hadn't been talking to Ira. Only her sisters and brothers made
her so nervous she acted dumb; among her friends, she was val-
ued for her good advice and smart ideas. And she hardly ever
stammered. But that was another world. Here, there was nothing to do but blunder through the minefield of her family's
scrutiny, avoiding suspicious objects when possible and turning
her face away from explosions.

They sat for a moment in silence. Ira, listening to the drum-
ming rain, hoped it would let up long enough for him to take a
walk around the pond. The dragonflies there had been the first
insects to interest him seriously, around the time he was three
or four, and he still had a sentimental attachment to the place.
He was thinking up a polite way to discourage anyone who
might want to accompany him when Mimi's voice abruptly interrupted his thoughts.

"Ira, do you like Meyer?" she asked without preface. Un-
braiding the section of hair she had braided, she repeated to

him her conversation with their father last night. Ira explained what lieder were and described his half hour with Meyer. He also passed on what Charlotte had told him.

"I knew he never molested her," said Mimi. A gloating smile twitched at her lips. "Charlotte. I don't like to bad-mouth people, but that girl is one twisted piece of macaroni."

"I think she feels pretty crummy about it. It was an honest mistake. I mean, it wasn't malicious."

Mimi gave him a high-eyebrowed, wide-eyed Oh? look.

"Not deliberately malicious."

"If you say so. Hey, you never answered my question. What do you think of Meyer, now that he's here?" She rearranged her legs, catching her ankles in her hands and pulling her feet up so her heels were near her thighs. "He's really pretty nice, don't you think? All I remembered of him from before was a couple of baby things and that awful time he visited when I was in high school. I must have told you — he asked me if I'd read Chairman Mao, and when I said no, he ignored me the whole rest of the night? He and Mark just sat in the den and yap-yap-yapped together till two in the morning, while I hid in my room and cried all over Claire."

"He was pretty strange then," Ira agreed. His own visit that year had been exquisitely painful, with Meyer interrogating him about his politics and showing no interest in any other subject. "Although frankly, in some ways, I think that was more the real Meyer than this is. He was always obsessed with one idea or another. And he generally would make us feel ignorant and useless because we weren't," he added, exaggerating a bit to comfort Mimi.

"But he's awfully friendly now, don't you think?" she persisted. "I think he wants us to forgive him. And I believe you should forgive people if you can," she added. This was in fact a major tenet in her rather miscellaneous but deeply felt personal code of right behavior, and it had long disturbed her that she could not forgive her own father his desertion. She looked attentively at Ira, but he said nothing. After a few moments, she suddenly plunged her fingers into her hair, viciously raking her scalp.

"But now he's leaving us again." Her face crumpled abruptly, and she buried it in her knees, her voice passionate but indistinct. "Forever. It would have been better if he had stayed away."

Meyer awoke feeling curiously improved, even invigorated. He lay still for a while, trying to focus his attention on the flow of blood through his body, to imagine the branching arteries, capillaries, veins, and to encourage the nourishing river through them. Around him sounded the muffled, rhythmless crash of heavy rain. Two weeks after he and Ruth bought this house, the first night they slept here, they had discovered the roof was riddled with leaks, one of the worst right over their bed. They woke up drenched at three in the morning and rushed around collecting children and pails, both of them inexplicably shaking with giggles.

His hand was on the buzzer when the door opened and Claire came in.

"You're up. I'm sorry — I just woke up myself." It was nearly eight, very late for Claire. She had had trouble going back to sleep after Mark's nightmare. At least she hadn't missed a good running morning. This rain was impossible. "How are you feeling? Use the john?"

He smiled. "I was about to call you." As she helped him across the room, he tried to describe his fits of energy during the night, and his sensation of returning health this morning.

The profound lethargy he had felt the day before seemed to have disappeared.

"Maybe it's another remission." She left him propped against the doorjamb while she moved a waist-high brass towel rack next to the toilet. So long as he had this to lean on, they had found, he could manage the bathroom alone.

A moment later, pushing awkwardly at the elastic band on his pajamas, Meyer wondered if she really believed a remission was possible. Standing, he felt as weak as yesterday; yet he half-believed it himself. Perhaps seeing the children again — ? "Hope is the worst of evils," he quoted in a murmur, "for it prolongs the torment of man." He dropped painfully onto the plastic seat.

When he had finished, Claire came in for him and walked him back to the bed. "Ed Agutter's due to stop by sometime late this morning," she said, fetching a basin of water and soap so he could wash. "We'll see what he thinks."

While he brushed his teeth, she offered to make him waffles, hash browns, fresh-squeezed orange juice, eggs, whatever he fancied. So far, guessing more from hints in his conversation than any direct request, she had made him a brisket, a Waldorf salad, egg drop soup and couscous; but he had never swallowed more than a mouthful or two before announcing that was all he could eat.

Now, though, he said, "You know what I'd like? French toast." He stopped and rinsed his mouth. "French toast with cinnamon."

"With all the cinnamon you want," said Claire, removing the basin and toothbrush.

Meyer must have fallen asleep while she was in the bathroom rinsing them, because later he didn't remember seeing her leave.

# ELEVEN

Anatole was waiting until nine so he could call someone and ask how the show had gone without him. For some reason, he himself had been up since six. He had shaved, dressed, gone downstairs and prowled through the kitchen, made himself coffee and toast, and sat in the living room for a while reading an old book of short stories someone had left lying open. About seven-thirty, he caught a glimpse of Ira on his way through the front hall, but he didn't say anything, and Ira passed by unaware of him. Anatole liked Ira, but he often had the feeling Ira thought acting an irresponsible profession, a silly job for a grown-up. He felt a kind of psychic guy-jostling in the air when the two of them were alone together, as if they were vying for a promotion only one of them could get. Sunny blamed Ira's insecurities, but Anatole couldn't see past his own insecurities far enough to know if she was right.

A little after eight, he climbed upstairs again, hoping Sunny would be awake. He wanted to tell her what he'd realized last night, outside with Charlotte, about his father passing as a Gentile and his own career as an actor. In the excitement of last night's wrangle, he hadn't had a chance. But she was snoring peacefully, lying on her side, her face almost hidden under a pillow. As he watched, she stirred, rolled over and half sat up.

"Fish-flavored ice cream," she mused aloud, then declared with more conviction, "Fish-flavored ice cream! We'll sell a million. Everyone will want to try some!" She subsided into the pillows, still sound asleep. Sunny often talked in her sleep, often sitting upright.

Anatole smiled, memorized what she had said so he could tell her later and shut the door again. He passed aimlessly along the corridor to Meyer's room. He had not yet even seen Meyer. The door was slightly ajar. He peeked in.

A cringing thrill ran through him. Propped against the pillows, eyes closed, hands folded over his chest, lay not a man but the awful vulnerability of human flesh. For an instant, Anatole knew that he, too, was a body — that whatever happened to his heart, his bones, his skin, his blood happened to him, to the idea, the essence of Anatole Bronski. It was simple. Simple and terrible.

He went in, careful not to wake his father-in-law. Noiselessly, he drew the door almost shut behind him. Sunny looked so much like the photographs Anatole had seen of Ruth that it had never occurred to him she might also resemble Meyer. Now he saw how deeply the skeptical curve from her nostrils to the corners of her mouth would one day be etched into her skin. He saw that her narrow nose would thicken, and that her earlobes would droop. For a brief moment, he felt as if he were married to the person in the bed.

He sat in the ladder-back chair. For another minute or two, he observed Meyer. Then, experimentally, he closed his eyes. He dropped his head back, let his mouth open slightly, encouraged his cheeks to pale to chalky whiteness. He synchronized his breathing with Meyer's. He let his cheeks sag. He let his hair and eyebrows fall out. He propped his heels in front of him and drained his limbs of strength.

Then he asked himself what he felt.

Isolated. Indifferent, but not unpleasantly so. He was slipping toward death as if toward sleep, rolling rather decorously down a smooth, gentle slope to not-being. Not-being was dark and tranquil. A needle of panic shot through his chest, but he willed himself to remain still, enervated, his eyes shut. Was this the panic of a healthy man playing at dying, or the elemental human terror of obliteration, so instinctive that no illness, no weakness could neutralize it? He was still trying to determine the answer when footsteps startled him, and he opened his eyes to find Claire in the room. She carried a tray. She must just have come in: The door was still moving behind her.

"Keeping him company," he whispered, struggling to right himself.

Claire stopped by the bed and gave her patient an expert glance — the glance a shopkeeper gives a shelf of goods when a neighborhood hooligan has just moved away from it. As if Anatole might have stolen Meyer's quilt, or stuck his glasses on him upside-down for laughs.

"Has he been awake at all?"

Anatole shook his head.

"Stirred? Talked?"

"No." He was on his feet by now, embarrassed at having been caught rehearsing dying, hoping Claire hadn't realized that was what he'd been doing. "Can I help you with that? Move a table or something?" he asked.

But she dismissed him. "Scurry along."

He was offended but too relieved to argue. Obediently, he scurried.

*

Jesse, lying on his stomach, hooked his ankle around Mimi's upturned foot and resettled himself against her sleep-warm flank. Under his arm, her rib cage rose and fell evenly. His face was close enough to her nostrils that he could feel the tickling exhalation of her breath. He had never slept with Mimi in a twin bed before. It was crowded, but he liked it, although technically, he hadn't slept much. He was used to getting up at five-thirty and he had been awake on and off the whole three hours since. One time, Mimi had wakened him — on a visit to the bathroom, from the sound of the plumbing. He fell asleep before she got back; when he woke again, she was sleeping. Between catnaps, he listened to the rain and desperately cast about in his mind for his next move.

In the beginning, when Mimi had objected to his view of marriage, Jesse had been confident that she would come around in a day or two. Of all the women he had been involved with, Mimi was the most adaptable about his — methods, was the term he preferred. Other girlfriends had made it a point of honor to impose their own methods on him. Several washed his dishes as he requested, or made his bed or turned his lights on and off as he thought best but insisted on reciprocal supremacy when at their homes, or equal input on neutral territory. If he objected, they accused him of being inflexible, a purist, a sexist, a control freak — even, on one occasion, a fascist. But Mimi seemed to have understood from the start, without even asking about it, that he simply couldn't stand to do things that seemed to him unsafe, unhygienic, wasteful, dishonest or impolite. His purpose was not to try to bend others to his will. That was an unwanted side effect. The point was, he had no choice.

As the days had gone by, though, Mimi had not changed her mind about marriage. If anything, she seemed to become more determined to change his. Jesse contemplated lying, pretending he believed a change in their legal status could bind them as one flesh. He would move into her apartment but (casually) keep his. Eventually she'd get over her obstinacy.

But he had discovered, without much surprise, that he could not do this. Three or four days ago, he'd opened his mouth, intending to say, "Okay, Mims, you're right. Let's get married and live happily ever after." When the words came, however, they were different. "Oh, Mimi," he had actually said. "I love you so much. Please don't twist me up inside."

And all the time, he was half enchanted, half tormented by the thought of the baby. It was a girl, he was sure of that. He already knew her dark curls, her tiny replica of Mimi's frog nose, her fat, translucent fingers. Now he moved his arm so his hand lay on Mimi's abdomen. Spellbound, he imagined the cells dividing and dividing.

The thought that Mimi could put a stop to all that with a half hour's brisk work at a clinic sent a shudder through him. Feeling him, Mimi opened her eyes.

She raised her head and put a hand to her mouth.

Jesse vaulted over her, hopped to his feet and scanned the room. His eye lit on the shirt he'd been wearing yesterday. He snatched it from the floor and handed it to her.

Mimi retched.

"Oh, sweetheart, let's get married," Jesse said, kneeling by the bed.

He groped in her purse for a Kleenex so she could wipe her lips and tongue.

Dabbing at her mouth, Mimi looked at him, her question in her eyes.

"We won't think about what it means, we'll just do it. Let's go now."

But she shook her head. Carefully, she folded the shirt into a neat bundle and set it aside.

Sunny woke at ten and found herself alone. She lay for a while and listened with pleasure to the rain pounding on the roof, a sound she could never hear at home because there were three apartments above them. Then she remembered the dead embryos and started to cry. One tear slid along her cheekbone and into her ear. It nestled there, surprisingly cold and wet. Over her objections, each time she had gone through IVF, Anatole had given names to the particles of life the doctors siphoned into her. The last two were Adrian and Gene — or Adrienne and Jean, if they were girls.

Or the late Adrian, Adrienne, Gene and Jean, since they were dead.

The realization that she was not going to give birth to children came to Sunny with a force, a cutting sharpness she hadn't felt before. Being infertile was the kind of idea you don't take in all at once, she had found — it was too big for that. Instead, she kept realizing it over and over, one time angrily, the next with amazement, the next with tears. . . . It was like a big house you got to know slowly. Yesterday, she'd stood in the empty living room, vast and echoey, smelling of fresh paint. Now she crouched in the attic.

She thought of a woman named Caroline who had been in her IVF support group, a short, muscular woman with big, healthy teeth and a bowl of shining, dark hair cut straight across her forehead. Unable to get pregnant, Caroline had had a laparoscopy. She learned her uterus, tubes and ovaries were enmeshed in a thick, thriving jungle of adhesions: endometriosis. Instead of being angry, worried or even despairing, she had been consumed with revulsion for her own body, which until then (she explained) she had always thought of as whole, well, perfect. She had compared herself to a house with termites. Amelia — they used first names only in the group, like criminals in a rehabilitation program — had almost died from her laparoscopy, which the doctor had botched, and which showed no endometriosis. But she was forging ahead. Meg, forty-two and already the mother of a little girl, was on her ninth IVF attempt. She confessed to rather liking the retrieval; she requested minimal anesthesia so she could enjoy the counting of her eggs as the doctor harvested them. Lydia, young and pale, with a single, endless blond braid down her back, had no firm diagnosis yet and was plainly ambivalent about belonging to the group at all — in Sunny's opinion, because she feared mere association with so many older, infertile women might somehow permanently make her one of them.

In spite of their differences, they were all lavish in their sympathy for one another. Even when Sunny admitted her intermittent terror at the thought of what a child might do to her life, her work, her relationship with Anatole — anxieties not one of them seemed ever to have entertained — they overcame their amazement and tried to help her talk it through. There were only two ways to forfeit their goodwill. One was to get pregnant. The other was to give up trying.

Mulling over the idea of a white-flag group for those who had fled the field of battle, Sunny finally made herself get out of bed, shower, dress. Before leaving the bathroom, she peeked into Meyer's room. But he seemed to be sleeping. Quietly, she shut the door again.

Downstairs, she found Ira, Mark, Claire and Charlotte sitting around the dining room table, their plates littered with crusts of French toast and orange rinds. A kind of electric current seemed to be running among them. Sunny noticed it at once, but she couldn't tell what it was. She sat down next to Charlotte and poured coffee from the plastic carafe. Claire offered to make French toast for her.

"Thanks, I'll get myself something in a minute. How's Meyer this morning?"

Everyone laughed.

"Bzz!" Ira said. "I'm sorry, I'm afraid you've lost this round of Distraction. Lucky for you, Miss Sonia Ginzburg of New York City, this was only a test round. You're still in the game."

"Distraction?"

"The object is not to mention — " Charlotte pointed at the ceiling. "Contestants try to distract one another by talking about other subjects, even though all they really can think about is — " She pointed again, nodded and winked broadly. Sunny looked around and was surprised to find even Claire laughing. This was the current she had sensed at the table: They were all slightly hysterical.

"He feels better today," Ira explained. "He ate two slices of French toast and fell asleep again. We decided to pretend we weren't all thinking about him for a minute. It was a game."

"And then I came in."

"Precisely." He spun a knife on the tablecloth.

"He couldn't really be" — Sunny looked to Charlotte, then Claire — "you know, permanently better?"

"No," said Claire, when Charlotte didn't answer. "But maybe for a day or two. It can happen." She looked at Charlotte for confirmation.

But when Charlotte spoke, it was to say, "I think I'll go sit with him. He might wake up."

Sunny choked on a mouthful of coffee. "What?"

She could feel the others shifting in their chairs.

Charlotte repeated the confession she had already made to Mark and Claire half an hour before.

"Nothing happened? Ever?"

Sunny glanced at Mark while Charlotte echoed in agreement, "Nothing."

Mark smiled and nodded, comfortably vindicated.

Charlotte, her cheeks beginning to flame, scraped her chair back, gathered an armful of plates and pushed backward through the swinging door into the kitchen. A moment later they heard her springy footsteps mounting the back stairs.

"Where's Anatole?" Sunny asked.

Claire said, "I thought he was with you."

"I saw him stamping around in the back meadow about half an hour ago." Mark reached across Ira for the sugar bowl.

"In this rain?"

Mark shrugged.

Sunny went into the back hall to look out the window of the mud porch. The meadow, swampy and somber, was empty. She returned to the dining room and looked out the front, into the driveway. He couldn't have gone far: The Triumph was still there, dull, dark and solid in an aquatic world. Next to it was a carpenter's van with a Manhattan address on its side.

"Is Jesse here?"

She sat down again while Ira filled her in.

"Hmm," said Sunny. She wondered how Jesse had found them and realized Mimi must have brought him up previously to meet Mark and Claire — the nearest thing she had to "folks." Mimi had never mentioned that to her. Mechanically, she reached for a paper lying on the table — yesterday's *Wall Street Journal* — and began leafing through it from the back.

"Look!"

Everyone turned at the sound of her startled yelp.

Excitedly, she poked her finger at the op-ed page. "Biological pest control and the pesticide industry. How do you like that?"

Ira's hand shot across the table and snatched the page away from her, almost ripping the paper. His face had gone white. "Who — ? Oh, Jesus." The others watched as he swiftly scanned the article. "Ladybugs, marigolds . . . ," he muttered. "Jesus." He whacked the paper shut and fell into a black silence.

"Not good news?" Claire finally ventured.

"These people don't know what they're talking about. I can't believe — This so-called information . . ." Ira tumbled again into disgusted wordlessness. He folded his thin arms and clamped them furiously over his chest. Across from him, Sunny realized too late how stupid she had been not to foresee this. A prominent op-ed piece placed by a rival organization — what could be worse? When he cooled down, she would talk to him about doing a piece of his own. She could help him. Meanwhile, to spare him further attention, she turned to Mark and asked for the details of Charlotte's about-face.

Anatole sat in the Triumph, grimly aware that cold rainwater was dripping off him onto the leather seats. He was glad to be ruining something. An hour ago, he had slipped into Mark and Claire's bedroom and used their phone — the only private one in the house — to call Cindy, the stage manager on *Crushed Velvet*. She had a four-year-old son and would certainly be awake.

Cindy had told him the play went fine without him.

As soon as she said it, Anatole knew, she realized it was the wrong answer. She started to backtrack. All she meant, really, was that there had been no disasters. Peter didn't go up on his lines, he managed to catch the letter opener in the fight scene when Mara throws it at him. Things like that. Of course it wasn't anything like when Anatole was in it.

Anatole, suddenly telepathic, was convinced Peter had sur-
passed all expectations and turned in a performance with an interpretation of his own. In the racket the rain made on the roof
of the Triumph, he heard the applause Peter got when he took
his bow. His bows.

And that faithless bitch, Mara. Holding his hand, going all
out, no doubt, to help him shine. Delighted, probably, to have
a break from Anatole, to be forced to skate along the rough ice
of an unfamiliar performance. He imagined her hugging Peter,
as she always insisted on hugging Anatole after each show.

"Tell everyone I'll be back tonight, would you?" was all he
had said to Cindy.

"Really?" came her surprised voice. "Is your father-in-law — "
She hesitated, looking for a delicate way to ask if he had died.
"Better?"

"He'll be okay for a while." And he had hung up. For a few
minutes longer, he sat there, trying not to call Mara, or Peter
himself. He thought of phoning his agent; but even with his
agent, he had found, it was best not to appear weak. He
thought of calling Dr. Rundback. He thought of waking Sunny
(who had insisted, needlessly, on having him miss last night)
and roaring at her. But in the end he got up and bolted outside
to march around in the rain.

Now, hunched in the Triumph, he realized he felt doubly
bitter about the missed show because Sunny was being so stubborn about IVF. He didn't really expect her to pursue the op-
tion of a donated egg — the whole idea was ludicrously unlike
Sunny — but he did hope the prospect (the threat) would rec-
oncile her to at least one more round of in vitro. He had a lucky
feeling about this next round.

He pulled his right leg out from under the steering wheel
and flung it over the stick shift. He would have to leave

Audubon no later than three to be at the theater in time for the show. Sunny would throw a fit when he told her he was going back. Maybe he should say he was leaving because of the IVF wrangle, rather than tell her the truth. In a way, that was true. Partly true. It was allied to the truth.

He decided to say nothing till one-thirty or two. If he could avoid being alone with her for a couple more hours, he would be able to announce his plans when it was too late to change them. Until then . . . He shifted uncomfortably on the wet seat. The floor mat by the accelerator squelched under his boot.

Ed Agutter was in his thirties, fair and plump, with earnest brown eyes, wispy hair and curiously small hands and feet. His discomfort as he looked around the circle of faces in Claire Ginzburg's living room was plain. He had told her he would prefer to give her his impressions and let her convey what he said to the others. If they had questions, they could phone. But she insisted they hear it from him firsthand. "That will be better," she had said firmly, leading him downstairs.

Now they were all assembled, Claire's husband and his family. Of all his responsibilities, explaining how things stood to the relatives of his terminal patients was the one he hated most. Even telling the patient was better. The families were always so hopeful, so desperate. They accused him of incompetence and demanded second opinions. They asked him to be honest, then cried out in pain when he was. If they were laymen (as, naturally, they usually were), they wanted exact odds on variables no one could predict. Every possibility meant so much to them, and they understood so little. They were black holes of need.

At last, haltingly, he began his explanation. "Your dad is feeling better today, but you may have noticed some tiny red spots on his skin. These are called petechiae. They are minihemorrhages, and they indicate he is entering what is probably the

last phase of his illness. Your dad has executed a living will in-
dicating he doesn't want life-sustaining treatment. Even if he did,
there would really be nothing we could do. He may live another
week. Probably not longer. You should be prepared for less.

"What will happen? He may develop an infection — pneu-
monia is common — and be unable to fight it off. He may
begin to bleed internally, into his intestine or abdominal cavity
or head — almost anywhere, really. Whatever happens, we'll
keep him as comfortable as we can.

"Think of today as the eye of the storm. He is eating and
talking, his pulse is okay, he's clearheaded. With luck, he'll have
a few more days of relative alertness. Eventually, though, the
anemia and, perhaps, fever may make him confused. At some
point, he will likely become comatose. From then on, there's
no reason to believe he'll feel anything. He will slide painlessly
out of life. You should understand" (Ed always closed his ex-
planations with an overview of the patient's illness) "he has held
up amazingly well against the disease overall. He put up a
whopping good fight. Now . . ." Ed spread his small hands in
what he hoped was an expressive gesture.

The Ginzburgs looked back at him in silence. The young
one with the reddish halo fought down tears, clutching the
hand of her husband, or boyfriend, a dazed look on her face.

"But he feels better today," she said finally. "He ate French
toast. Don't you think . . . ?"

Ed shook his head no. The woman with the pale cornflower
eyes leaned across the coffee table to pat her on the knee. But
the dermatologist (she had met Ed at the door and warned him
about the petechiae, which she confirmed had not been there
yesterday) remained surprisingly silent. Usually doctors felt
the need to add something.

Claire's brother-in-law — Ira? Isaac? — asked, "Does he
know what's going to happen? Meyer himself?"

Ed was relieved when Claire answered. "The general outlines. Sure, he knows."

"Will he realize it while it's happening?" This from the tearful sister, whose tears now spilled over onto her rounded cheeks. Her husband (or boyfriend, Ed somehow suspected) pressed the inside of his arm against hers.

"It depends. He may not. Or he may," Ed told her. "I've tried to prepare him without frightening him — though frankly, he's pretty darn well-informed. Eventually, he'll likely lose track of where he is. If he needs it, the pain medication may contribute to this, make him feel dreamy. He won't feel anything more alarming than falling asleep." He shifted uneasily in his armchair, conscious that he had gone a bit beyond the real scope of his expertise. For all he knew, Meyer would hear trumpets and feel the fiery wrath of Jehovah on his neck.

He felt his own neck and shoulders relax as his listeners began to move, looking more at one another than at him. Apparently, the dreaded business was over. The younger son raised his eyebrows and pushed his glasses up his nose in a Well-I-guess-you've-told-us-everything-you-can kind of way. The dermatologist uncrossed her legs, leaned back and exchanged a glance of bleak solidarity with Claire's husband, Mark. Finally, Claire herself stood up. She thanked Ed and walked him to the door, parroted his instructions and asked him the name of the doctor who would be on call that night. He drove back to the hospital feeling that, on the whole, the visit could have been worse.

In Ed Agutter's wake the Ginzburgs sat, chastened, sobered.

"He makes it sound so gradual, dying," Sunny finally said. She had been unable to locate Anatole, though she had searched the house and the Triumph was still standing in the rain. When she had glanced into Meyer's room, she had found Charlotte watching their father sleep. His frame barely disturbed the blankets. "So mundane. Well, I guess it is. But doesn't it seem like it should be more — I don't know — defined? Epic? Definitive. This sounds like you feel crummy, pop a Darvon, take a nap and — P.S., you don't wake up."

"Better that way," muttered Mark.

"I guess."

"The modern American way of death," Ira said. "It does seem to lack dignity. More like putting a cat to sleep."

"That's exactly what I thought last night!" exclaimed Mimi, astonished, as if the two of them having stumbled on this comparison was one for the record books. "Except I was thinking a dog."

A classic *pigletiste* response, Sunny gloomily noted to herself, wondering briefly if it would be worthwhile to ask Vanessa Redgrave about her views on animal rights.

"He doesn't want heroic struggle," Charlotte said. "Anyway, what modern death really lacks is suffering. We've always been nicer to animals."

Bolstered by Jesse's nearness, Mimi objected, "What's right for animals isn't necessarily right for people. How would you like to be fed once a day, or have to be walked on a leash?"

Jesse squeezed her against him. He was sorry about her father's condition, but it certainly was making Mimi friendlier. It occurred to him to try to get a dying benison from Meyer, a mandate to marry his daughter.

Claire came back, preceded by a whoosh of chilly air from the front door, and resumed her place on the camelback sofa next to Mark. She took his hand and rubbed it.

"I wonder if we should all sort of go in and tell him goodbye," Sunny ventured, when no one else had spoken for a while. "In case this good period doesn't last." She noticed without interest that someone else had been reading her *Best Short Stories* book: An issue of *Harper's* had been slipped between its pages as a place mark.

"Don't you think that might scare him?" asked Jesse.

Sunny looked at him. It was the first time he had spoken since they sat down with Agutter — the first words, probably, he had ever addressed to her that weren't purely the result of a sociable or practical or merely polite impulse. She was less than pleased by his implied criticism (especially since it was just). At the same time, it was a responsible, even sensitive objection. Her opinion of him improved.

"I didn't mean all at once," she lied, then added more truthfully, "And of course, not say good-bye out loud. Just each of us to ourselves."

When no one answered, Claire gave a murmur of assent. It was obvious each of them would deal with any final leave-taking in his own way. She was, naturally, most concerned with Mark.

"First, though, I'd like to change Meyer's sheets," she said, as a plan took form in her mind. "Sweetie, would you help me?" She stood, Mark's hand still in hers.

She had to tug before he would stand up and follow her, but once they were on the stairs, he came willingly enough, only lagging in the corridor. She patted his hand as they reached Meyer's door.

# TWELVE

Sunny was in the kitchen making coffee for the others when the sound of footsteps coming down the back stairs caught her ear. It was Anatole, his hair wet, all slicked back, unnaturally black. He looked startled.

"Where have you been?"

"Out walking. I needed to think," said Anatole. In fact, he had left the Triumph to sulk for an hour in a corner of the gloomy barn until hunger, boredom and dampness finally dislodged him. He had sneaked upstairs to change and was hoping to rustle up some food before anybody saw him. "I sat with your dad for a while," he added, letting the juxtaposition of this remark with the sentence "I needed to think" do his lying for him. "He was asleep, though. How are you today?"

Sunny wanted to make him feel guilty for having disappeared, but she couldn't seem to muster the appropriate recriminations. Instead, "He's in the last stage," she said, her voice cracking with sorrow and frustration. Her sinuses prickled as they always did just before she cried. "Dr. Agutter was here."

Anatole crossed the room and put his arms around her. To

her annoyance, she moved forward as if responding to a magnetic pull and clung to him. "Twenty-eight years, and then we get a week. That selfish bastard . . ."

Her words trailed off into wet burbling. She sobbed against him. Anatole cradled her head and petted her hair, kissed her forehead, murmured, "Okay. Okay." Teeth nearly chattering, she repeated Dr. Agutter's prognosis. Anatole drew her to the breakfast nook and sat her down. There, she described how she had waked in the night and talked with Meyer.

The kettle screeched.

"I'll do it." Anatole stood up.

"The coffee's in the freezer." Her words sounded fuzzy, muffled.

"It's so infuriating," she said, as he patted the filter into place. "Why did he have to turn up? Now we're all wrenched around. Ira wants tea," she interrupted herself. "In front of you, to your left."

He opened the cupboard.

"Constant Comment. Sugar, no milk." She was silent a moment before going on, "By the way, Charlotte recanted."

"Did she?" said Anatole. He felt perversely disappointed.

Sunny snuffled deeply, wishing she had a tissue. She watched as Anatole poured the water, gathered mugs, spoons, lemon, a pitcher of milk. His hair had begun to dry. His thick socks made a whispery noise as he padded over the linoleum. He sat down next to her and stroked her hands, which were splayed and pressed against the maple table, while the water finished dripping through the filter.

Sunny sighed. Why on earth had she insisted on his missing last night? He had gone onstage in the midst of worse crises than this — hers and his own. He had gone on with raging fevers, with a pinched nerve in his back. Once, Sunny got stuck on the subway during a track fire — two hours in a smoky car on the Number Nine between Fiftieth Street and Times Square. Having no idea where she was, Anatole had been beside himself with worry; but he still went on. Hours after Max's triple bypass, with Max still in the recovery room, he had played Gaston, the lisping Frenchman, in *Heavens Above*. And God knew he had worked often enough just after they learned (again) she wasn't pregnant.

Chagrined, disappointed, and too late, she recognized in last night the tracks of the ruthless tractor that was her character. It bumped over all in its path. With a crunch, she ground over the bones of Anatole's professional reputation. Over their marriage. Over his love for her.

Repentantly, she said, "You know, it occurs to me you might still be able to make it to tonight's show if you went in soon."

She felt his body tense, but all he said was "Hmm," on a high, pondering note.

"I know you don't want to miss another night."

Carefully, "True," Anatole said.

"The only thing is, I really would like you to come back. I'm scared to sleep up here alone. I swear I'll have you back in the city by one-thirty tomorrow afternoon."

Anatole turned her face up, tilted it and kissed the bridge of her nose. "You could come with me," he said. "Stay in the city, do the interview Monday, come up here again and write it."

Sunny shook her head. "That might not work out so well," she said, an obscure superstition preventing her from being more explicit.

Anatole kissed her nose again. Though it shamed her, she knew even as he did it that she would never apologize to him for last night. If she admitted blame, she reasoned, he would realize she was the slow poison in his life and leave her. Whereas if she said nothing, she could rely on his abundant, free-floating guilt to cloud the question in his mind. This was always her reasoning when she knew she had wronged him. Her apologies to him were few.

He carried the tray to the living room. There, Charlotte, Ira, Mimi and Jesse had been rejoined by Claire, who had picked up her needlepoint frame and was idly tapping it against one knee as if it were a tambourine. Mark was still upstairs.

Sunny asked Anatole to go back to the kitchen for another mug.

"And you might as well call and let Peter Cavanaugh know he can crawl back under his rock." She turned to the others. "Anatole's going to drive down and do the show tonight," she explained. Suddenly inspired, "Come to think of it, Claire, why don't you go, too?" Between the kitchen and the living room, she had already had time to grow uneasy about having asked him to drive back tonight. Especially so late, especially if the rain kept up. It was the kind of selfish request God might punish with an accident. The rainy night, the panicked scream of tires, the car careening out of control . . . But Claire would drive for him and keep him awake. Claire was a good driver. "You've never seen the show. You should. And you could drive him back, so he can sleep. It would really be a favor."

"You might even enjoy the play," Anatole put in tartly. "Some people find it entertaining. They pay to go!" Twice he had offered house seats to Mark and Claire; twice they had responded with excuses. In fact, they had not come to see him in anything since they'd moved up to Audubon.

"I'm sure I would enjoy it," said Claire vaguely. But she began to dither about taking care of Meyer and making dinner.

"Don't be ridiculous. If you don't get out now, who knows when you will?" insisted Sunny. "We'll all be gone by tomorrow night, and you'll be left doing everything again. Charlotte can keep an eye on Meyer, and the rest of us can certainly cook dinner."

"I don't know . . ."

At this moment, Mark came in. He had already left Meyer when Claire had returned (after a very long absence), and Meyer had been asleep; but from the pink glow of Mark's forehead and cheeks, she deduced he had managed to have the talk he wanted. Mark always scrubbed his face with cold water after a painful discussion.

As soon as he understood Sunny's proposition, he urged Claire to accept.

"You come, too," she answered, catching at his hand. "You need a break yourself."

"I can't go to the theater tonight." From his tone, it was clear he meant he could not indulge in such frivolity when his father was so ill.

"Then how can I?"

Yet everyone pushed at her.

"Go, go," said Mark. "It'll make me feel better to know you're out of here."

"Come," invited Anatole. "Keep me company."

"Especially on the drive back," Sunny hinted.

"Can you do it, Charlotte? Monitor him, and all?"

"God help my patients if I can't."

"Then I guess . . ." Claire shrugged. She didn't believe Anatole would come on to her when they were alone. If she read him right, he was one of those men who only flirted under surveillance. At the same time, she couldn't conceal from herself that the simple prospect of being alone with him for a whole evening — of having his smell, his bulk, his attention to herself — excited her. "Okay." Her voice sounded small in her own ears. Weakly, she smiled up at Mark.

When Claire had dragged Mark up to Meyer after Agutter's visit, they had found him strangely excited.

"Ed told you?" he asked.

Mark nodded uncertainly. Claire began to bustle around the bed, efficiently shifting Meyer this way and that.

"It won't be long."

Mark accepted a couple of pillowcases and set about changing his father's pillows. The expression on Meyer's face was weirdly playful, puckish. "You almost sound pleased," he said cautiously.

Meyer seemed mildly embarrassed, as if he had been caught in a social lie. "It is a great adventure," he said defensively. "Greater, in my opinion, than life itself." He had told Mark his views on death before; Mark had both suppressed his skepticism and made it abundantly clear.

"Damn," interrupted Claire. "No top sheet. Let me check the linen closet."

She hurried across the hall and was back in a moment.

"Not a clean sheet in the place. Full house. I'm going to wash this one by hand and throw it in the dryer on high, okay?" Spreading the quilt over her father-in-law, she swept the linens she had stripped off into her arms and left. "Stay here for a bit, will you, Mark?" she tossed over her shoulder. "I won't be long."

Mark exchanged a glance with her as she left. This is it, her look said, don't blow it. He lingered awkwardly by the end of the bed. "Can I get you some soup?" he asked, helplessly compelled. "Cocoa? A sandwich, a cream soda?"

"Ha! Cream sodas," said Meyer, swept with nostalgia. "No, I thank you." He lapsed into a contemplative silence, his eyes fixed (so far as Mark could tell) on a knob on the dresser.

"Dad."

After a pause, Meyer's gaze traveled to meet his.

Mark stood at the end of the bed, his left hand clutching a

wooden pineapple, his right balled into a fist in his pocket. He struggled against the reflexive courtesy. I'm sorry, part of him wanted to begin. I'm sorry you're so sick, I'm sorry we have so little time, I'm sorry to dump this on you at a moment like this . . .

That's all Meyer's fault, he told himself firmly. Suppose Eliot had something to say to me. Wouldn't I want him to say it? Nevertheless, it was with the sensation of leaping into a bottomless abyss that he forced himself to open his mouth and start, "You know, this past winter, I left Claire. Just like you left Ruth. I was forty-six, the same age you were." His voice was tight but surprisingly even, controlled.

Meyer said, "Did you?" as if he were impressed — as if the knowledge made him like Mark more.

"Yes. I shouldn't say 'you know,' because in fact, no one does know except Claire. Even June — she was still home at the time — Claire didn't even tell her what was really going on." He moved restlessly to the ladder-back chair and took hold of it from behind with both hands.

"It was kind of stupid, actually. Very stupid, because the stuff you would normally run away from—the job, the daily grind—most of that was over for me. I had quit my firm, we had moved up here. I had already run away, but I ran away all the same. How do you like that? Like father, like son."

Meyer cleared his throat, but Mark waited in vain for him to speak.

Finally, Mark went on. "Anyway, what I'm saying is, seeing myself do that made me feel closer to you. But it also made me" — he steeled himself — "hate you. Because, what an ugly legacy to pass on to your son, you know? And yet at the same time, I could see it. For the first time, I could see why you went. There was a woman in my case, too." He lowered his voice and hurried on, in case Claire should come back sooner than he expected.

"A file clerk in the Sullivan County Record Room, in Monticello. Lizbeth. Moody, nervous, incompetent — totally the opposite of Claire, see what I mean? Very young, younger than Mimi. She goes out to clubs at night to dance. She smokes grass, she drinks margaritas. Her friends are other clerks, and shop assistants and manicurists. And in February, I left Claire and June to move in with her. I was like a crazy man, an insane man.

"But, you know, Meyer, as I hear myself say this, actually I'm beginning to wonder if this happens a lot — more than people know, I mean. Like with us. I was gone almost three months, but Claire covered up for me, she kept it a secret. Do you think this happens a lot, more than people realize?"

He stopped. He had asked the question deliberately, because Meyer had no reason not to answer it. It wasn't a personal question, or a loaded one. Just a simple, direct inquiry to get his father to say something. He used to ask witnesses questions like that occasionally.

At last, Meyer conceded, "Probably," then backpedaled, "Possibly."

Satisfied that he was at least listening, Mark resumed. "So maybe it's not a case of the acorn not falling far from the tree. I don't know. Whatever, common or not, I went. And I'd be lying if I said I regretted it. I've been with Claire since I was 17. I never had . . . you know, relations with a woman except — " He paused to glance guiltily around. Was that a footstep outside? The rain muted everything. He glanced at the half-open door. No one. "I never knew you could feel like that — that there were such feelings, that anyone could feel that. I guess I was lucky, because afterwards, Claire took me back. She's quite a wonder, Claire. People underestimate her.

"But what I'm getting to, is that the whole time I was with Lizbeth, maybe I didn't care about Claire, but I was terrified I'd end up losing touch with Eliot and June. That I'd lose stature in their eyes. Or maybe they'd even refuse to see me out of loyalty to their mother." He heard his voice grow more heated and stopped to calm himself. Meyer looked politely interested. "I guess I don't need to spell this out, but my question is, How could you stand to let us fade into your past? How could you physically tolerate that? The flesh of your flesh." Moved by his own oratory, Mark repeated the phrase, his voice straining, "The only flesh of your flesh."

Meyer's gaze broke from his son's and wandered up to focus on some point in the air over Mark's left shoulder. He was silent a long moment. In fact, he had a sixth child, Josh — in Tacoma, so far as he knew. Mark and Claire knew about him. They had talked about him when Meyer arrived; but the matter must have slipped Mark's mind. He seemed upset. Not wanting to correct him now, Meyer closed his eyes and tried to think, but the huge imminence of death distracted him as it had throughout Mark's story of — what was it? Marital infidelity, he thought. How unfortunate that Mark had waited until now to relate it. A few days ago, this morning even, he could have concentrated better. But now, although he heard the anguish in his son's voice, he had no idea what to say to soothe it away. He found himself curiously unable to focus on Mark at all. What was his question? He was waiting for an answer to whatever it was. Meyer wondered if "Probably" would do again. But no, this had been a how question — how Meyer could . . . could have done something. Given the passion in Mark's voice, it seemed out of the question to ask.

"I don't know," he said at last, then added an all-purpose "I'm sorry."

To his dismay, though, Mark only seemed to get more upset.

"Okay, I'll tell you how," he said. Now his voice was harsh with anger. Meyer opened his eyes. Mark was spasmodically gripping and releasing the back of the chair. "I think I do know. And the answer is, you had no business having kids in the first place. You didn't deserve children, and you didn't deserve Ruth. You were always so amused, so playful. When you weren't holed up in your study. When I was a kid, my friends used to say they wished their dads could be like you were, full of interesting facts and lines from books. And no discipline. But I think that's a crock. I think that was a cop-out. You lived with us like a boarder in a rooming house. You never took any real responsibility. You were never *there*."

Yes. Yes, this was familiar; this was almost what he had talked about in the night with Sonia. "That's right," Meyer said. "That's true."

For a moment, Mark was silent, staring at him. Then, "How can you lie there and say that so nonchalantly, 'That's right'?" he demanded. "These are your dying words to me, I'm right?"

Meyer blinked, confused. Had Ed Agutter told them he was dying now, this minute? And were these such bad last words to a son? He couldn't remember what was at issue. Suddenly, he felt drowsy again; a cloud of sleep was drifting toward him. But he rallied himself. Fathers and sons. Fathers and sons.

"Did you know my father was fifty-two when he married my mother?" he said. "A childless widower. She was forty. They never expected children. They were so amazed when I came, they could hardly keep their hands off me. Sometimes, Papa would take me to work and let me roll in the bins where the furs were kept . . ."

Meyer stopped. Where was he going with this story? He must have had a point, but what was it? It occurred to him that these really might be his last words. Perhaps, wrapped in this drifting cloud was death itself. His thoughts turned dimly to a book on his night table, but he couldn't remember now which book or why it was on his mind. His son Mark was here. What should he say? "You're a good man, Mark," he said. "You'll take care of them." And again, "You're a good man."

He closed his eyes. Surely those were acceptable words. They were true, and they were pleasant. Never say anything unless it is two of these three: true, necessary or pleasant. His mother had taught him that.

The room faded.

Meyer was sleeping by the time Mark straightened out the quilt. Claire would be back soon, but he checked the night table anyway, to be sure the water glass was within reach, the buzzer and the tissue box at hand. He switched off the bedside lamp. The rain beat steadily on the glass of the windows; slightly loose, the panes hummed back. The room was filled with a pearly gray light. Mark bent and almost kissed his father's white forehead before he left.

# THIRTEEN

"Mom never had a nervous breakdown," Sunny was saying. "Mom?" she added uncertainly. She sat in the rocking chair by the fireplace, rocking ferociously. Meyer was sleeping. Claire had gone upstairs to change, Anatole to the kitchen to eat something and make his call to New York. Mimi and Jesse, hands locked together, still huddled side by side on the love seat. Ira, sunk deep in his armchair, had removed his glasses and sat hunched over them, folding the earpieces in and out. Mark and Charlotte faced each other across the coffee table, Mark slumped limply in a corner of the camelback couch, Charlotte hugging her knees to her chest in the center of the corduroy sofa.

"Yes she did," repeated Charlotte. "When she was sixteen." She looked to her brothers for confirmation.

"Yeah." Reluctantly, Ira agreed. "She told me about it the year I turned sixteen. She locked herself in a room with a knife and a mirror and wouldn't come out for a week. If that's a nervous breakdown." Ira gazed moodily at the nearest of the coffee table's ball-and-claw feet.

"She called it that," said Charlotte.

"What was the knife for? To keep people out?" Mimi asked.

"To mutilate herself. Well, that's what she told me," Charlotte defended herself, as Mark glared at her and Sunny yelped, "What?"

"Did she do anything?" This from Sunny.

"I think she scratched up her skin a little." Charlotte looked uncomfortably to her younger brother. "Isn't that right, Ira?"

Ira heard his name and realized he had not been listening. Somehow, his whole consciousness had become absorbed in the world under the coffee table, the curving grain of the wooden legs, the syncopated V's in the circling pattern of the rag rug. Automatically, he said, "Right." He shook himself mentally, forcing his attention to return to the conversation. This kind of microcosmic spacing out — the dreaminess he'd been known for as a child — rarely occurred except when he was with his family.

"It probably wasn't that big a deal, when you think about it," Charlotte went on. "Just a sixteen-year-old girl in a snit. If it happened now, she'd stick a ring through her nostril and call it a day."

"You know, this is really starting to bother me." Sunny stopped rocking and straightened up, her feet flat on the floor. "There's all this family lore you Bigs know, and Mimi and I don't know anything."

As she spoke, Anatole appeared in the doorway and pointed interrogatively toward the stairs. Sunny waved him away, and he disappeared.

"What else have we never heard?" she went on. "Did she sip gin from her teacup? Bury her fingernail clippings in the park?"

"You're getting the wrong idea, Sun." Ira slipped his glasses on again. "You know what Mom was like."

Mimi said, "I don't. I don't remember much at all, really."

"You were" — Charlotte paused to count — "in high school when she died. Surely you must have noticed something."

"You know what? You can back off, Charlotte," Mimi said. She extricated her hand from Jesse's to point a finger at her sister. "You think I'm some kind of — rug or something you can talk down to however you want. Well, back off, I'm war — telling you."

Charlotte threw her hands up in mock surrender. "Yes'm."

"I don't even know what she was like, and I was finishing college," Sunny said. "If you think about it, Charlotte, I'll bet your understanding of her wasn't so all-fired profound when you were in college. Not to mention high school."

"In point of fact, I was nineteen the summer she flew me home to babble at me about Meyer. And I learned more about her in those two months than in the whole eighteen years before them."

"Like what?" Mark demanded. Charlotte had never mentioned any such revelations to him.

"Like — well, like nothing she ever expected me to blurt out in front of" — Charlotte glanced around the room — "all and sundry."

" 'All' being the sacred Ginzburgs, I suppose, and Jesse being 'sun-sun — ' "

At the same time, "What happened to Miss Let's-Keep-the-Facts-Straight?" Ira laughed. "Come on, spill it."

"Oh, for goodness's sake." Flustered, Charlotte crossed her ankles, hugging her knees still tighter against her chest. "She told me about their marriage, that's all. How they met, what Meyer was like. You know, going over the past. It was the summer Mark and I worked at Milt's Retreat."

"And?" Sunny prodded.

"Oh, God. Let me think. She told me that before we were born, he used to roll up notes and put them in the ring of Daisy's collar — remember Daisy, Mark?"

He nodded. Daisy had been a dachshund, and not a very nice one. Mark mainly recalled fearing her.

"Daisy would wander around the house, until eventually, maybe hours later, Ruth would notice her and find the note and read it."

"And what would it say?" asked Sunny.

"They were love notes."

"Oh!"

They all considered this. It was difficult to connect Ruth with love notes. The Ruth they knew generated a literature of leaflets, of bulletin boards ("Mothers! Join us! Rally to demand a traffic light at Riverside and 77th!"), of letters to the editor. Her communications to them when they were away were terse and cheery (". . . Got to run, hon! Eat your Wheaties. XO, Mom.")

"What else?"

Charlotte sighed. "Oh, let's see. She told me Meyer used to make strudel, everything from scratch. It was the one thing he enjoyed cooking, but he stopped making it when Mark and I were little. And he used to do imitations of Granny and Grandpa Zellerman behind their backs. The Zellermans always looked down on the Ginzburgs, you know. They thought they were lumpen, because Zellermans have been here for generations and the Ginzburgs were born in the old country. So Meyer would walk around right behind Granny and Grandpa Zellerman on Passover, for instance, and mimic their fancy ways. Ruth had to pretend not to see, of course, but he was so funny once, she peed in her pants."

"Really?"

"And he called me Juicy Fruit when I was a baby — " Charlotte's stern cheeks colored, "because my diapers were always full. And . . . let's see. What else? During the war, when Meyer was in Alaska, he once sent a drawing of a snowflake copied from life, out in the cold, with a magnifying glass. His letter said he was enclosing the flake. But the army censored the drawing. All she got was a black blotch.

"And — hmm, occasionally, as he got into his thirties, Meyer used to have quick fits of depression, when he would hide from everyone. For a day or two, or three, he wouldn't eat or wash or even get up. Mom would tell us he was sick, but he wasn't. Remember she used to say Dad had a 'touch of the grippe'? Well, that's what he was in the grip of. Come to think of it, he was probably a little manic-depressive."

She paused briefly before going on. "Anyway, Mom thought maybe she hadn't been understanding enough about these depressions. Something about them rubbed her the wrong way, she said, so she was always angry when he fell into them, not sympathetic. That's what she said.

"And that was what got me. That was what was so wild. The whole time she was telling me all this, she was in agony. She still thought Meyer was the cat's pajamas. She couldn't be pissed at him. She couldn't say, 'That fucking asshole left me with five kids and no money, and fuck him.' It was always, 'How could I have lost the love of this fascinating man?' She insisted she had caused him to leave. Some fault of hers, something about her that was impossible to live with. It couldn't be him, it had to be her." Charlotte sighed again. "Such a smart woman, too."

Mimi stirred uneasily. She had always admired her mother's lack of bitterness toward Meyer. Growing up, Mimi had had several friends whose mothers had divorced, then tried to poison their children's minds against their fathers. Though Ruth hadn't talked a lot about Meyer, when she had, it was usually the way you would talk about a friend you still liked but had somehow lost touch with — affectionately, but as if their time together were part of a distant past.

Now Mimi wished she had let Ruth finish whatever it was she had started to say about not missing sex with Meyer. In her experience, no one made sense unless you had some idea of their sex life. Charlotte hadn't mentioned that part of Ruth and Meyer's relationship, and Mimi certainly didn't want to ask if she knew anything on the subject. Maybe they didn't have sex, except to have children. Maybe Ruth felt guilty because she was prudish; Mimi had had that feeling once, with a boyfriend who thought she should behave like the girl in *The Story of O*. Luckily, the feeling of guilt hadn't lasted more than a week after they broke up.

She thought of how much Ruth liked to cook and eat, the way she used to wriggle down into the grass here in the summer and drowse in the sun for hours. Definitely, she enjoyed her senses. In fact, Mimi had always assumed she'd inherited her own considerable desires from her mother. Was it possible Ruth had been too demanding? There were times when Jesse teased Mimi about that. She glanced at his face (turned away from her now to look at Charlotte) and tried to imagine him leaving her because she wanted too much sex. The thought made her smile. Whether by chance or because he felt this, he turned, saw her and smiled back. He took her hand again and gripped it, holding it against his thigh. Mimi tried to scowl, but all she could think of was his angular shoulder against hers, the warmth of his thigh through his jeans. She tried pulling her hand away, but Jesse held on to it.

"Funnily enough," Sunny now said, "I had an idea about this very point last night. I was thinking how Ruth's omnicompetence made us crazy, and it struck me it might have driven Meyer crazy, too."

Even before her words ended, Charlotte threw her hands in the air. "Oh, terrific. God forbid a woman should be capable. That's a nice, progressive theory, Sunny. What do you do, miss a deadline now and then to keep Anatole interested?"

"Charlotte, please, please tell me you haven't become one of those people you can't say the truth to in case it contradicts received liberal wisdom," Sunny shot back. "I'm so bored with that."

"It has nothing to do with received wisdom, liberal or illiberal," said Charlotte, remembering at the same time the hormonal theory she had expounded to Ira. Were it ever to come up publicly, she would certainly disavow it. "It's a question of thinking along the lines of certain stereotypes, certain old myths. Which is stupid, and will lead to stupid conclusions."

"Well, she did drive us batty. That's not a conclusion, it's a fact."

"But we didn't abandon her."

"You did." This came from Mark, who had straightened his shoulders a bit and now sat forward on the couch, pointing at Charlotte. "You ran to California."

"Oh, please. Now what? I had to grow up. Excuse me."

"Whatever you had to do, you left Ira and me to pick up your slack. Not that it's so awful, but it wouldn't hurt you to take responsibility for your actions."

"I was seventeen."

"Ira was thirteen."

"Ira can speak for himself." She turned to him. "Speak, Ira."

"Arf," said Ira.

"No, really. What do you think? Did I abandon you?"

He shrugged. "It was *sauve qui peut*. You saved yourself."

"But at your expense?"

He made a face, twitching his eyebrows together and bunching his mouth up on one side. That heightened mental acuity he had programmed himself to feel this morning had been a reality on and off throughout the day. He felt it now. Mark was using him as a human shield to make a surprise attack on Charlotte. If Ira confirmed the charge that Charlotte was a deserter, it was Ira who would bear the brunt of her anger — Mark and Charlotte were too tight for Mark to get stuck with it. But if he denied it, Mark would use that one day as evidence his baby brother was a wimp. For her part, Charlotte was more interested in proving Mark wrong than in whether or not she had actually caused anyone harm. It was a classic no-win situation. He turned his empty hands up. "My records don't go back that far," he said, shaking his head.

Dissatisfied, Charlotte nevertheless sat back, her lips pressed together.

In the silence, after much inner debate, Mimi said, "It seems to me that it would be natural to keep loving someone after you loved them for twenty years. You know?" She turned hopefully to Sunny. "To want to, I mean. I mean, if one day Ruth said, 'Oh, that Meyer, he always was a bastard,' then she would lose her whole image of him, her idea of this man who took up twenty-five years of her life. You know?"

Sunny looked politely confused. Mimi bit her bottom lip. For once, words were coming easily to her. But they weren't the right words. She wasn't expressing herself clearly.

"I mean, if you love someone," she tried again, "that love itself is like a possession of yours. Your emotion of love, that's what you cher — value," she concluded, seeing even in Sunny's attentive face only a vague comprehension of her idea. In her head, she knew exactly what she wanted to say — she thought Jesse probably got it, too — but you had to spell things out to Sunny and Mark and the rest of them in complete sentences or they didn't understand you at all. In that sense, it suddenly occurred to her, they were the stupid ones. "Loving someone is a joy," she said, taking a last stab. "It makes you feel strong."

The uncomfortable silence that often followed one of Mimi's contributions to the family's conversation was broken by Anatole's arrival. Vibrant with energy now that he was to leave, he came in and crossed the room to stand behind Sunny's chair, his fingers on her shoulders.

"Charlotte, Claire says would you go upstairs for a minute so she can talk to you about Meyer's medication?"

Charlotte unfolded herself and stood. As she went, she said, "I think Ruth was like a lot of women. She enjoyed feeling guilty. With Meyer gone, she had nothing to do but obsess about him. It gave her the illusion of continuity, of still having a man in her life." She paused in the doorway. "When what she should have done was go out and find another man. Such a smart woman, too," she repeated. "You can bet when Alec left, I didn't agonize over what I'd done to push him away."

Under the clatter of her footsteps taking the wooden stairs, Anatole stage-whispered to the room, "Sounds like a safe bet to me. I'll bet old Alec agonized over why he didn't leave sooner, though."

Mimi snorted with laughter.

"Don't be rude about Charlotte," said Sunny, reaching up for his wrists. "She's your sister-in-law."

Behind her, Anatole bowed. "Terribly sorry."

Sunny leaned her head back and looked, upside down, at her husband. She was amazed — as she was often amazed — by his willingness to forgive her. If the tables were turned, if he had prevented her from taking an assignment so he could have eight extra hours of moral support, she would have smoldered over the injustice for months. Yet there was nothing in his face but gladness to be going, and love for herself.

All the same, she sometimes worried that his resentments were assembling somewhere deep inside him, accumulating and accumulating until they reached a critical mass and blew up in her cowardly face.

# FOURTEEN

As they swept past Liberty, rain flying at the windshield and sluicing off over its metal edges to splash the side windows, Claire realized she had never seen Anatole drive before. In fact, she had only been in a car with him once, years ago, the winter before he and Sunny were engaged.

The car had been a taxi, and it was the first time Claire and Mark met Sunny's new boyfriend. They took the train in from Larchmont, went to Sunny's apartment for a drink with her and Anatole Bronski, then all hopped a cab to a restaurant in Tribeca. In the cab, Mark sat in front, Anatole between the two women in back. Claire remembered the insistent (deliberate? unavoidable?) pressure of the side of Anatole's upper leg against hers. As the cab jounced down Seventh Avenue, he told a long story about ordering *salade niçoise* in Nice. Claire looked sidelong at him, laughed, asked what happened next, exchanged glances with Sunny, who had heard the story before. At the same time, she fought a slight nausea from the motion of the rattling, overheated cab. She also fought a dizzying attraction to Sunny's boyfriend.

She had never met a man who radiated such confidence, who was so vigorous, relaxed, playful. So — tuned in, was the phrase that kept recurring to Claire. It had nothing to do with his fame — which was less then, in any case, than now. Anatole seemed equipped with different senses than other people. More senses. It was as if he could dance along the invisible currents that flow among people in a social situation, as if he breathed intuitions and emotions rather than air. Certain messages, certain moments, were definite and material to him that to her — to almost anyone else — were hypothetical, cryptic, ephemeral. He was a dog who heard inaudible whistles, who read eyes, gestures, smells. In a way, not unlike a nurse or doctor, except that instead of noticing shortness of breath or a telltale tremor he picked up — what? Claire couldn't say. Psychic clues that eluded her.

Later, she went home convinced that he also gave off such data, in a way even outsiders like herself could mysteriously understand. She thought he had conducted silent one-on-one conversations with herself and Mark simultaneously with the audible one. He warned Mark he wouldn't be deterred from marrying Sunny by Mark's (obvious, Claire feared, even without extra senses) mistrust of him. And what had he told Claire? That in another life — or maybe this one — he would have whisked her far away from everyone else and made love to her hour after hour, languorously, deliciously.

On and off in the years that followed, he had given her the same message again — sometimes explicitly, by flirting, sometimes (even more disconcertingly) when she was trying to discuss library funding or the spread of rabies in raccoons.

What confounded and embarrassed her was that she didn't know if he was truly attracted to her or only did all this as a sort of gallantry, to amuse and flatter her. The way the young Jimmy Cagney, or James Stewart, for example, used to "flirt" with his movie mom over her apple pie. His behavior certainly didn't seem to bother Sunny. Claire wasn't around him enough to know, but she imagined he behaved this way toward lots of women. And she was sure there was nothing serious in it: He didn't pine for her when they were apart or even, she suspected, think of her at all. But did she actually arouse him? That was what she couldn't figure out.

It galled her that she was so inexperienced, so tone-deaf as to be unable to make at least an estimate of his sincerity. She was sure he could judge quite shrewdly the effect he had on her. Of course, he was an actor, and therefore professionally interested in the effect he had on other people. He was a career manipulator. Actors were famous for indiscriminate, insignificant shows of affection. Put all these factors together, and it was only natural Claire felt completely lost. If Anatole had been a doctor, she assured herself, she would have had no trouble identifying the nature and extent of his interest in her.

As it was, however, she was baffled. It seemed to her that each time they met, he was able to bring her close to him or spin her away as if she were a yo-yo, as if he could choose the degree of closeness and understanding between them, set it like a thermostat. While by contrast, any attempt on her part to stand on her dignity, or (rarely) approach him emotionally, dissolved unnoticed and without result.

Not that any of it mattered anyway, in the end. In twenty-five years of marriage, the closest Claire had come to infidelity was to harbor a wordless, short-lived crush on a kidney transplant patient (once) and a teacher of Eliot's (twice). Those few times colleagues or drunken husbands of friends had pawed at her outright, she had shoved them away and threatened disclosure if they tried it again. Apart from all of which, if she were planning an indiscretion, she would certainly choose someone other than Sunny's husband. It just galled her, that was all. It made her feel childish.

Now she watched his profile against the rain-spotted

window, with the bare trees and tatty billboards of the Quickway sliding past behind him. He drove actively, glancing often
in the mirrors and aggressively overtaking other cars. He kept
his hand on the stick shift even on the highway, as if he might
need to change gears any second. Did he care at all, she wondered, that she was with him? On the way home, would he ask
her opinion of the play? She must remember to say something
nice about his acting. He would expect that. She'd seen him act
only three times before, twice in movies and once in a musical
that closed the week after it opened. If what she had seen was
representative, she didn't care much for his work. He seemed
artificial to her, phony. But no one shared this opinion, neither
critics nor friends she had asked, so maybe it had to do with
knowing how different he was in private life. He was the only
actor — the only public person — she knew.

She took a last look at his profile, his large, handsome nose,
the slightly exaggerated hollow between his cheekbone and his
jaw. Then, fearing he would feel her gaze, she swiveled her
head as if to survey the fleeing countryside. Instead, though,
her eye was caught by her own reflection, shimmering and
askew, on the rain-streaked windowpane. How small, how de-
mure she looked! Her hands were folded in her lap; her feet
nestled primly together in gleaming black pumps. She stared at
herself, simultaneously relieved and appalled by the disjunction
between her collected appearance and her drifting thoughts.

Suppose she were to open her mouth and say, "Anatole, do
you desire me?" Or, "Anatole, I always find being alone with
you disturbingly erotic." Only those few words, spoken aloud,
just that little puff of breath, and the gulf between her inner
and outer selves would be nothing, would be transformed to
smooth, continuous ground. She turned her gaze to his hand
on the stick shift. It was huge and ruddy, and looked warm. A

few dark hairs curled up from the backs of his fingers. His knuckles were bony and slightly raw. She would never speak any such reckless, true sentence. Instead, "What made you decide to go back to the city tonight?" she heard herself ask. "I thought Sunny told me you were going to skip this performance."

"Sunny had an attack of generosity," he answered, without turning his head. "That happens to her from time to time."

Claire gave a half laugh. "I'm sure it isn't as bad as that."

Now he glanced at her, smiling in a way she hadn't seen before — or maybe she had, but it was in a movie. Yes, in *Pressure Drop*, when his boss tells him the firm is letting two architects go. A knowing smile, both cynical and wounded.

"You're a funny person, Claire," he said. He turned his eyes back to the road. "You know perfectly well what we all are, but you don't like to say it. Why is that?"

"What do you mean, 'what we all are'?"

"What we are," he repeated. "Sunny is selfish and judgmental, and she can't stand to be confronted with her faults. Actually," he added, struck, "she's similar to Meyer in that. And I'm insecure and vain. Volatile. We all have our flaws. Except for you, maybe. Maybe that's why you don't like to point ours out."

He fell silent, and Claire listened for a while to the crisp, metronomic click of the windshield wipers. She felt disconcerted by these bald assessments of Sunny and himself. What, she wondered, did he think of Mark? At length, "I have plenty of flaws," she said.

He looked at her again, smiling this time in a more familiar way. "Oh, yeah? Like what?"

She hesitated. "I'm not always honest."

Anatole hit himself on the forehead. "Not always honest! Why, I have half a mind to stop this car this minute and put you out on the highway. But how do I know you're telling the truth?"

"I can also be officious. I don't like to give up control."

Anatole downshifted, heading for the road shoulder. "That's it, then, I'm not taking any officious, controlling bitch to New York — "

"Don't you dare pull over." Laughing, Claire pushed at his right arm and nudged the steering wheel.

"Jesus Christ, it's true. You're a hellion. Get your hands off the steering wheel, you pushy, power-crazed — "

"Be careful. Really, Anatole, look out." She put her fingers to his face, which was turned toward her, and forcefully pressed at his chin and cheek until he was facing forward. Then, as he resumed control of the car and picked up speed, she put her hands back in her lap and told herself to keep them there.

They drove on for another mile or two without speaking.

Then, "Claire, how happy are you, really?" he suddenly asked.

The atmosphere in the car changed at once. Claire forgot they were traveling and felt instead as if they were holed up together in some cozy sitting room. She considered his question. Until the advent of Lizbeth, she had been quite happy, both in the sense of feeling at peace with her past decisions and in terms of day-to-day pleasures. Now she had no peace.

"Happy," she said.

Anatole said, "Hmm. 'When we are happy we are always good, but when we are good we are not always happy.'"

"Who said that? Dickens?"

"Oscar Wilde. Unfortunately, I don't think he was right. It's the easiest thing in the world to be happy and bad." He paused, longing to tell her about the struggle to get Sunny pregnant and the impasse they had come to this weekend. But to tell Claire was to risk making the issue a subject of family debate, a development he believed could only work to his disadvantage.

Claire nibbled at her lower lip. She felt she was supposed to inquire whether Anatole was happy — he had asked her — but she didn't want to. Instead, before she could even think to herself, I'm going to ask, she asked, "Anatole, are you faithful to Sunny?"

"What?"

"If you don't want to tell me, don't," she backpedaled immediately. "I would never say anything to her, of course."

He gave her a brief, curious glance. Then, "Unfailingly," he said. "In word and deed. I told you that yesterday."

"Really!"

"Really."

"Of course, you've only been married three years."

"Why do you ask? Are you unfaithful to Mark?"

"Certainly not," she said, and thought instantly, God, I'm a prig.

"Then he cheats on you."

She looked at him. It seemed to her that his very hair was vibrating with curiosity. Anything she told him now she also told Sunny, if not Mark himself.

"No, not that either." She floundered for a moment and went on, "I just wonder how people manage. Especially in your field. So glamorous," she murmured, grinning a nervous liar's grin. She began to tuck her short hair behind her ears, smoothing it over and over. "You realize Mark was my high school boyfriend. To me, sex is Mark." She heard the sadness in her voice and stopped talking, afraid if she went on she would give Mark away. If she hadn't already.

"That seems very sweet to me."

Claire felt herself starting to cry. Making an effort, she breathed in deeply and focused her attention on the neon sign of a roadside lodge now coming into view. "Boy, it's really coming down."

Anatole took a fast glance at her. That she was blinking away tears was obvious, but whether the tears of the betrayer or the betrayed he wasn't sure. A moment later, he had checked the time and made his calculations.

"Let's stop for coffee." He cut across to the right lane and out onto the exit.

"Here? We just left home."

"I didn't have enough coffee." He coasted into the parking lot of the Mohawk Lodge, shut off the engine and looked at Claire. She was hunched down, ostensibly groping for her folding umbrella. He waited until she straightened, put his hand gently on her arm and looked into her eyes with what Sunny called his Deep Searching Gaze.

At that moment, even he didn't know what he intended by it. To some extent, he was really moved by Claire's unhappiness. At the same time, he was excited by the prospect of family scandal. His magpie's instinct for studying and appropriating the emotions of others had also been aroused. Finally, the Searching Gaze was one he had practiced for many years and often used professionally. He resorted to it as a police officer puts a hand to his gun, whether it is there or not. The truth was, Anatole had made use of his emotions in his work so often that they didn't always have a natural shape anymore. They were too well exercised, too disciplined — like a ballerina's outward-turning feet.

In any case, Claire declined the implicit invitation to search back. He had caught her eyes, but she refused to see him. Just as if he had been a man exposing himself to her on a bus.

"Well, let's go if we're going," she said, opening her door. She ducked out into the rain.

In the lodge's empty coffee shop, they took a booth by a window facing the highway. Anatole asked for coffee, Claire for a Diet Coke.

"So you're sticking to your story?" he said, as the waitress left with their order.

"Don't embarrass me."

"I'm sorry. Whoever it was, you or Mark, it must be painful."

"Please, Anatole." Looking down, she polished her spoon with her thumb. She noticed she was quite disappointed to learn (or, at least, to be told) that Anatole did not fool around after all. It came to her that she had been hoping he might make a move on her — and hoping she might reciprocate. Just this one, very particular time, to get a tiny bit even with Mark.

Now, feeling Anatole's eyes on the top of her head, she looked speculatively at his hands, his surprisingly slender wrists, his sweatered arms. Was it possible he was as true to Sunny as he claimed? She had known men who flirted wildly only until they succeeded in hooking the interest of their prey. Then, satisfied, they desisted. Sometimes they even quietly, condescendingly turned to the women they had targeted and warned them off, as if the women had been the initiators. As she often had over the years, she wondered what Mark was like in this regard. Certainly he behaved unexceptionably when he was around her, but his office staff, she had often thought, was strangely devoted to him.

And then there was Lizbeth.

The waitress returned. While she had been behind the counter, she had realized why Anatole looked familiar. Claire watched him sign his place mat and twinkle up at Mona (as the name tag on her shirt proclaimed her) as he handed it over. Mona, sixteen or so, with a flat, moon face and dirty hair, attempted to twinkle back. But she was nervous and self-conscious, and her lips twisted instead into an unattractive smirk. Claire felt a tug of sympathy for her. She recalled June at that age, only a year or two ago. No doubt she was cursing herself for not having washed her hair that morning, for being dressed in a worn flannel shirt and jeans instead of her best outfit. As if her appearance mattered — as if, had she been witty instead of awkward, lithe instead of clumsy, Anatole might have remembered her, come back for her, eloped with her.

As the girl reluctantly retreated to the counter, a wave of self-pity swept over Claire, and the tears she had successfully squelched a few minutes earlier came flooding from her eyes. At the same time, a sob rose irresistibly from some hitherto unknown depth inside her. It coursed through her chest, gathering panic and shame as it went. She heard herself erupt in a sort of choked gasp before she buried her head in her hands, willing herself to cut it out.

A moment later, Anatole was on the vinyl seat beside her. A moment after that and she was cringing under his arm, her forehead pressed to his itchy, woolen chest. She gurgled, "I don't know why — Excuse me . . ." From high above, as it seemed, Anatole answered, "Don't be crazy, don't be silly . . ." Meanwhile, even as she thought, The last person I'd choose to fall apart on — ! And, Gee, won't this be something for Mona to tell her friends! the tears rolled on, the sobs gushed up one after the next.

As soon as she had enough control over her body to do so, she sat up and whispered hoarsely to her glass of Coke, "Can we get out of here?"

"Of course."

Claire felt him fumble in his left pocket for a bill to throw on the table. Then he lifted his arm from her shoulders, plucked her damp coat up from where it had fallen behind her and helped her wriggle into it.

"Ready?" said his voice low in her ear.

She nodded, her hands still over her face. She felt him slide

away from her and forced herself to uncover her eyes enough
to sidle out after him. Praying that Mona would think she had
just told him she had cancer or lost her job — anything but the
truth — she allowed him to fold her under his arm again and
stumbled out into the rain.

In the car, she huddled, rain- and tear-damp, blowing her
nose in a handkerchief Anatole took from an inside pocket. (A
monogrammed handkerchief, she thought, even as she took it.
He would!) She felt profoundly humiliated. A vague idea
nagged at her that Anatole would disapprove of Mark now —
would feel that Claire couldn't have built up such a cache of
wretchedness if Mark serviced her properly, drew off her emotions now and then. Cleaned them out, like a lint filter.

But when she finally looked up from the handkerchief, Anatole was grinning at her.

"What?"

"I don't know. It's a low-rent taste, I guess, but I love it when
people's feelings get the better of them. When someone blows
up in a rage, or if a shopper can't help snatching the last pair of
gloves on special out from under the next guy's hand. It makes
me feel hopeful." He added, "I'm sorry. I don't mean I'm glad
you feel awful. I'm really sorry you feel awful."

And to her astonishment, she saw his face fill with tender
concern. Not the theoretical concern of someone who is trying
to understand how you feel, but genuine distress.

"Have I ever told you how much I admire you, Claire? You
and Mark are such fine people. In ways Sunny and I can never
be." Again, he wanted to tell her about trying to have a baby, in
particular about his conviction that Sunny's unmotherly nature
was part of what was holding things up. If she were more like
Claire, she'd be six months along by now.

Claire sniffled, wadding the hankie into a ball in her hand.
He had certainly never told her anything about admiring Mark

and herself. If she had to guess, she would guess he was making it up this minute. All the same, it was as pleasant to hear as if it had been an empirically verifiable fact.

She thanked him.

"I mean it."

As she remembered it later, he then swooped across the stick shift and put his arms around her. At first, she thought he was hugging her, for comfort. But the side of his nose grazed the side of hers as it slid past, and his mouth — both cooler and softer than she would have expected — abruptly materialized against hers. She felt his smooth teeth behind his lips, which were parted, and the bone in his upper gum. Then the blunt tip of his tongue. Some part of her brain took a skip. At the same time, another part remained observant, detached. His kiss was disappointing. She was mostly aware of how alien his body was to her, how strange it was to be touched in this way by someone who was not Mark. "Wrong man, wrong man," said an inner voice, making not a moral judgment but a practical distinction.

After he drew away, she couldn't remember how she had responded physically, if she had responded at all. Certainly her body was calm, almost inert, now. It was as if it hadn't happened.

"Let's never do that again," she said.

"Okay." He had been thinking during the kiss of Sunny. He thought he might have drunk enough in that one sip to transform her. The next time he kissed her, he would exhale all of Claire's milky sweetness into her mouth.

Beside him, Claire was already preening herself on having provoked a certifiably passionate overture from Anatole Bronski. And with her eyes red, yet. That would give Mark a headache. Sunny too, for that matter. Not, she remembered regretfully a moment later, that they would ever know it had happened.

# FIFTEEN

It was five-thirty when Claire and Anatole crossed the George Washington into Manhattan, early enough for a quick stop at the apartment on Riverside Drive. The doorman nodded at Claire, apparently not surprised that she was not Sunny, and in they went, sharing the elevator up with an elderly man in a yarmulke.

Claire had rarely visited here, and when Anatole first opened the door for her, she felt momentarily disoriented. She had forgotten the apartment was backwards, to take advantage of the view of the Hudson. A long hall led past a small bedroom and the kitchen before opening into the living room. The master bedroom, with the same view, was beside it.

Behind her, Anatole snapped on a light and the hall lit up. Claire stood uncertainly, looking around for somewhere to put her dripping umbrella. To her left was a wood-framed mirror with a row of hooks, fully loaded with scarves and jackets. To her right was a narrow, marble-top table covered with unopened bills, magazines and flyers. There was also a white paper bag, open at the top and full of what Claire could not help recognizing at once as fertility drugs: ampules of Metrodin and Pergonal, alcohol wipes, half a dozen syringes.

She jumped a little when Anatole, still behind her, said, "Give me your umbrella." She handed it to him, awkwardly averting her startled face. He dropped the umbrella, along with his own, into a corner of the hallway outside, then closed the front door. He moved past her, down the corridor, turning lights on as he went.

She hesitated, afraid he would turn around. He disappeared into the kitchen but popped out a second later.

"Come in, don't just stand there," he said, beckoning. "I'm going straight to the theater, but you're welcome to stay here until seven-thirty if you want."

Obediently, she moved down the hall as he headed toward the master bedroom, off the living room. "I want to grab a few things I'd like to . . ."

His voice faded. She waited a moment, in case he came right back out, until she heard him rattling drawers, looking for something, from the sound of it. She darted back down the corridor to the hall table, crumpled the top of the paper bag and shoved it for good measure back among some copies of *People* magazine. Then she sprinted to the living room, where the leaded casement windows gave a view of misted lights and rain.

Poor Sunny, she thought, crossing the room to get a better look out the windows. How old was she? A wave of gratitude for her own early marriage flooded her, and a fleeting, joyful memory of being pregnant. She wondered how long Sunny and Anatole had been trying. She stared down at Riverside Drive, the West Side Highway and the sullen river beyond it. Poor Anatole. Maybe that was why he had kissed her.

They had gotten over the awkwardness of that kiss surprisingly easily. There had been perhaps ten minutes of silence between them before a pack of bikers passed the Triumph and

Anatole started to tell a story about some Hell's Angels he'd found waiting for him outside the stage door at the theater one night. After that, it was almost as if nothing had happened.

By the time he barreled back out of the bedroom, Claire was sitting on the living room couch, apparently absorbed in a Xeroxed *Vanity Fair* profile of Vanessa Redgrave.

"Sunny's interviewing her Monday," he said, reading over her shoulder.

"I know. She mentioned it." Sunny's habit of "mentioning" the names of her glamorous interviewees had given rise to many jokes among Mimi, Mark and Claire. She turned to look up at him. He had changed his sweater, and a fawn leather bag like a pocketbook was slung over his right shoulder. "We're all set?"

Anatole repeated his invitation to stay behind and relax. "I'll give you a key and you'll lock up when you leave for the theater. There isn't much in the kitchen, but you can probably find something for dinner."

Briefly, Claire imagined spending two unsupervised hours in Sunny and Anatole's apartment. Rummaging through Sunny's study. Touring their bedroom. Checking the inventory in their medicine chest. Sunny might be less intimidating if Claire knew more of her secrets. She already liked her better since having seen the Pergonal.

But the temptation lasted only a moment. "No, actually, what I'd love is to go have some Thai food. There's a place on Ninth Avenue not far from the theater where maybe you could drop me? We don't have Thai food in Audubon yet," she added, "only the world's worst Mexican restaurant."

Twenty minutes later, Anatole left her on the street across from the Bangkok Grill. She hopped out of the car, wrestled with her umbrella, and bent down again to wish him luck through the open door before remembering you weren't supposed to do that. She closed the door, and the Triumph pulled away.

The restaurant was almost empty. A smiling hostess urged her to sit in the window, living testament to the restaurant's popularity, but Claire insisted on a table near the back. As soon as she had ordered, she used the public phone in the tiny vestibule to call home.

Unfortunately, Charlotte answered.

"Don't think I can handle things?" she asked.

"Actually, I wanted to talk to Mark."

But Charlotte returned after a long interval to report that Mark and Sunny had driven into Livingston Manor to try to buy some saffron. When Claire asked, as casually as she could, how Meyer was, Charlotte snapped, "He's fine. He ate an Eskimo Pie. Everything's under control."

Claire hung up, her concern about Meyer replaced by annoyance at Charlotte, and ate in solitude as the restaurant slowly filled with chattering couples. She felt regal and rather mysterious, munching *mee krob* and *satays* ferried to and from the kitchen for her by a reed-thin man. Afterwards, slogging through the rain on West Forty-seventh Street, a high school thrill, the thrill of a cheerleader whose boyfriend makes a touchdown, ran through her at the sight of the marquee. Anatole's name was above the name of the play. In the lobby, she overheard a heavily made-up woman raving about how fabulous he had been in *Winter Apples*. Claire would have to tell him.

The play itself seemed to pass much more quickly than it should have, though by her watch it was no shorter than most shows. Anatole's character, Jimmy Damrosch, was a would-be dramatist who had charmed his wife and their friends with his gift for words and his extravagant, whimsical manner but who in the practical world destroyed himself at every turn. His wife — the actress had a long list of stage credits in the *Playbill*, though Claire had never heard of her — was a school librarian. She had always put her husband's desires ahead of her own, always thought of him as the valuable, "creative" one, who would rise to prominence one day and dwarf her small, drab accomplishments. In the second act, she was forced to the realization that he would never complete anything, was in fact incapable of success. At the end, she left him.

Anatole's role might have been written for him. He teased, he did pratfalls, he broke down in tears of rage and grief. He bellowed, nuzzled his costar, spewed out puns and riddles and *bons mots* (including Oscar Wilde's about happiness and goodness). Claire recognized his swashbuckling greeting to her in the kitchen yesterday and wondered if it had originated with him or the script. Closely as she watched, though, she found it impossible to decide if he was good in the part, or even to feel the flow of the play as it moved from its bright early scenes to the ever more gloomy late ones. She had had the same problem with Eliot four years before, when he went through a rock 'n' roll–playing phase: She could never tell if he had talent or was making a fool of himself. She could not (or would not) divide her desire for him to excel from her judgment long enough to know.

When the play was over, she waited as instructed by a door at the foot of the stage until a woman named Cindy came out and took her inside. Anatole was behind the door, in a harshly lit, rough-walled corridor. He was drenched in sweat. He loomed at her, twice as big as she remembered, smiling, buoyant, then trotted her along a maze of hallways to his dressing room. Following him, Claire thought of the runner's high she sometimes got. He talked a mile a minute, hardly pausing for her answer when he asked how she liked the show. Relieved, she hurried after him, nodding as he introduced her to this or that passing technician or actor and murmuring, "Yes" or "Really?" as required. When they finally got to his dressing room, she was taken aback by how tiny it was — a rectangular, brick-lined cell. On one wall was a counter and a lighted mirror. Opposite stood a rickety chest of drawers, a small metal wardrobe rack and a couple of coat stands. Anatole told her to sit down and danced off, a white terry-cloth robe over his arm, to take a shower.

Claire sat on a wooden stool and looked at herself in the lightbulb-studded mirror. One of the nicest things about living in Audubon, she had found, was that she hardly ever thought about her appearance. In Larchmont, she must have checked her reflection eight or ten times a day, a behavior that now struck her as almost pathological. Not that she'd let herself go; in fact, she liked what age had done to thin and refine her face. And she was fitter than ever. Even in this hard glare, she looked well.

She studied herself thoughtfully. As much as she had wondered about her, Claire had never seen Lizbeth — had never even condescended to ask Mark what she looked like. She had imagined her feverishly, however, sometimes nervous and small, sometimes big and curvy. She had dressed and undressed her, changing her hairstyles the way a little girl plays with a doll. Except that little girls pretend their dolls are their babies, or their grown-up selves, while to Claire, Lizbeth was Satan.

"Lizbeth." She spat the name at the mirror, disgusted all over again by its insipidity. "Hi, I'm Lizbeth," she practiced aloud.

For Claire, one of the most painful aspects of Mark's desertion had been its timing: just when June was about to leave home, just when their lives were finally coming back into their own hands. After they'd moved away from everyone she knew to Audubon. What choice did she have in those months but to carry on with June and hope the affair would fizzle out? What else could she have done? How contemptible of Mark to trap her that way and wander off to pursue his pleasures. Yet it was unthinkable to her to build a whole world with him, then go off herself and live alone. When he praised and thanked her for having "taken him back," fury leapt and eddied in her head.

She gave a start as the door breezed open. Anatole shot back in, so fresh from his shower that his eyelashes were spiky. His hair was plastered straight back from his face, giving him an unusually vulnerable look. The thick terry-cloth robe was wrapped around him. He smelled of a cologne she didn't know.

She jumped up. "I'll get out of your way."

"No, no. Turn your back. I'll be dressed in a jiffy."

"No, it's fine—" She reached past him for the doorknob, but he intercepted the movement, taking hold of her wrist.

"Don't be so squeamish. This is the theater, my girl." And he sat her back down on a stool in front of the mirror.

"Put your head down on the counter and close your eyes. No peeking."

Sheepishly, Claire folded her arms among the scattered lipsticks, pencils and powders, and rested her head as she was told, shutting her eyes. But as if of their own will, they popped open a few seconds later. Anatole's image was in the mirror, white, naked, facing away from her.

"You're looking." Too late, she caught sight of the hand mirror nailed to the wall behind her, only a few inches from his nose.

She screwed her eyes shut. "It was an accident." She heard the jingle of what she guessed was the loose buckle of his belt — still threaded through the loops of the jeans he'd worn to the city — and the swish of toenails on denim as he pulled them on. Then a zipper and, without warning, he was leaning over her bent back, his mouth next to her ear.

"You know what Freud said. There are no accidents."

She blushed. To her horror, a shiver of voluptuous pleasure traveled through her, warming her blood. "Where did I just hear that?" she asked, a quiver in her voice betraying her, as Anatole straightened.

"My intelligent wife."

He went on getting dressed. Claire, her head and arms still in a heap on the counter, worked at calming down. This had been inevitable, she assured herself. It was meaningless. She hadn't had sex with Mark since he left her — in that sense, she hadn't yet "taken him back." She was a walking time bomb, that was all.

After a few minutes, she felt Anatole sit down on the stool next to hers. She opened a single eye and peeped over her folded arms into the mirror. Fully dressed, he was gazing at her huddled reflection. He looked alert, interested, sympathetic. A little sad. Smudges of makeup like the ones she had noticed yesterday showed under both his eyes. Without looking away from the mirror, he slid his hand over her forearm until it covered her hand.

"I'm sorry about that kiss in the car. It was stupid of me. I hope it didn't upset you," he said.

"That's okay," mumbled Claire into her arms. She didn't want him to apologize too much and take it away. She lifted her chin and set it on her upper arm, so that her whole face showed in the mirror.

Anatole gave a quick smile, then broke his gaze into the mirror to look at her directly.

"Who was she?" he asked.

Claire thought of saying, "Who was who?" but the wish to have it out was too great. She had told no one till now.

"Just a woman. A clerk in the county records office. A young woman."

"Is it still going on?"

"Not between them, no. But in me."

He sighed. He lifted his hand from hers and with both his hands began gently to massage her shoulders. "Has this happened often?"

Slowly, she sat up and tilted her head to lean into his kneading fingers. "Apparently not. Mark says this was the first time."

He said nothing.

"Anyway, sorry to dump this tawdry mess on you."

"Don't be so silly."

Her head dropped forward, and he examined the fine arrow of down on the nape of her neck. He wondered why indeed he had acted on the impulse to kiss her in the car. That had been foolish, and maybe unkind. In part, it was a confusion of his professional with his personal prerogatives — an actress would not have read the kiss as Claire might have done. In part, it was that selfish desire to steal a mouthful of her essence for Sunny. It might also have had to do with his threadbare sexual life these days. When infertility comes in the door, as Sunny had once grimly joked, pleasure flies out the window. Whatever his motives, though, one point was not in dispute (the very point he feared Claire hadn't understood): He had never had any intention of carrying things further.

Absolute fidelity — emotional and sexual — was the bedrock of Anatole's life with Sunny. It was magnetic north. The ozone layer. If he compromised it, he would descend into the hell where Sunny had found him. At that time, he had been living with one woman and sleeping with two others. Somehow, after traveling a circuitous conversational route he could not retrace later, he had actually told Sunny all this during their first interview, which was supposed to be about his role in *Winter Apples*.

The next night, he phoned her, ostensibly to ask her not to print a joke he had made about the director. After the article appeared, he called again, to thank her. He invited her to dinner. She accepted.

Her life then seemed so simple to him, so beautifully pure. She lived alone. She worked hard. She saw him with a fierce clarity that seemed to cleanse him. When, almost mechanically, he tried to seduce her, she laughed at him and sent him home.

Within a week, he had broken off all three relationships and moved alone into a new apartment. Sunny made him endure three months of abstinence before letting him touch her. Then she had him take an AIDS test. By the time they slept together, he was convinced the world held no happiness for him unless he abjured other women forever.

"You won't tell Sunny, will you?" asked Claire, her head still bowed.

"About what happened in the car?" He could promise that. Sunny knew that little breezes of lust still shook him now and then; so long as they blew through and departed, she didn't want to hear the details.

"No. About Mark," said Claire.

Anatole pondered what it might feel like to keep a secret of this magnitude from his wife. His hands stopped moving on Claire's shoulders. "I'll try."

"That's as good as saying you'll tell her." Claire raised her head, ducked her shoulders out from under his hands and turned to face him. She saw at once that he would repeat every word she had said. She stared at him, confused. Sunny's marriage to him, treated by the family as something of a joke, was obviously stronger in some ways than her own.

Her eyes narrowed. She felt her nostrils quiver. For a moment, she hated Anatole. In his way, he had seduced her — into confiding in him, into exposing herself to him. Then she re-

membered the long years when Sunny had been alone, or seeing someone "because he was there," as she used to put it, or
clinging for dear life to some sullen, surly bastard of the type
she used to favor. Claire could be a little happy for Sunny, recalling all that. And a little sorry for her, remembering the
Pergonal.

"Tell her for God's sake not to say anything to Mark," she
finally added, as Anatole remained mute. "Or Ira, or Mimi.
Anyone."

"Can do."

On the way home, Claire drove, switching the wipers on and
off as the unsteady rain required, thinking at first about how
much of herself she had revealed to Anatole, then, after all,
how little. In some ways, she thought, there was no confiding
to other people, no reaching out. People were sealed packages.
Mountain villages cut off by snow. Even to someone with extra
senses, like Anatole, Claire was as inscrutable as an egg. No
matter how much she said — if she had talked all night, if they
had climbed over each other for hours in a bed at the Mohawk
Lodge — he could never have known her. He could not understand what Mark's betrayal had done to her. She would have
walked off afterwards intact, remote as Jupiter.

This was a line of thought she had developed since Mark's
defection. Before then, she would have said she knew Mark.
Now she wondered who she had known. Whoever it was could
never have done what Mark in fact had done — certainly not as
Mark had done it. The phantom or figment she'd thought she
was married to had vanished forever, along with the person she
had been accustomed to think of as Claire Ginzburg.

# SIXTEEN

Charlotte had lied when Claire phoned from the city. It was true Meyer had been able to sit up and talk with Ira and Sunny for twenty minutes or so, and later with Mimi and Jesse. Charlotte had sent Ira into Audubon to buy an Eskimo Pie, a taste of Meyer's she remembered from forty years ago. She sat with him while he ate it — most of it — around three o'clock. But he fell asleep soon after, and two hours later he woke with a headache he said was like nothing he'd ever felt before.

"Do you think — ?" he asked, when she'd come in answer to the buzzer.

Charlotte looked hard into his faded eyes. The petechiae on his neck and arms had multiplied visibly even since the morning. His pulse was perceptibly weaker, and his breathing was worse.

"It's possible," she made herself say. It was possible this was the onset of a stroke.

Meyer smiled, and she knew it was. His smile was lopsided. Now she saw that his left eyelid drooped.

He screwed up his right eye and shut it experimentally.

"How about a painkiller for that headache?"

"I'm going to have a stroke," he said.

You are having a stroke, thought Charlotte, but she could not bring herself to say anything more aloud. She stalked down the corridor to the bathroom Claire and Mark had built onto their bedroom, found the Demerol Ed Agutter had prescribed, shook two out and carried them back. Leaning against her, her father choked them down.

She called the hospital from the relative privacy of Claire and Mark's bedroom and caught Agutter as he was leaving for home.

"Of course I'll come if you really feel you need me," he said, when she had described the headache, the drooping lid. "But you know there isn't a thing I can do that you can't."

Community General was in Harris, fifteen miles out of Audubon, and Agutter lived twelve more in the wrong direction. It sounded to him as if she had the situation well in hand. She had a good supply of Demerol? Well, that was what he would suggest. Yes, it certainly sounded like a stroke. Comatose? By midnight, maybe. Maybe not till morning. Then he might linger anywhere from an hour to a day to who knew? He was sorry, truly. Charlotte realized, with some shame, that she was making him say what she already knew for the simple comfort of hearing someone else say it. Soon she would have to say it herself, to her sisters and brothers.

She took his home number, thanked him and hung up. For an hour, she hid in her room, checking Meyer occasionally, while downstairs the others clustered here and there, calling to each other, throwing open doors, clumping in and out of the house. Twice, she heard someone come up and peek in at Meyer. When the phone rang, she sprang for it, hoping Agutter had relented. But it was only Claire.

At seven, she looked in on Meyer again — he was still asleep — and made herself go downstairs. Mark and Sunny were back from the Foodmart. In the kitchen, Jesse Fabrizio was presiding over the preparation of a vat of bouillabaisse. Ira, his pale eyes streaming, chopped onions; Sunny measured spices. Mimi and Mark stood by the sink, washing fish. Jesse moved among them, supervising. As Charlotte watched, unnoticed, he first told Ira to mince the onions smaller, then brought a knife to Sunny so she could level the spices off properly. Charlotte stood in the doorway, dimly aware of a tingling, slightly buzzy sensation in her skin. Finally, she coughed, loudly, so everyone would hear.

Except for Jesse, who seemed engrossed in picking off every flake of papery skin from a head of garlic, they all looked up.

Charlotte looked back at them, feeling that surge of mixed exaltation and giddy fear that accompanies announcements of the kind she was about to make. The moment, the scene, froze before her. She would remember each detail — the smell of heated olive oil, Sunny using a pinkie to pull a wisp of hair from the corner of her mouth, the chirp of the tap as Mark abruptly shut it off — remember them forever, though she wasn't aware of them now.

"Meyer is dying," she heard herself say. "He's having a stroke — bleeding into his head. From now on, he'll be less and less lucid. Then he'll lose consciousness. Then he'll die."

By the time she had finished speaking, she felt angry. She usually did feel angry when she was sad. Her mad-for-sad gene, she called it, when she explained it to Kyle, who was on the receiving end of the switch more often than either of them liked. There followed a second of deep silence, during which the others all seemed to come toward her, though no one moved.

Mark was the first to find his voice. "What kind of time frame are we talking here?" He groped without looking for a dishtowel. "Hours? Days?"

Charlotte explained. Maybe hours. Maybe a day. "He's sleeping now, but one of us should sit with him in case he wakes up and needs more Demerol. Or in case — something else happens," she concluded, her training momentarily failing her.

"Like what?" asked Mimi immediately.

"Like he suddenly feels like waltzing and wants a partner." Charlotte looked from Mimi to Mark to Sunny, 'I ask you!' blazing in her eyes.

"Like he dies," Sunny said gently, going from the counter to the sink to put an arm around Mimi. Jesse arrived at her other side at the same moment. For a few seconds, they held her between them. Mimi swayed a bit, recovered her balance and straightened. Feeling her gravitate toward Jesse, Sunny moved away.

"Oh, buck up, Mimi. Even you must have understood this was going to happen. Why do you think we're all here?" Charlotte came into the kitchen, piercing the invisible scrim that had seemed to separate her from her family. She reached behind Mark to pull a paper towel from the roll beside the sink and handed it to Ira, whose face glistened with onion-pricked tears.

"Leave her alone," he said, taking it.

"But she's ridiculous. Look at her." Charlotte seemed to be appealing to Jesse. "Here's a completely foreseeable event — foreseeable and foreseen — that affects all of us equally. And here's Mimi, pale but brave and staggering around like Greer Garson in *Mrs. Miniver.*"

"You really are an asshole, Charlotte," said Sunny.

At the same time, taking a step forward, Mimi said, "The fact that you foresee something doesn't make it hurt less when it happens." One of her fish-wet hands was still touching Jesse's hip. "If you saw that a brick was about to fall on your head, it wouldn't hurt you any less when it hit you." She made a

hiccuping noise that Charlotte took for a suppressed belch and
Jesse knew might be the beginning of throwing up. He came
forward to stand next to her again.

"I'm going to go up and sit with Meyer," Mark announced
suddenly. "Charlotte, come show me what to do."

"No." Impatiently, Mimi shook Jesse away. She moved toward the butcher block table where Ira and Charlotte stood
side by side. "I have something to say to Charlotte now. Mark,
go up by yourself, if you're going."

But Mark, at the doorway now, stood frozen like the rest of
them, staring.

"You think you're so supe-supe-so much better than me."
Mimi stood with both hands on the swollen, scarred wood, her
face a bare ten inches from Charlotte's. "You look down on me
because you're a doctor and I'm only a singer. And a waitress,"
she added conscientiously. She hiccuped again. Her complexion had taken on the greenish tinge Ira had noticed that morning. "And because you're smart in a certain way that I'm not.
You all think that, you all look down on me for that." She
looked around the kitchen, glaring at each of them except
Jesse. He stood by the sink, beaming encouragement at her.
His expression was rapt, Sunny thought, almost ecstatic.

"But that's where you're all so narrow and stupid your-
selves," Mimi went on, "all four of you. You laugh, you make
jokes, but you don't have fun. You're not joyful. Now your
father is dying, but that just makes you more — " For the
first time, she floundered a bit. "More sophisticated," she
finally spat out sarcastically. "Because you don't know how to
be sad, either. Maybe alone, maybe in private or with your husband or wife, or over your careers. But you can't turn to each
other to share normal grief. You never did about Mom. And
you know what? I pit-pit" — with a great effort of concen-

tration — "I pity you," she finally brought forth. She lowered her voice and leaned even closer to Charlotte's transfixed face. "I really do."

"Well, save it," Charlotte advised. She backed away uneasily. "What does she do for an encore, sing 'People'?" she asked Mark, and was about to say more when Mimi suddenly ducked her head and rushed toward the sink. At first they thought she was going for Jesse. But a moment later, she had flung the fish out of the basin and stuck her head into it. Jesse placed his palms on her heaving back.

"Take it easy." Charlotte sounded alarmed. Sunny realized she must take this vomiting for a psychosomatic reaction and bit her lip to keep from spilling the truth. A moment later, though, leaving Mimi washing her mouth out at the tap, Jesse explained it himself.

"She's pregnant." His tone was both defiant and reproachful, as if Charlotte had tried to prevent the pregnancy or, knowing of it, had deliberately launched her attack in spite of it. "We're getting married," he added recklessly.

Mimi shut off the tap. "That hasn't been decided," she said, while at the same time Sunny and Mark both erupted into noisy congratulations.

"How far along?" Charlotte asked, in her doctor's voice.

"Seven weeks." Jesse put his arm around Mimi, who pulled slightly away.

"She shouldn't be drinking, then," said Charlotte.

"I'm not sure I'm going to have it. And please address me directly."

"Of course you are," said Sunny, while Jesse gave a squawk of anguish and clutched weakly at Mimi's hair.

"If you're sure you're not going to have it, that's one thing," Charlotte said. "If you might," she went on implacably, "don't drink. Believe me, if you knew what fetal alcohol syndrome can do, you wouldn't."

Mimi, her mouth clean and dried by now, looked at her, shaking her head. "I guess you just don't know any other way to be." She took Jesse's hand. "I've had enough of this sad puppy. Come on, let's go sit with my father."

# SEVENTEEN

For a few minutes, Sunny, Ira, Charlotte and Mark moved silently around the kitchen. Sunny put the spices away; Mark rinsed and dried the fish, muttering to himself that he would broil it.

The tedious rain slapped the windows. Sunny thought about her father and wished Anatole were here. When her thoughts turned to Mimi again, she glared at Charlotte, who had sunk into a corner of the breakfast nook.

"You don't have to look at me like I threw the kittens down the well," said Charlotte. Her head was dropped forward into her hands, and she was rubbing her temples intently, on her face a strange look of inward concentration. "I didn't know she was pregnant."

"Who did?" Mark meant this as a rhetorical consolation, but when the other two said nothing, it became a genuine question. Sunny and Ira exchanged glances.

"Ira and I, apparently," Sunny said.

"Did you?" said Mark, pausing in the act of slicing a lemon. "How do you like that?"

But Charlotte, to whom this question was addressed, was

completely absorbed in what she had finally realized was going to be a full-blown hot flash. Her face and neck burned, her temples were moist. Her brain felt as if someone had shaken a bottle of seltzer inside her skull, then let it explode. "Menopause," she said to the curious stares of the others. "Ignore me."

"Charlotte, you're menopausal?" Instinctively, Sunny shrank away from her. This was something different from wrinkles. This was the death of fertility, the shadow of death itself. And Charlotte was only seven years older than she was. "Aren't you early?"

"A little."

"Want some ice or something?" Mark feinted in the direction of the refrigerator.

"No, no." Charlotte waved a hand at him. "It'll go away in a minute. Actually, maybe a glass of cold water, "she amended, as her flush deepened.

Sunny drifted warily toward the bottom of the back stairs, then watched Mark fetch the water and sit down across from Charlotte while she drank it. Ira also sidled up to the breakfast nook and hovered anxiously, as if Charlotte might slip into convulsions. She drained the glass and looked up at them, laughing.

"I'm not going to melt." She pulled her sweater off over her head and tugged at her turtleneck collar. Her underarms were dark with sweat.

Spooked, Sunny could think of nothing except getting away from her. First the attack on Mimi and now this freakish (Sunny hoped it was freakish), premature, permanent lunar eclipse. She knew these were reactionary, misogynous thoughts; but she didn't care. She had to flee her older sister's force field.

"I'm going up to Meyer," she announced abruptly and sprang up the stairs before anyone could stop her.

At the top of the steps she paused, holding the newel post.

Then, more as an aid to contemplation than because she had
to, she went to the small bathroom next to Ira's room and peed.
Jesse's murmuring voice reached her as she passed Meyer's
half-open door, but it didn't stop and she hoped they hadn't
heard her. She needed time alone. In the bathroom, she sat,
idly exchanging a sober glance with her ghostly reflection in
the now-dark window beside the toilet. How could she have
been so stupid as to ask Meyer about Sheila instead of the more
than twenty years before Sheila? Now she would never know
his side of the marriage, his memories of Ruth. Unless . . .

Would it be unpardonably crass to interrogate him now? It
wasn't as if she were interested in his will, or his personal life.
She only wanted to learn what she should have learned years
ago — would have, if Meyer hadn't deserted them. Not that
she would take his word for gospel, any more than Ruth's. She
just wanted his point of view.

It was the kind of judgment she found impossible to make.
She wished she could discuss it with Anatole. Her watch said
seven-forty. Anatole would not be pleased to receive a call from
her so close to curtain. She rose with a sigh and decided to go
in and play it by ear. Meyer might sleep from now until — forever — anyhow. She washed her hands and doused her face for
good measure, then went out into the corridor.

Jesse's gentle murmur still flowed out from Meyer's room.
Ears straining, Sunny quietly moved closer.

". . . a transparent vacuum without circumference or center,"
she thought she heard. "At this moment, know thou thyself;
and abide in that state. I, too, at this time, am setting thee face
to face."

The voice paused. Sunny peeked around the door.

Jesse was sitting on the ladder-back chair, reading aloud
from a paperback book by the soft glow of the bedside lamp.

Mimi had carried a bentwood rocker in from what was now Eliot's room and was rocking slowly at the foot of Meyer's bed. She caught the slight movement of the door as Sunny crept in, turned to look and put a finger to her lips.

Meyer was lying on his back, his eyes closed, his arms straight along his sides on top of the quilt. For an instant, Sunny thought he was dead. Then she saw the hem of the sheet rise with his chest. Jesse began to read again. "O nobly-born Meyer Ginzburg, the time hath now come for thee to seek the Path in reality. Thy breathing is about to cease . . ."

Mimi read Sunny's face and leapt up. She drew her by the elbow back out to the corridor.

"*The Tibetan Book of the Dead*," she whispered. "Meyer had it. He asked us to read it to him."

"Why?"

"I don't know. Jesse said it's to help him focus his spirit or something. We have to read it over and over, the same paragraph. Jesse knows all about it," she added.

"Is Meyer even awake?"

Mimi shrugged. "It doesn't matter if he's awake or not, he wants us to read it. There are other parts we read later, when he — gets worse. Oh, and he also said we shouldn't cry or pray for him, any of us."

No fear of that, thought Sunny. This was the Meyer she remembered, the Meyer of obstacles and evasions, the Meyer of the arcane, the abstruse, the occult. The Meyer you could only be close to on his own terms. Aloud, "Because — ?" she asked.

"Because it would hin-hin — "

"Hint?"

" — hinder his spirit's journey."

Sunny beckoned her to move a few steps farther from the door. From inside, they could still hear Jesse's flowing words. He had come around to the vacuum again.

"Sorry about Charlotte jumping you downstairs." Sunny put a hand on Mimi's shoulder. "She's a pig."

"She's a demented pig."

"Mims, why don't you marry Jesse?"

Mimi's large green-brown eyes turned away, toward the half-open door, then back. She raised her eyebrows.

"I don't know what your objections are," Sunny went on, "but I think he's a keeper. A person. Plus he's obviously crazy about you."

Mimi gave a small, unreadable smile and abruptly leaned forward to peck Sunny's cheek. "Want to come sit with us?"

For half an hour, the three of them sat while Jesse read. Meyer opened his eyes when Mimi and Sunny first returned to the room and again several times as Jesse's voice droned on, but Sunny, perched beside Mimi on a wooden chair from Ira's room, couldn't tell how much her father took in of his situation. His gaze was unfocused and still. If he was looking at anything, it seemed to be the hallway light coming in through the partly open door. Then his lids would close again, and they would wonder if he was listening or not.

When Jesse's voice began to grow thin, he held the book out to the two women. Sunny, afraid if she opened her mouth she would scream, declined. She was filled with wrath at being made to assist her father in his last conscious hours exactly by avoiding meaningful discourse. Whatever meaningful discourse he might have been capable of, anyway. Mimi stood and took Jesse's place.

"Read it like you just thought of it now," he murmured, handing her the book. Sunny noticed he managed to brush Mimi's fingers with his own. "Not like it's something you're reading."

"If I do that, I'll stammer," Mimi whispered back. She had always been able to read aloud from a text without any difficulty, but her throat froze the moment she tried to recite the same words from memory.

"Do your best."

Mimi sat down. At the same time, Jesse motioned to Sunny to leave the room with him. She did, keeping him company as he gulped a handful of water from the sink in the little bathroom. She followed him into the room he and Mimi were sharing.

"Sit down." He patted the bed next to him.

Sunny sat.

"Are you familiar with *The Book of the Dead?*"

She shook her head.

"If you like, I can explain."

Sunny hesitated, debating whether or not it was a good idea for her to make an effort to understand Meyer. After a long pause, she said, "Okay."

"See, when you die," Jesse commenced, gesturing with his hands folded together and his index fingers extended against each other, "the first thing that happens is your soul immediately becomes one with the eternal, the immutable light." His hands parted and his fingers fluttered like flying leaves. "The clear light of the void. You lose your ego. You realize you and the universe are one. It's bliss. But then, your spirit starts to sort of spew out all its own illusions — or some people believe these illusions are manufactured and shown to you by actual deities and demons. Either way, instead of being clear, you see images, fantasies. You follow that so far?"

He stopped and looked at her, hands clasped again, the blunt tips of his index fingers just under his chin. She couldn't make out whether he believed what he was saying or was filling her in as a courtesy, since he happened to have read the book. His brown eyes wore their habitual expression of deep, insightful serenity (a misleading expression, from what Mimi told her, but sufficient nevertheless to make Sunny feel hopelessly worldly and tainted). But his tone was as matter-of-fact as if he were saying, See, the first thing after you leave the highway, you'll pass an old Esso station and come to a fork in the road. She nodded. He went on.

"At first the fantasies are okay, they're pleasant. But they start to get terrifying. Finally, your soul is drawn to carnal things. This is the end of what's called the *Bardo* state, the time between death and birth. I'm skipping a lot of stuff, of course, but the last thing is, you see a mating couple and enter the womb, and that's how you come to be reborn. The point of *The Book of the Dead*, though, is to teach you how to resist the illusions and not be reborn. Then you don't have to come back to the world; instead, you reach Nirvana. See?"

"Mmm," said Sunny. "Sort of like Chutes and Ladders." She recrossed her legs.

Ignoring her, Jesse went on. "Meyer wants us to read the passage we're reading because it reminds him how to keep his thoughts with the eternal. Actually, the book calls for people to read to the corpse for days. But I guess Meyer knows no one's going to do that."

"I'm certainly not," Sunny agreed.

Jesse was looking sideways at her foot, an expression of pain on his face. She thought her cynicism had offended him but realized a moment later that it was because she had inadvertently allowed the side of her boot to rest on the bedspread. Mimi had said he was funny that way. She moved her foot. Jesse relaxed.

"Listen, thank you for telling Mimi to have the baby."

"There's nothing to thank me for. I think she should."

"She has to," he blurted out passionately, then reddened. "I mean, I hope she will. Not that I don't believe in a woman's right to choose," he added.

Sunny slid back and pivoted so she faced him, and on impulse took his clasped hands in both of hers. Clearly, he perceived her as so rigid, so hard and narrow of thought, such a walking bureaucracy, that her prejudices had to be propitiated even as his heart flew into his throat. And if he perceived her so, to some degree, Mimi must, too.

"You make me feel a hundred years old," she said, but what she meant was, Have the social accretions of only twenty years — less — so coated and disguised me that you can't see who I am? But there was no shedding her identity, no chance of casting it suddenly off so that Jesse could see how dearly she loved Mimi, how tenderly she desired the flesh of that baby to live. She had built up her role in life, her persona (smart, acidic, capable) with care, at times with much difficulty and determination, until now even she could not breach it. This agglomeration of habits, attitudes, poses, pronouncements, tones of voice, clothes, affiliations — this carapace, this fastness, this prison — was Sunny Ginzburg.

She saw Jesse's eyes drop uneasily and realized her snatching his hands had puzzled and worried him. With a quick pat, she released them.

"Mimi's just scared," she said. "And upset about Meyer. She'll come around." She stood. "Let's go back in."

Mimi looked up gratefully as they returned. She was stumbling over the word *Bardo*, which meant nothing to her, and had just resorted to spelling it out when the others entered. She looked imploringly at Sunny, then held the book away from her and squinted at it angrily as her reluctant tongue negotiated the next words. When at last she reached the end of the paragraph, Sunny went to relieve her.

As she sat down, her father opened his eyes. He looked sharply at her. "Sonia."

"Yes."

"Sonia, my head."

"Should I call Charlotte? Do you want us to stop reading?"

"No, but my head, it's so strange." He closed his eyes again. "Read."

She raised the book but gave Jesse a glance that sent him out of the room for Charlotte.

Then, "O nobly-born Meyer Ginzburg," Sunny began, "the time hath now come for thee to seek the Path in reality . . ."

# EIGHTEEN

By nine-thirty, everyone in the house — even Charlotte, who seemed to hold each distasteful word at arm's length as she brought it forth — had taken a couple of turns at reading to Meyer. When not reading, they wandered around downstairs, or sat keeping Meyer and the reader company. By ones and twos, they ate a dinner of tepid fish and baked potatoes in the breakfast nook. Several times, Meyer opened his eyes; once, while Ira was reading, he asked for a drink of water. But his breathing was shallower and shallower — almost panting — and no one was surprised when, around a quarter to ten, he complained that his brain was bursting and asked for more medication.

Charlotte, who had gone to call Ted, was summoned from the phone and came in frowning, the bottle of Demerol in her hand. In theory, Meyer wasn't due for a second dose till eleven-fifteen at the earliest. Too much medicine in him at once could make him stuporous. All the same, after observing him briefly, she shook out two more pills and held him while he got them down.

As she and Ira settled him under the quilt again, Meyer

mumbled, "The next passage." His voice was weirdly strained and thinned.

"The next passage?" Ira looked helplessly around. By now they were all crowded into the room. Sunny thought her father was narrating what he saw, perhaps, as other dying people are said to cry, "The light!" or "Beautiful!"

But Jesse explained, "He wants us to go on and read the next part of the book. I'll find it."

Everyone watched him thumb through the pages and listened while he began: "Now the symptoms of earth sinking into water are come . . ."

One by one, as his voice murmured on, the others left the room. Ira went first. Meyer seemed to have fallen asleep again anyway, and to Ira the atmosphere around the bed had become almost intolerably charged. Mark soon followed, then Sunny and Charlotte together.

In the living room, Sunny fell full length onto the corduroy couch. For the past hour or so, she had had the impression of stately music playing inside her head, a grave hum of cellos as sinister as the buzzing of many bees, yet also beautiful. The evening's events seemed curiously predetermined. Like a play. Her father's deterioration proceeded at its own pace. It could not be stopped; neither could any of his children refuse his allotted role. A horrible downward momentum had them all in hand; yet, like the private music, it was beautiful as well as dreadful — right, fit, meet. She wondered if only a hard person would think of all this at such a moment.

Charlotte, coming in behind Sunny, hesitated a moment before dropping onto the corduroy couch next to Sunny's feet. She was damned if she was going to let them shun her.

Ira spoke first. "I guess this is it, huh?" he said. "There wouldn't be anything else we could do for him?"

Charlotte shook her head. "Not a thing."

"Morphine?" Ira suggested.

"Doesn't want it."

Ira was silent, then he spoke again. "You know, it's stupid, but I had sort of started to think he might have something to say to us, you know? Some reason he came back besides having nowhere else to go."

No one spoke.

"He didn't tell any of you anything, did he?" Ira went on. Sunny, her eyes closed, her arms raised and crossed over them, could hear in his voice how embarrassed he was to feel compelled to ask. But he was compelled. "No revelations? Confessions? Retractions?"

"He told me he was sorry he hurt us," Sunny offered. "But he also basically said he couldn't have done anything else."

"He told me the reason he left had nothing to do with us. It was all him."

Ira looked inquiringly at Mark, but Mark only raised his eyebrows and looked bleakly back.

"He seems so tiny." Ira took his glasses off and cradled them in his hands. "An insignificant speck in an infinite universe. This is stupid too, but I always somehow believed Meyer was a thinker of stature, you know? A poet-philosopher. But really it seems his ideas are just a jumble of this and that. I thought — without thinking about it, I guess — that he was . . . rigorous, somehow. Brilliant, even." He paused. "Well, it made a nice story to grow up on, anyway."

Sunny lifted her arms and opened her eyes to look sympathetically at him. Then she hitched herself back, folded her arms under her head and found herself gazing into Mark's tired brown eyes.

Mark sighed.

He wishes Claire were here, thought Sunny, and realized a moment later that she was glad Anatole wasn't. Though she would soon begin to worry about his safety on the road back — the rain still pounded steadily at the windows — it was a kind of luxury just now to be a daughter, a sister, not a wife. Several times since her marriage, and especially since the trouble with fertility had begun, she had felt a strong sense of Ginzburg tribalism when she got around her family. It was as if they had traded her to Anatole for a cow or a couple of goats. Close as she was to him, he was now and would always be Other, while the people here were forever Kind. She disapproved of this instinct in herself. It seemed childish and in some way disloyal to her husband. Still, there it was. Tonight, with her father dying upstairs, it was more powerful than ever.

"Did anyone ever find out where he's been since that time he came to see us in New York?" she asked abruptly. "When I talked to him, I was so busy . . ." She left the sentence unfinished.

"Claire and I worked out a kind of skeletal narrative between us," Mark volunteered, when no one else answered. For some reason, Meyer had been reluctant to chronicle his doings outright. If they asked him directly, he said he was too tired, or joked that the tale was too dull to recount. Mark had put considerable effort into piecing together such scraps of history as Meyer had let fall. "He was in Mexico City for a while, then Paris. That solidarity group he wanted money for when we saw him never really took off, thank God, but he spent a couple of years among various Latin expatriate revolutionaries. Early in the eighties, he and a partner developed a computer program you use for composing music, but they couldn't market it properly, and eventually the product was superseded. Tom McBride told me about that. Evidently, he did make some money though, because after that, he bought a plot of land outside Santa Fe. He lived on it in some kind of old-fashioned trailer called a land yacht. He told Claire that. Then he completely gave up the written word for a year — no reading, no writing — to see what was left. He met Tom McBride soon after, at a book fair in Albuquerque, and eventually sold what he owned in New Mexico to move to Boulder. His illness must have eaten up whatever money he had. By the time McBride called, Meyer was living in the back of his bookstore. Well, you know that. And that's about all we learned."

For a while, no one spoke. Sunny wondered if Meyer had still been in Santa Fe when she got married or if he had already moved to Colorado. She wished she knew what Tom McBride had that her own family didn't. Then an incident she had all but forgotten popped suddenly into her head.

"Remember in nineteen fifty-eight, that blizzard when Mom had to go to the hospital?" she asked, breaking the silence. She wriggled back to prop herself higher against the arm of the couch. "Meyer carried her all the way down to Roosevelt Hospital. He probably saved her life."

"Actually" — Charlotte drew her legs up and held them tight by the ankles — "he probably didn't. She was bleeding because she'd had a miscarriage, but it's not as if she were hemorrhaging. She told me about it that summer I was back here."

"Charlotte, does the phrase 'cease and desist' mean anything to you?" Sunny asked.

"Well, I'm sorry. I'm sure he meant well, but it seems pretty clear she had already expelled the major clot and was starting to heal by herself. All Meyer actually did was jolt her around in subfreezing temperatures for an hour when she felt like shit. Healthwise, it wasn't the greatest course of action."

Sunny looked to Ira for help, but he refused to let her catch his eye. "How about 'less justice and more charity,' in the words of the great Archy?" she asked.

"In the context of keeping history straight, no, charity doesn't mean anything much to me. I happen to believe that in the long run, it's best to be as factual as possible. Especially when it comes to personal relations."

"Haven't you noticed that it isn't possible to be factual about personal relations?" Mark asked her. "Meyer thought he was saving Ruth's life. Meyer's intention was to save Ruth's life."

"I always thought he did save her life," mumbled Sunny, while Mark went on: "So in this case, what everyone thought, what we all believed — that is the relevant fact."

"Not from a medical point of view, it isn't."

"We're not having a medical discussion."

"Well, if you're going to have any kind of sensible discussion about an emergency trip to the hospital, I don't see how you can ignore the medical — "

"Charlotte, drop it," Mark broke in. "Let it go, give it up. You are mistaken. You are not correct. Everyone here knows you're wrong, and in fact, you are wrong. That can happen, even to you. So leave it. Okay? Shut up."

Sunny, braced for a nasty return storm from Charlotte, was surprised to see her release her ankles and run her hands through her hair, shake her head and laugh.

"I'm being rigid and overbearing, aren't I?" she said, cheered and relaxed by this brief resurgence of the old, caustic Mark, the pre-Claire Mark. "Sorry. It's a problem I have. I get hold of an idea and I — I don't know, I'm like a dog with a bone." She patted Sunny's feet and added, "Meyer was heroic. He did a fine thing."

Sunny pressed her lips together and pulled her feet away. It would be a pleasure to say good-bye to Charlotte tomorrow.

The others returned to the subject of the blizzard, recalling what they had done to keep warm and pass the time, but Sunny only half-heard them, her mind still on Ruth's miscarriage. Though she had often consoled herself with the fact that Ruth was forty when Mimi was born, she realized now that in all her calculations, she had managed to block out her knowledge of Ruth's miscarriage. Could a disposition to miscarry be inherited? For the first time, Sunny asked herself what Ruth would have advised her to do about her infertility.

Her thoughts were interrupted by the arrival of Mimi herself, crossing the hall from the dining room with a full glass of milk in one hand and a plate covered with food and cutlery in the other. She hadn't been downstairs since the incident with Charlotte. Now she sat on the love seat, her plate balanced on her knees.

"Meyer's sleeping."

Charlotte stood up. "I'll go take a look at him."

"Jesse is with him," said Mimi, but she avoided Charlotte's eyes. Charlotte left. Mimi assembled a huge forkful of buttered potato and fish.

"Starving," she announced before piling it into her lavish mouth.

She chewed and swallowed, then eagerly gulped from the glass of milk. Her cheeks and chin had a pearly luminescence. Her movements were quick and greedy. Eating for two, thought Sunny and blurted out, "You will have the baby, Mims, won't you? You couldn't abort it."

Mimi paused, a mouthful of baked potato poised in mid-air. "Well, I could," she said. "But — not that it's any of all of your biz-biz-beeswax — I'm not going to." A dark rose color rushed into her cheeks, and she slipped the fork into her mouth to help fight a rising smile.

"Yes!" said Sunny, and immediately loathed Mimi. She wished Anatole were here.

"And Jesse?" Mark asked.

"I'm sorry. Did I . . . ?" Mimi put down her fork and pulled the collar of her velveteen sweater away from her neck, peering over her shoulder and into its interior as if checking the label. "Nope, still says 'Mimi Ginzburg.' Thought for a minute there I'd turned into June or something. Is there any particular reason you feel I owe you this information?"

"I only want what's best for you." Mark began to rock in short, stiff jerks.

"Half a marriage is better than none," Ira said encouragingly.

"Is it?" Mimi picked up her fork again. She resumed eating. Apparently, the discussion was at an end.

For half a minute, no one said anything. Mimi's fork clicked and skidded; the rocker creaked; the rain rattled the windows. Then Charlotte's footsteps, slower than usual, sounded on the stairs.

She appeared in the doorway, face strained, hands fisted in her pockets. Her low voice cracked a little. "He's in a coma."

"What?" The creaking rocker stopped.

"He's out. Comatose." Abruptly, Charlotte sat down again on the sofa by Sunny's feet. She looked at her knees. "It's just a matter of time."

# NINETEEN

As had occasionally happened to him in the past, Meyer noticed he was looking down at his body on the bed from a distance of three or four feet. Next to what might have been his ear, had he not been utterly incorporeal, was the white glass globe of the ceiling fixture. On a chair beside his bed sat Jesse, Miriam's boyfriend; Meyer, gazing down upon his dark head, the hair pulled smoothly back into a ponytail, saw the tiny whitish spot where the boy would one day start to bald. Jesse was holding Meyer's copy of *The Tibetan Book of the Dead* and reading aloud.

It came to Meyer that he had used all his learning, his fitful erudition, to keep away those he loved instead of bringing them near. This had been an error. Ruth entered his mind, then Leanne, the mother of his son in Tacoma, and he knew he had left both women when he should have stayed. He saw he had torn them in two. This also had been an error. He noticed his children bleeding around him, though they were alive. He saw that his parents had been good and kind, and he had cared too little about them. He knew he himself had been generous sometimes, but too often to strangers rather than to his own.

He had loved knowledge, but not deeply. And people — but, again, not deeply. These were his errors.

A moment later, he was in the living room above his children. He didn't know how this had happened; he had never gone from place to place before when out of his body. His children, except for Miriam (and Josh, of course, who was not in Audubon) were talking about the blizzard of '58, when he had carried Ruth to Roosevelt. He had forgotten that day. Charlotte was arguing with the others. Secretly, Ira was in agreement with her, though he said nothing. Meyer warmed to them, especially Charlotte, who couldn't bear to let a half-truth go by. He never had been able to either. He hoped she would learn.

Sonia was worrying about whether she could have a baby. She would not, he realized. But this would be all right for her. He tried to communicate this to her, but although her thoughts were as clear to him as the words the others said aloud, she seemed not to notice his at all. For the first time, he wondered if he were dead. The thought proved unexpectedly jarring, and with a nauseating lurch he was back upstairs, reentering his body.

It was the last fact he knew.

# TWENTY

Claire and Anatole turned into the muddy driveway at two in the morning. Claire was at the wheel. After the hill at the top of the drive, she shut the lights off, switched into neutral and coasted the last few yards to park behind Ira's Rabbit. It was very dark outside. The rain was less steady now, yet it fell heavily enough to coat the windshield in a moment. They had run out of conversation some thirty miles back. Claire thought Anatole might be asleep.

But he wasn't. He sat up smartly and, unbuckling his seat belt, thanked her for her company. Jimmy Damrosch was still in his voice. "You made an expedition of what would have been a dreary chore."

She opened her door; the interior light sprang on. Anatole's hair had dried into its habitual lush waves. He looked exhausted. "Thank you," Claire whispered. "Don't slam your door."

They walked quietly up to the house, the wet, pebbly earth squelching under their feet. There was one light on downstairs and another in the bathroom next to Ira's room, but the rest of the windows on the front of the house were dark. Claire worried about Meyer. Charlotte or no Charlotte, now that she was back, she wished she hadn't left him.

By the time she unlocked the door, Sunny was in the foyer. She wore a white flannel robe and green Chinese slippers. From the state of her hair, Claire guessed she had been in bed, if not sleeping.

She bounded up to Anatole and threw her arms around him. "He's dying. He's in a coma."

Claire dropped her purse and ran up the stairs, forgetting to muffle her footsteps. She had been crazy to trust Charlotte. Down the hall, Meyer's door was shut, but a bar of light shone along the bottom. Claire threw the door open. Charlotte, swathed in a crimson dressing gown, was slumped in the rocker that belonged in Eliot's room. At Claire's entrance, she opened her bleary eyes.

Sleeping. Charlotte had been sleeping. Claire felt Sunny and Anatole materialize behind her.

"What's going on?" Claire's voice was harsh, piercing.

Charlotte blinked at her, straightened and looked for a few long seconds at Meyer. "He had a stroke."

"No." Claire strode to the bedside, gently took Meyer's pulse and picked up the bottle of Demerol from the nightstand. It rattled. "How many has he had?" she demanded in a dangerous whisper.

"You think I drugged him?" Charlotte stood. She was a good six inches taller than Claire. She looked down at her. "What exactly do you take me for?"

"He was fine when we left. I mean, not fine, but — You said he ate an Eskimo Pie this afternoon."

"And he did."

"So when did this so-called stroke happen?"

"Probably it was already happening then. If you mean when did he lose consciousness, about four hours ago. Look, if you don't believe me, check his neck. Go on," she added, as Claire stood immobile. "Go on."

Finally, Claire turned to Meyer again and carefully, deftly slid one hand under his ashen head. Sunny grabbed Anatole's arm, squinting with incomprehension and suspense. Claire seemed to try to raise Meyer's head. A moment later, she slid her fingers back out from under it and turned once more to Charlotte.

"I'm sorry. Please forgive me," she muttered.

"Incredible." Charlotte, her face white with anger, sank back into the rocker.

"What was all that about?"

At first, neither woman answered. Then, "His neck is rigid. That's a stroke," Claire explained.

"Oh." Sunny realized now that she had unconsciously been hoping Claire's return would somehow alter Meyer's condition, that he would miraculously perk up with her around. She tucked herself under Anatole's heavy arm and rubbed her cheek against him.

"You called Agutter?"

"Yes, of course."

"Did he say he'd come?"

"There isn't a thing he could do."

Slowly, Claire unbuttoned the rain-misted coat she had forgotten until now. "You've been sitting with him?"

"We all have," said Sunny.

"I'll take a turn. I'm wide awake." She draped the coat over the footboard of the bed. "You get some sleep, Charlotte."

It was agreed Claire would watch him until four, then wake Sunny. Ira had already sat with him and had gone to bed; Mark was due to take over from Sunny at six. They had all agreed Mimi should be spared night watch.

With Anatole's arm still draped around her, and holding his broad hand in both of hers, Sunny said good night to the others and headed down the hall. Anatole smelled of makeup and, despite his habitual postperformance shower, sweat. She could tell he didn't know what to say to her, now that the crisis had come. She felt sorry for him. Before she married, she had believed that husbands and wives were somehow immune from this kind of helplessness — that Anatole would know her so well, and she him, that welcome, comforting words would come instinctively at such times. She had already learned how far off the mark that expectation had been. There were dozens of occasions — far less difficult occasions than this one, too — when she had no idea what to say to help him, when she was reduced to probing tentatively with one suggestion and another to find an acceptable direction, or when her silence (her companionable, supportive silence, she thought) had been interpreted by him as indifference or worse. Similarly, he had often astonished her with his clumsy, almost brutal attempts at consolation. Nevertheless, she clung to him, to his sheer mass and density, to his ticking, sighing, pulsing heat.

As they undressed, she roused herself to ask how the show had gone; sometimes she found it a relief to put the focus on him at such moments. And in fact, as he slowly, hesitantly embroidered his account with more and more detail — the first-act curtain, his entrance in the dream scene — she felt herself relaxing. She climbed into bed with him and lay listening not so much to his words as to the vibrations in his chest as his voice rumbled through it. To her subsequent amazement, especially since she knew she was to be wakened two hours later, sleep came quickly.

Next door, in Meyer's room, Claire sat with her face buried in her hands. She had been evil to suspect Charlotte of drugging her father. And stupid, too, to say as much. Mark always teased her about her dislike of Charlotte; he said she envied the closeness he and Charlotte had shared as adolescents. She yawned.

Right this minute, Anatole might be telling Sunny about Mark's affair. In a way, she hoped so.

Meyer's breathing was quick and whispery. Claire rocked, wishing June were still home.

Across the hall, Ira lay sleepless in the dark, his sheets twisted damply around him. Why did he feel no sadness about his father's abrupt deterioration? In fact, he felt nothing about the illness, the stroke, except anger. The whole weekend, he had worn what he hoped were the right concerned expressions, said what he guessed were the things he might be expected to say. But what he felt was rage. He wondered if any of the others (Mark? Sunny?) were being similarly dishonest. He hated Meyer for forcing him to this hypocrisy, and himself for cooperating. He should have gone home yesterday. He shouldn't have come at all.

A while ago, there had been some commotion in the corridor, footsteps, raised voices. He thought Meyer had died. For a few minutes, he lay still, ears straining, expecting his door to be opened at any moment, expecting a set, tight face to appear and give him the news. But no one came. The voices faded. Perhaps Meyer had died but it had been decided that there was no point waking the house, that the bad news could wait until morning. It was possible. It was possible.

He did not get up to check.

At the end of the corridor, Mark lay dreaming of a blizzard of white metal flakes. They clicked as they fell. They were sharp, dangerous, like razors. They accumulated in lethal heaps and drifts in front of their old house in Larchmont.

Mimi stumbled across the hall into the lighted bathroom to pee. She had a fuzzy recollection of having already gotten up to go once before tonight, but she was too sleepy to be sure. She hoped no one else was around; all she was wearing was a T-shirt that stopped at the top of her hips. At the glare of the bathroom light, she flinched. Her brain felt drugged and heavy. She had been dreaming Meyer was back among them and about to die. There was a droning in her ears of voices chanting the same words over and over.

Oh. This was not a dream.

She flushed the toilet and staggered hurriedly back across the hall. Jesse had rolled to the center of the warm cocoon of their narrow bed. She shoved him over with her legs as she slithered back in, and he stirred and mumbled, "Baby."

In the next room, Charlotte slept what she thought of as doctor sleep. It was a skill she had learned in her internship: Half of her slept, half remained alert. To learn to do both simultaneously, she had had to practice, like a pianist who learns to play a different time signature with each hand. The great drawback of doctor sleep was that it wasn't, finally, very restful. She was glad her responsibilities as a dermatologist rarely required it of her anymore. Still, it was there when she needed it. Like swimming. She could also set her mind to wake her at any given hour.

Secretly, Claire had intended to sit up till six, through Sunny's shift. But she soon knew this feat would be beyond her. Her back ached, even the skin of her face seemed to ache with weariness. She longed for sleep. To her surprise, she also longed to lie in bed next to Mark. She felt she had betrayed him a little tonight, and it made her feel fonder of him — or if not fonder, at least it made her want to assert her right to sleep next to him. If he knew Anatole had kissed her, he would be angry, and that imagined anger somehow made him attractively dangerous. At four, she checked Meyer's pulse once more — it was very low — and stole into Sunny and Anatole's room.

It gave her an odd, thrilling sensation to stand unseen in the dark of their room. One of them snored softly. When her eyes had adjusted sufficiently to the dimness to make out which body was Sunny's, she put a tentative hand on her shoulder.

Sunny turned and sat up. The snoring continued.

"It's four," whispered Claire. "Can you — ?"

"I'm there." In seconds, Sunny was on her feet, had picked up her robe and slippers, and was following Claire from the room.

"Any change?"

Claire shook her head.

"Anything I should — ?"

"Not really. Call me or Charlotte if something does happen, but I doubt . . ."

Standing outside Meyer's door, Sunny shivered. The air in the hallway was cold after the snugness of bed. On an impulse, she kissed Claire. "Thank you for keeping Anatole company. It was a help to him, I know."

"I enjoyed it." For an instant, Sunny's impulsive embrace had made Claire suspect she knew about Lizbeth. But now she thought not. "Anatole is a lovely man," she said.

"Do you really think so?"

Claire laughed at her tone. "Yes."

"That's the nicest thing anyone in this family has ever said about him," Sunny whispered. "I always think everyone thinks he's a pain in the ass."

"No," lied Claire.

"But he really is lovely, when you know him. Claire, your eyes are closing. Go to bed."

*

Later, Sunny was glad she had been the one with Meyer when he died. Not that she realized it was happening until it was over: His breathing simply got fainter and slower, and then stopped. Sunny wasn't focused on the sound at that moment, and it might have been a minute or longer between the time he died and the time she knew he had died. Earlier, when she first went in, she had drawn the ladder-back chair up close to the bed, close enough to sit and lay both her hands on one of his. Though she knew he didn't want them to do such things, she couldn't help hoping her own warmth and vigor would some-how revive him. She had sat there, holding his hand and watch-ing for signs of returning strength, for almost half an hour.

But her father showed no response, didn't even stir or sigh, and at last she gave it up. She was in the bentwood rocker thinking about how the rain had finally stopped and how muddy the driveway would be in the morning when she no-ticed the sound of his breath was gone.

She woke Charlotte, but not with any hope anything could be done. Then, trembling with cold, she slipped back into bed with Anatole.

# EPILOGUE

"That seemed short to me, that trip."

Mimi heaved herself out of the Rabbit into the chilly April afternoon. She stood in the small, crowded parking lot of the Cold Spring Cafe, arranging the folds of her cape so they covered her front better.

"Must have been shorter in the front seat." Thoroughly carsick, Sunny waited impatiently for Anatole or Jesse to extricate himself from his seat belt and get out so she could. She hated being carsick. She always got carsick riding in the back. But, of course, since Mimi was so huge —

A wild idea that her queasiness could be morning sickness leapt in her brain. Immediately, she worked to stamp it out. She and Anatole hadn't even made love at the right time this month (though perhaps what she had always thought was the "right" time was wrong for her, and this "wrong" time just the trick she needed?). Anyway, the chances of her getting pregnant without even trying were next to nil (though not trying was exactly what folk wisdom said you needed to do . . .).

At last, Anatole got out and she could clamber from the Rabbit behind him. It was almost May, but the air off the river was cold, bracing. A couple of lungfuls and her nausea was gone. Carsick. Carsick was the diagnosis.

"There's Mark and Claire," said Ira, pointing to the silver Prelude across the parking lot. "They must be inside."

"Ira."

Claire's voice intercepted him as he moved ahead of the others toward the restaurant. She and Mark were coming up from the small deck behind it, above the river. In a few weeks, the café would start serving out there again; now, the painted metal furniture was chained together.

"We got here ten minutes ago ourselves. It's jammed inside."

The seven of them came together, a quickly milling bunch with the lumbering Mimi at its dense center, like the nucleus in an illustration of an atom. Claire exchanged kisses with Ira, Sunny and Anatole. She squealed over the size of Mimi's belly, then shot an apologetic glance at Sunny. Sunny and Anatole had officially announced their infertility over New Year's; now they were deciding whether to adopt.

Extending his hand to Anatole, Mark asked how *Crushed Velvet* was doing.

"*Aunt Addie's Bouquet*, you mean," said Anatole, squeezing Mark's narrow hand until the bones cracked. "*Crushed Velvet* closed in January."

"Oh, sorry. Yes, of course."

"It's a great play." Jesse stuck his hand out to Mark to force Anatole to break his death grip. "Anatole's great in it. We saw him Friday."

Released, rubbing his right hand gently with his left, Mark sidled over to Mimi and murmured in her ear, "Charlotte called this morning. She said to remind you it can take half an hour from when you ask for the epidural to when you start to feel it, so think ahead. She really feels crummy about last fall, Mims."

Mimi's full mouth flattened. Charlote could mind her own business from now until the end of eternity, as far as she was concerned.

A black Jeep nosed into the parking lot, threatening to mow down the Ginzburgs. Ira shepherded them all to one side.

"We'll do the ceremony first," Mark said, as the Jeep passed them and roared off toward the other end of the lot. "Unless somebody's starving."

Everyone agreed it would be much better to do the ashes first. Even Mimi, who had been continuously ravenous for seven months (and had the pounds to prove it) felt it would be impossible to eat knowing the ordeal that was ahead.

Ira, his hands shoved deep into the pockets of his battered bomber jacket, asked where the ashes were. Awkwardly, with an obscure sense that stashing it there had been sacrilegious, Claire produced a small metal canister from her purse.

Everyone fell silent. The tin gleamed in the bright spring sunshine.

Mimi swallowed. "My fath - fath — He said not to cry," she whispered hoarsely to Jesse. Jesse put his arm around her.

"There's a public dock down that way." Ira took the lead again. About a month ago, he had driven up here with Kyoko. They had hiked along the wintry bluffs and poked around in the antiques stores. He would have brought her today if it hadn't meant taking two cars, he said to himself, which was almost true. Ira was the one who had suggested Cold Spring for this event. Now he hoped it wouldn't ruin the place for him. On the felty inside of his pocket, he began to sketch his sign — the two straight lines on either side of a squiggle — with his index finger.

The dock was only a few hundred feet from the back of the café. They walked in ones and twos, suddenly solemn, along a concrete path. The river stretched blue and choppy alongside them; on the opposite shore, a spidery green shawl of new, tender leaves clung to the highlands. This close to the water, the day felt almost raw. The short wooden pier was deserted, and Mark led the way to the end.

Sunny drew her hand out from under Anatole's arm and wrapped her blazer around her more closely, hugging the cloth to her chest. That morning, Josh Meachum had phoned the apartment. Sunny had tracked him down in December, using information from Tom McBride. At first, Josh had said he had no interest in anything to do with Meyer, who had never been more than a name to him. Claude Meachum was his father. Some weeks later, though, a photograph had arrived of a tall, gangling young man with an almost uncanny resemblance to Meyer, leaning against a vine-covered brick wall. With it had come a request for pictures of the Ginzburgs. Sunny had sent them. After the date had been set for scattering Meyer's ashes, she had dropped a note to Josh to let him know.

Now, standing in a ragged circle with the others near the end of the pier, she told them what he had said this morning — that he sent his regards, or respects, or whatever one ought to send, and was sorry he couldn't be with them.

Mark formally relayed Charlotte's hellos and love to everyone, then took the canister from Claire, who at once jammed her hands into her pockets for warmth. They all watched as Mark bent his head and set his fingertips on the tin to open it. The wind picked up wisps of his gingery hair and sent them flying above him. Sunny wondered what the ashes of a man were like. Were they really ashes, like in a fireplace?

Mark looked up. "Not going to open. I need a screwdriver," he announced.

Everyone smiled and shifted to examine the thin-lipped lid

of the canister, which was wedged in tight, like the lid of a paint can.

"Would a pen — ?" Ira reached into his shirt pocket.

"Here." Jesse whipped out a fat Swiss Army knife. With a practiced flick, he extended the screwdriver blade and gave it to Mark.

Mark pried the canister open and offered it first to Sunny, perhaps (she thought) from a conscious effort at feminism, perhaps because she had been with Meyer when he died, perhaps from some more muddled combination of gallantry and family politics. She took Anatole's hand, squeezed it, let go and went to her brother. The ashes were mostly powdery, white and gray, but they had flakes and little solid lumps in them that she decided not to think about. She scooped up a small handful and closed her fingers over them so they wouldn't blow away. The fine ashes were gritty under her fingernails.

"Is that safe?" She heard Jesse's startled voice behind her. "Touching that? We couldn't — Mimi couldn't get infected?"

Sunny knelt at the very end of the weathered wooden dock, while behind her, Claire murmured reassurances to Jesse. Poor man, thought Sunny, what a nightmare for him to be invited to handle human dust.

The Hudson looked greenish and not very clean from this angle. The wind made tiny whitecaps on its surface here and there. Sunny hesitated but, feeling the eyes of the others on her back, held her arm out over the river and opened her hand. The ashes whirled briefly in the wind. Some were blown back under the dock. She tried to love her father as she watched the rest drift gently down.

As she returned to the others, Mark held out the canister to Ira, who went to the end of the dock in his turn. Kneeling, he was surprised to hear himself burst into sobs. Reluctantly, he accepted a handkerchief from Anatole on his way back.

One by one, Mimi, Claire and Anatole made their pilgrimages (with a hotly muttered apology, Jesse declined to participate). Mimi, already in tears when she started, returned to hold out her arms to the still sniffling Ira. Their embrace around her belly was doubly awkward. Claire did her business with swift efficiency, Anatole slowly, taking careful note of each sensation.

At last, sweeping them all with his eyes, Mark went forward with the canister. He set the metal lid on the dock beside him and released two handfuls of ashes low into the gusty air. Then he upended the canister and shook it until it was empty. He hit the bottom twice, then, without thinking, flung the whole container into the water and dusted off his hands.